"It's a challenge," Jeremy said. "But let's be hopeful about the station's future. I won't leave you alone with this, Brooke. You can count on me."

Her shoulders relaxed. Her gaze caught and held his. "You don't know what this means to me."

"I think I do." He leaned forward, cupped her face with both his hands and kissed the top of her forehead, just like he kissed his kids at the bus stop. Only this was different. This gesture made his heart stop. When he drew back, he kept his hands on each side of her face. He stroked her cheeks with his thumbs. Her skin was moist from the tears, but soft and silky.

And then she leaned just slightly toward him, but it was enough for him to know that she was feeling something, too. He hoped it wasn't just gratitude. He hoped she felt just a bit of what his senses were telling him now.

Dear Reader,

As the title of this book implies, this is a love story about honor, and I examined my own beliefs about honor as I wrote it. I admire Brooke, the heroine of this story, for her drive, ambition and uncomplicated ideal for her life—work hard, achieve, never give up. And then she meets Jeremy, our hero, whose dilemma comes when he must risk a successful future that directly confronts a moral question from his past. His decision isn't an easy one: pursue fame and security or lose everything he has worked for. As the two characters in this book fall in love, they realize their ideas of right and wrong, self-gratification and self-sacrifice must be examined.

A weighty plot? To be sure it is, especially when innocent children and a lost relative become intertwined with the main characters' attempts to do the right thing. I hope you enjoy this journey of self-discovery. I'd love to hear your thoughts. You can contact me at cynthoma@aol.com.

Thanks for reading.

Cynthia Thomason

HEARTWARMING

A Man of Honor

———

Cynthia Thomason

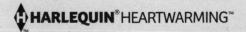

Recycling programs
for this product may
not exist in your area.

ISBN-13: 978-1-335-51093-8

A Man of Honor

Copyright © 2019 by Cynthia Thomason

Printed in U.S.A.

Cynthia Thomason inherited her love of writing from her ancestors. Her father and grandmother both loved to write, and she aspired to continue the legacy. Cynthia studied English and journalism in college, and after a career as a high school English teacher, she began writing novels. She discovered ideas for stories while searching through antiques stores and flea markets and as an auctioneer and estate buyer. Cynthia says every cast-off item from someone's life can ignite the idea for a plot. She writes about small towns, big hearts and happy endings that are earned and not taken for granted. And as far as the legacy is concerned, just ask her son, the magazine journalist, if he believes. You can contact Cynthia at cynthoma@aol.com and cynthiathomason.net.

Books by Cynthia Thomason

Harlequin Heartwarming

Twins Plus One

Baby Makes Four

The Cahills of North Carolina

High Country Christmas
Dad in Training
High Country Cop

Visit the Author Profile page
at Harlequin.com for more titles.

This book is dedicated to my son,
John Thomason, a journalist and writer whose
words always come from his heart as well as his
brain. Honorable men do exist and I am proud
to know one.

CHAPTER ONE

BROOKE MONTGOMERY CROSSED the newsroom at her usual hurried pace, grateful that none of the staff stopped her with any of the myriad of questions she answered every day. She had assignments to get to her writers before noon so the stories would be ready for the five o'clock broadcast.

Could be worse, she thought. *And usually is. Sometimes I hand my writers breaking news at four o'clock with only minutes to spare.*

She then expected them to compose literate copy before Fred Armitage, WJQC's anchor for the last fifteen years, stared at the camera with his serious expression and said, "Good evening, ladies and gentlemen. Once again we have news."

Brooke heard scuffling behind her. She glanced over her shoulder to see Cissy Littleton approaching her. "Brooke, wait, did you get the news about horses being mistreated out in Chandler Acres?"

Without slowing down, Brooke waved her papers at the young production assistant, who also filled in as an occasional copy editor. "It's here, Cissy."

Cissy caught up to her. "Good, because you know I love animals."

"You should have the material for the tele-prompter in an hour," Brooke said. "If we have time, the horse story will be on. Just read through it for mistakes, but don't add any personal feelings about the fate of offtrack horses. We run a legitimate news program here. If I know you, you'll make a pitch for every citizen to adopt a seven-hundred-pound animal."

"I'll be good, I promise," Cissy said. She suddenly grabbed Brooke's elbow. "Holy cow, Brooke, do you see that man with Milt Cramer coming into the newsroom? He makes Milt look like a troll."

"Milt is your boss, Cissy. Nice way to speak about him."

"He's your boss, too, and I've heard you say worse."

"You have not," Brooke retorted. "Unless it was two hours into happy hour at Pickler's."

"Brooke!" Milt called out to her. "Come over here. I want you to meet someone."

Brooke shoved the papers into Cissy's hand. "Get these to the writers immediately."

"In a minute," Cissy said. "I want to know who the mysterious stranger is, too. He looks famous, doesn't he?"

Brooke watched Cissy tuck the papers under her arm, then they walked over to Milt. In truth, the man's handsome face, perfectly square jaw, sandy blond hair and minor imperfections from scars on his face did look vaguely familiar, like someone she ought to know. But wouldn't she have remembered a guy that good-looking, who stood at least six feet three inches tall?

"Glad I caught you, Brooke," Milt said. "I want you to meet the greatest wide receiver the Carolina Wildcats have ever had."

A conversational buzz began in the newsroom and seemed to spread in all directions. All keyboard tapping stopped, and Brooke felt as though she was the center of attention. Though, of course, she wasn't.

Milt identified her. "This is Brooke Montgomery, our head producer."

Brooke wiped her hands on her navy slacks and haphazardly tucked loose strands of hair into the topknot at her crown. Her comfy shoes and falling hairstyle were typical stress factors of her day as producer of the five o'clock news.

She took the hand the greatest receiver offered her. "Sorry, I didn't get your name," she said. She didn't follow football and had no idea who he was.

"He doesn't need a name," Milt blustered. "Brooke knows who you are," he said to the "greatest." "She thinks her job is to check every fact."

She looked at Milt. "That *is* my job, Milt."

The man smiled. "I'm Jeremy Crockett," he said, still holding her hand.

"Saddest day of my life when he retired last season," Milt said.

Okay. Brooke had heard his name before. "Nice to meet you."

"I'm Cissy Littleton, Brooke's personal assistant," Cissy said, reaching for Jeremy's hand and forcing him to turn his attention to her. "Nice to meet you."

Brooke let her get away with the exaggeration. Wannabe assistant was more the truth. Milt didn't correct her, either. He probably didn't know what job Cissy currently had. Milt didn't pay much attention to the staff directly under Brooke's supervision. He just let Brooke run the tight ship she commanded on a daily basis.

"Same here," Milt's idol responded to Cissy.

"I'm showing Jeremy the station," Milt explained.

"Well, fine," Brooke said. She was used to people touring the newsroom, but usually the guests were middle-school kids who didn't get WJQC's owner as a guide. "I hate to rush..." Brooke nodded at Cissy to get her to move to the writers' area. "We've got stories to finalize and a deadline looming."

"Sure, I understand," Jeremy said.

"Brooke, I'd like to see you in my office later," Milt said. "I expect things will have calmed down by three o'clock."

Unless all hell broke loose, as it often did.

"Come up to see me then," Milt added.

"Okay," Brooke said. She acknowledged Jeremy one more time. "Hope you enjoy seeing how a newsroom operates." She walked briskly away without waiting for a response. She hoped she'd shown acceptable enough manners to excuse herself.

Cissy trailed behind her. "Can you believe it? A Carolina Wildcats football player right here in our newsroom."

"Yeah, that's something all right." They'd reached the glass doors that separated the top writers from the rest of the newsroom mayhem. "Don't you have something to do, like deliver those rough copies?" she asked Cissy.

"I do, but I can't stop looking at him. Can't you just picture him in those tight pants football players wear? I'll bet he looks scrumptious."

Brooke gave her a warning look.

"Okay, I'm going." Cissy grabbed the door handle, her attention still on Jeremy.

"I've got to review some videos," Brooke said after taking time for a last glimpse at the amazing Mr. Crockett. A wide receiver... Brooke thought he was a guy who caught the ball passed by the other guy—the quarterback, right? She could believe the guy was good. He had strong hands. Today, Jeremy's legs were covered in beige khaki, so did not resemble the swoon-worthy image Cissy flipped for. But Brooke had to smile. She bet his legs did look pretty good in those tight pants.

AT THREE O'CLOCK Brooke waited outside of Milt's office for his assistant to announce her presence.

"Send her in." Brooke heard Milt's booming voice over the telephone. He sounded happy so she didn't expect bad news.

He stood when she came inside his office. "Have a seat, Brooke." He came around his desk and leaned on the corner facing her. "How about that visit from Crockett today?" he asked her. "Made my week, I'll tell you."

"Happy for you, Milt." Brooke sat stiffly in a leather chair. "What was Jeremy doing here, if I may ask?"

"You may, and I'm glad you did. Hold on to your stockings, Brooke. I have news."

Stockings? No one wore stockings anymore and certainly not in eighty-five-degree Charleston, South Carolina, in May.

"I hired him," Milt said.

Brooke had to quit thinking of stockings and reorient herself to the sound of Milt's voice. "What? You hired him? A former football player? For what position?"

"He's going to take over for Armitage in six weeks when the old boy retires."

Brooke had to concentrate to keep her jaw from dropping. Milt hired a jock to do the evening news? What credentials did he have? How much confidence would he inspire from listeners who were used to calm, collected, though sometimes dull Fred Armitage? "I'm not sure I understand," she said.

"Jeremy is going to deliver the evening news. Quite a change from the format we're used to around here. But Jeremy will add life and vigor to the broadcast."

"Pardon me for asking, Milt, but what does Jeremy know about broadcasting the news?"

"Nothing." Milt hooted, no doubt at the expression on Brooke's face. "That's the beauty of my plan. He's new. He's fresh. And no one would dare call him stodgy." Milt's face grew serious. "I recognize one very important fact, though. He'll need some training."

"I would imagine so."

"But we have six weeks."

Brooke started to speak but bit her lip. After a moment she said, "What do you mean 'we'?"

"That's why I called you in here, Brooke. Who knows more about the news at WJQC than you do?"

No one. Brooke could agree with that. Who knew more about the news than Jeremy Crockett? Almost anyone, Brooke feared. "What are you suggesting, Milt?" She held her breath.

"I want you to train him, Brooke. Take him under your wing."

This was not happening. Didn't Milt watch her run track around the station on a daily basis?

"Teach him everything from a producer's viewpoint and skills," Milt continued. "And then go on to camera work, voice modulation. When he's absolutely perfect, then go into budgetary concerns, legal matters. The whole enchilada, Brooke. I want Jeremy to be a champion here, too." Again Milt chuckled at his humor. "I'll bet that's something the man can understand."

"Milt, I don't have the time to tutor your golden boy. I barely get my work done as it is. I'm always under pressure. There seems to be one emergency after another in the news-room. I couldn't possibly—"

"Come on, Brooke. I need you to do this. We all do. The future of WJQC could depend on it."

"Isn't that a bit of an exaggeration?"

"I wish. We're facing a financial crisis here. I haven't told anyone because I don't want people to panic. If you care for this station and the employees as much as I think you do—"

"That's not fair, Milt. Of course I care about everyone who works here."

Milt's voice dropped. All humor had been sucked out of the room. "You owe me, Brooke."

She couldn't help it. Her voice rose in disbelief. "I owe you?"

"You bet you do. You owe me hours of work. It's either that or you should consider paying the station half of your salary the last few months."

"What are you talking about?" Brooke worked her butt off for WJQC. Except maybe for those few times she… No. Milt couldn't know about that. She'd kept her personal business private.

"I've seen you at your desk talking on the

phone. Didn't sound like WJQC conversation to me. In fact, I walk by and you immediately hang up. I caught you doing personal internet stuff during WJQC time. You can't think I haven't seen your computer screen in the middle of the day while you're looking up names and dates. Heck, Brooke, you've even been canvassing prison records. I don't know what's going on, and I don't want to know, but one thing's for sure. You owe me for time and dollars lost while your mind hasn't been on your work."

Brooke couldn't argue with the truth. But she could plead the obvious. "Has my work suffered?"

"If you mean has the news gone on at five o'clock every day, then yes, it has. Was it the best you could offer our listening audience, then who knows?" Milt crossed his arms, clearly frustrated. "You can't deny the simple truth that our ratings have dropped. Other stations are getting the jump on us with breaking news. Advertisers have gone elsewhere in alarming numbers. At first I thought it was all Armitage's fault, but he just reads what you put on the prompter. So whose fault is it really?"

"Milt, you know that a newscast is a combination of many facets. I'm just one. Besides, I didn't know our stats were so shaky."

"Now you do, and so does the board of directors. It won't be long until the lowliest employee is aware of the situation around here. My butt's been in the fire lately, and major changes are needed."

"But isn't hiring an ex-jock going a bit too far?"

Milt's gaze was fixed on her face, almost pleading with her. "I expect you to be a team player. And right now that means joining forces with Jeremy Crockett. I truly believe that he could be the future of WJQC. He'll add the spark we need to attract new viewers, ladies especially." Milt managed a slight smile. "He's single, you know. And from the way the women are drooling over him, he's not bad on the eyes."

"I wouldn't know," Brooke said. "And I never thought that putting a has-been jock on the news at dinnertime was the answer to ratings problems."

"He's not a has-been. He quit the team this year for personal reasons. Otherwise he'd still be playing. And as for the ratings, I think Jeremy could be the answer to our problems."

"Or he could be an even bigger problem," Brooke said.

"Well, sure, we can't put a buffoon on the air. Not that Jeremy is that. He's been to college, but he's raw. He needs training from the ground up, and you're going to give it to him."

Brooke had tangled with Milt before. His bluster didn't scare her, but this time was different. "And if I don't?"

"Now, Brooke, we're getting into sticky territory. But I'll level with you. Along with other changes I've been contemplating around here, your position is one of the decisions I've been mulling over."

"You're thinking of firing me? After ten years?"

"I'm thinking of everything that can help WJQC back to the top. You've been slacking off, so you could be a big reason for the ratings slip. I know Armitage is no ball of fire. He's old. He's tired. But you should be giving one hundred percent and you're not. You're still the best news producer in the business as far as I'm concerned. Or you used to be.

So I'm asking you to step up and do the right thing. Make this football player the face of the nightly news."

"Or you will fire me?" she asked again just to clarify.

Milt nodded. Just a single dip of his head. "Your performance lately gives me just cause. At the end of six weeks we'll reevaluate your efforts around here. If Jeremy isn't camera ready and pitch-perfect, I'll get someone that can make him into a dang news genius."

She exhaled a deep breath. "You do realize that I could go to almost any station in the country and get another job?"

"Possibly, but not in Charleston. The city you claim to be so fond of."

He had her there. Charleston had always been her home. She loved the vibrancy of the downtown district. She loved the history, the culture. She definitely didn't want to leave. She swallowed and said, "And if he is camera ready?"

"Then you'll go on as producer and even get a nice Christmas bonus this year."

Not working at WJQC? Brooke had never even considered it. The station was her second home. She loved her job, every frustrating, tense moment of it. She was good at it. "Are we finished?"

"We are."

She stood.

"Oh, one other thing…" Milt said. "Don't discuss this conversation with Jeremy. It's between you and me. He doesn't need to know about our plans. You just become his friend, offer to tutor him. Don't let him know there are conditions attached."

"Heavens no, Milt," Brooke said. "Conditions that include my continued tenure at WJQC."

"It's nothing personal, Brooke. It's business. Jeremy seems like a nice guy. I don't want him to know that you're helping him for any reason other than your willingness to boost WJQC. I want Jeremy to believe from day one that we're all a big happy family around here. But you can sleep on this, Brooke. Let me know first thing in the morning."

Milt narrowed his eyes. "And, Brooke, don't ever underestimate me again. If you're not giving WJQC your all, don't think I won't know it. Because I will. Whatever's happening in your personal life, leave it at home."

Brooke exited his office. Her palms were damp and her knees were wobbly. It's not like Camryn hadn't warned her. The twin sisters had always had a secret radar that let them know the other was going off the tracks. And Camryn had told Brooke often enough that her obsession with finding their half brother was going to cost her big-time. And losing this job was definitely big-time.

If only Milt had warned her before, when he'd first suspected she was using company time for a personal matter. Now he was loading her up with extra work, an ultimatum and a project that might never prove successful. And she had no choice but to give in because if Jeremy failed, the loser would be Brooke.

She left early that day, to think, to wander the city she loved so much. She went to the Charleston Art Gallery, where a Lowcountry exhibit was opening that night. The paintings calmed her, made her appreciate all that South Carolina had to offer. When she went home, she knew what she was going to do.

CHAPTER TWO

DRESSED IN A beige tailored suit with a purple silk blouse, Brooke hurried to her door at seven thirty the next morning. After a long and restless night during which she'd accepted that she would do what Milt wanted her to and do the best job she could, she'd been up early to plan her approach to her newest project.

Why?

For many reasons. Admittedly, she loved this mid-size condominium on the third floor of a historic building just six blocks from the Battery. She had a mortgage on the condo and twenty-five years before she would pay it off.

She couldn't give up the elegant lifestyle she had chosen for herself. A renovated Civil War–era building with antique Colonial furnishings and treasures she had collected for years. Extralarge closets that held nice clothes, numerous pairs of shoes and twenty handbags.

And that wasn't even considering that WJQC

was important to her. Her time there had evolved into more than a career. Her friends—other enterprising women in Charleston—often took a backseat to news deadlines and her WJQC family. She remembered when Milt's third grandchild had been born. Trish, the makeup woman, had been her first good friend and still was. Was she willing to sit by and watch Trish and others at the station lose their jobs?

No. She would do what she could for Jeremy Crockett and hope he was a good student and willing to do what was necessary because he needed to learn a lot in just a matter of weeks.

Despite the unpleasant nature of Milt's ultimatum, Brooke had hesitated to ask her sister for advice. She knew what Camryn would say. *Don't do anything foolish, Brooke. Stay the course.*

She knew what her parents would say, so she didn't call them. *Follow your heart, dear. You can always move back in with us.*

Ah, no to that last prospect. Even more than her walk-in closet and a location near the Battery, Brooke valued her independence. Her parents were great. She loved them, but living under their roof? Not going to happen.

She opened her front door to head to the stairs and her assigned street-parking space when her cell phone rang. She checked the digital readout, saw a name she recognized and immediately went back inside, dropped her briefcase and purse on a chair and sat down.

"Gabe, I hope you have good news."

The private investigator who had been helping her track the whereabouts of her half brother, Edward, spoke the first words she'd heard from him in over a week. "Hey, there, Brooke. How are you doing?"

His cheerful attempt at a polite greeting was almost irritating, though it didn't take much to irritate Brooke this morning.

"I'm fine," she lied. "Are you back from Tennessee?"

"Just got back this morning," he said. "Sorry, but no good news to report."

"Not again. I was so hoping this lead would turn up something."

"Well, me, too, kid, but it was a wild-goose chase. That Eddie McClaren I found in Riverside prison in Nashville isn't our boy."

She'd sent Gabe to the prison to personally interview this Eddie McClaren, a man the same age as her brother, and a criminal with a rap sheet that began back in his adolescence. She didn't know what she hoped Gabe would find out to be honest. "Are you sure? Did you talk to him?"

"Of course," Gabe said. "The guy opened up without much prodding. Turns out he was born in South Carolina like I discovered, but the papers for adoption weren't okayed by his biological parents until he was seven. He was in foster care before that but his mother and father held on hoping he would correct his behavior. Didn't happen, and he stayed in the foster system." Gabe tsked. "Sorry, Brooke. It all seemed to add up until I actually spoke with the guy. He knew his parents, still is in touch with them. And his mother isn't Marlene Hudson."

Brooke closed her eyes and sighed at this latest disappointment. Of course, Marlene wouldn't be in touch with her son. She had wanted no part of a relationship with any of her children. The twins' older brother had been given up for adoption by their biological mother, Marlene, when the boy was only three. His memory of them, if any, would be spotty. "So where does this leave us?" she asked the investigator.

"I'll keep following leads if you want me to. But, Brooke, my per diem ran out on this trip. I'm going to need an advance if I'm to keep the search going."

Four times Brooke had come close to believing that Gabe had found her brother. Four times she'd had to choke back her disappointment and transfer funds to Gabe's bank account. But close was better than nothing, and Brooke couldn't give up. Not yet. Edward had to be out there somewhere. "How much do you need, Gabe?" she asked.

"Six hundred will keep me going."

"Okay. I'll arrange for the funds to go into your account." Gabe had come to her with excellent references, and she truly believed he was doing his best to locate her brother. But, realistically, how long could she keep paying him?

"Okay, kiddo," Gabe said. "I'll report back in a few days."

She disconnected and let her thoughts wander to Camryn. She knew how her twin would feel about this latest transaction. She'd call it foolish and a waste of time and money. Camryn had never understood Brooke's obsession with finding their half brother. Camryn had even balked at the idea of visiting their biological mother when Brooke had traced Marlene Hudson to Myrtle Beach. But true to their similar nature of always supporting each other, she had gone with Brooke. And she had even sympathized with Brooke when Marlene treated them coldly.

After talking with Marlene and realizing that the woman wanted nothing to do with her daughters, Marlene had let slip that the girls had a half brother. That bit of news was all Brooke needed to cope with Marlene's bitter and hostile reaction. From that day on, she had focused her sights on finding this Edward.

Cam would never understand. She was happy with the family the girls had found with Linda and Craig Montgomery and didn't want to know the woman who had given them up. That was fine for Camryn. She had two wonderful daughters, a husband and two stepsons who adored her. Brooke was basically a serial dater and didn't plan on having any kids of her own. She wasn't exactly jealous of Camryn.

Her life decisions were her choice, but still she experienced loneliness sometimes.

She needed to know about Edward. Since that fateful day in middle school when she'd tried to sketch her family tree and found it pitifully lacking, she needed roots, a background, a story that was truly hers. She wanted a family tree that meant something. Unlike her sister, Brooke would probably never have children, but Edward was out there somewhere, a connection, a blood relative who might love and support her just as she would him.

Brooke headed off to work. She needed this job, this income, to maintain the lifestyle she'd come to love and to keep paying Gabe. And so, more than anything, she needed Jeremy Crockett to succeed, and perhaps, if she worked his butt off, he would.

JEREMY SET TWO cereal bowls on the kitchen island and filled them with Lucky Charms. To balance his kids' dietary choices he cut up a banana on top and gave each child a glass of orange juice. "Come on, guys. The school bus will be here in fifteen minutes," he hollered up the stairs to the second floor of his house.

Two sets of footsteps sounded on the maple staircase of Jeremy's three-thousand-square-foot home in upscale Hidden Oaks, a suburb of Charleston. He'd closed on the home a year ago, having chosen it for its expansive backyard and gated security. Didn't hurt that a creek ran across the property line of his three-acre estate, providing him with the opportunity to fish for rainbow trout. Not that he had yet. As soon as he felt secure in his position as anchor for WJQC, he might actually have time to enjoy himself.

Oh, sure, he'd signed a three-year contract. A fair offer, his attorney had told him, with a loophole or two in Jeremy's favor if the job didn't work out. Milt Cramer couldn't fire him without due cause and without paying a sizable buyout. But Jeremy didn't want out. He'd spent the last year examining his options, and now it was time to settle on something. He wanted to succeed at WJQC. He had altered his entire life to make this move. Plus, he had ideas for the news. Maybe inject a line or two about sports figures, funny or heartwarming stories to lighten up the day-to-day tragedies and tedium.

Jeremy accepted that he was a rookie. He knew what that meant on the football field, and after yesterday's visit to the station, he knew what it meant in the newsroom. He had a lot to learn. Milt had told him that the pent-up bundle of nerves in the navy pantsuit Jeremy had met yesterday knew more about producing the news than anyone in the business, and she would educate him from A to Z.

What was her name again? Not good to forget the name of the one person who stood between you and abject failure. "Brooke," he said aloud. "That's right."

"Who's that?" his six-year-old son asked.

"Just a lady I met yesterday."

"Are you going to marry her?" his nine-year-old daughter said with an obvious slanted eye of disapproval.

"What? No, of course not. I don't even date anyone, as you well know."

"Good. You should still love Mommy—" she directed a glance at her brother "—even if she is dead."

"Stop talking about Mommy dying," Cody wailed.

"Well, she did, even if you don't want to talk about it," Alicia added.

"That's enough," Jeremy said, his frustration growing. He was trying with his kids, trying to help them cope, but sometimes it seemed like a losing effort. "I will always love Mommy," Jeremy assured them. "And we all miss her."

"Then how come you didn't marry her," Alicia said.

Jeremy sighed. "Alicia, we've gone over this. Not marrying your mother was a very complicated decision."

"But people who love each other get married."

Jeremy shook his head. "Look, there's something you don't know. Your mother…" He stopped. Now was not the time to unravel the twisted strands of his relationship with Lynette, especially since the school bus could be pulling up at the gate. Besides, why burden a little girl with the truth? Fairy tales weren't real. "We'll talk about this later, okay? Please, get your backpacks and I'll walk you down the lane to the bus stop."

The stroll along the cool, shady path to the bus stop was pleasant enough this morning. Jeremy was grateful that his two children were teasing each other and pointing to a pair of chattering squirrels.

"Have a great day," he said when the bus arrived. He kissed each child on the forehead, watched the bus drive down the two-lane road and headed back inside.

This parenting business was difficult. He'd never realized how hard it could be. Lynette had done all the heavy lifting regarding raising their two kids. Jeremy was the "fun parent" who Skyped every day, told funny stories and showed up every couple of weeks to buy tickets to theme parks and video arcades. But no one thought Lynette would die on a ski slope in Durango, Colorado, over a year ago. And no one thought Jeremy would take over as a full-time dad to two grieving kids.

Lynette was everything Jeremy had wanted for his life partner. Well, almost everything. She was a good mother. She was supportive of his career choice. Lots of pro-football wives resented the holidays they spent with no husband at the head of the table. Lynette never complained. She was happy to see Jeremy when he came to Colorado, and she was the first to wish him good luck on the field when he left.

The only problem was, they weren't the typical husband and wife. They weren't husband and wife at all. Over the ten years they'd been together, Jeremy had asked Lynette to marry him at least a half dozen times. The answer was always the same. *Why spoil a good thing?*

The problem wasn't him. She loved him. The problem was marriage in general. Unlike Jeremy, Lynette had grown up in a privileged household, though no one would have guessed it upon meeting the down-to-earth woman. But she had her own money, her own interests, her own friends. She simply didn't want to marry, and didn't think she needed to.

And so the two remained faithful to each other without the license that Jeremy would have liked, but Lynette preferred to live without. They had two children and consulted each other about every major event or decision in the kids' lives. Jeremy didn't believe that Lynette had ever experienced the first twinge of jealousy when he went out of town to stay in hotels and greet fans. She didn't have to, and she knew it. And he never questioned her loyalty.

And when she had a freak accident on the ski slope that horrible day, Jeremy had gone to comfort his children. Unfortunately, he didn't know how to comfort himself. That had been fourteen months ago. He'd flown to Colorado at least once a week to visit Cody and Alicia at their grandparents' home until he'd purchased the house in Hidden Oaks and accomplished his goal of settling down. For the last year, he hoped he'd been providing his kids the secure life they needed.

He wanted to give them a good life, and quitting football and taking a job where he wouldn't risk a concussion or a broken bone every week seemed the fatherly thing to do. He'd already spent a decade as a professional athlete, had plenty of money, and taking a pay cut to work at the news station wouldn't cause any unnecessary stress to his bank account. At this point in his life, he considered himself a quiet, thoughtful man who took his responsibilities seriously. But it occurred to him that maybe he was a little dead inside.

Back in his bedroom, Jeremy put on trousers

and a button-down shirt. He decided to skip a tie. He wasn't on the air yet, wouldn't be for a while, and when it was time he'd go through the dozen or so suits he had in his closet, add new ones and discard the old. For now, he'd keep it casual and hope that Brooke would see his determination in ways other than his dress.

"Marta, I should be home by six," he said to his housekeeper.

"We'll be fine, Mr. C. I won't give the children any unhealthy snacks."

"You're already more qualified to be a parent than I am," he said.

Marta chuckled. "I've been a parent four times, sir. It's not like I don't know all the tricks."

Finding Marta had been a gift. Recently widowed, the strong woman with a hearty Scandinavian background needed something to occupy her time. She liked the idea of moving into the house in Hidden Oaks for the company, and so far she was proving to be everything Jeremy needed in a housekeeper. The kids didn't exactly love her, but they listened when she spoke in that deep, no-nonsense way she had.

The drive into Charleston was forty minutes. Jeremy didn't mind it. His SUV had a great sound system and Sirius radio caught him up with news of the day, a necessity now that news was his future. He parked in his assigned spot when he arrived at the station, happy to see that his name was already on the placard. He was three spots closer to the door than WJQC's news producer, Brooke Montgomery. Only the head meteorologist and Fred Armitage were between them. He hoped that special consideration didn't cause any friction between him and Brooke. He'd gladly give up his parking space if she'd teach him what he needed to know.

Jeremy got out of his car, smoothed the front of his shirt and headed for the door. The primary thing on his agenda was finding Brooke to see when they could meet today. Might as well get started on the first day of the rest of his life.

BROOKE HAD ONLY four miles to drive to the station in downtown Charleston, although the trip took thirty minutes or more because of traffic. But that was okay. Each morning she had a chance to catch up with her sister, Camryn. Brooke initiated the hands-free device on her car phone and punched in the single digit that would connect her to Cam on her farm. Last night, Brooke had decided to level with Camryn about what was going on in her life. Not to would not have been possible.

"Hello, Brooke," Camryn said. "How are things this morning?"

"Great. Wonderful. How's Esther?"

"She's fine. Just got on the school bus."

Brooke adored her nieces. She asked about the other one. "And Gracie? How is she?"

"Grace is up at the house with Reed. Oh, she's happy and healthy. And chubby as all get out."

Brooke was grateful. After suffering two miscarriages, Camryn had been stressed out through this latest pregnancy. Near the end of her term, a couple of months ago, the baby came early, but everyone in the family celebrated the healthy birth.

"I'm sure you knew how I would answer that question so I'm guessing you have something important and personal on your mind today," Cam said, guessing correctly.

"I do. It's Milt—he's come up with this bizarre idea to improve our ratings."

Camryn sighed. "What did he do now?"

Brooke gave her a quick rundown on the new hire and the ultimatum Milt had given her to turn the jock into news-announcer gold. "Milt has stars in his eyes," Brooke said. "He genuinely believes this ex-football player will turn WJQC into the top-rated show at the five o'clock hour. And he wants me to be the one to perform the miracle of ridding his brain of all the athletic stuff and filling it with local and worldwide current events."

"I'd say he picked the best news producer in Charleston to do that," Camryn said.

Brooke smiled. "Well, yeah, he did. But here's the deal—if I don't do the possibly impossible, he's going to fire me."

"That's not fair. I know lots of ex-athletes have become broadcasters, but most of those have gone into some related sports field. Tackling real news is a different story. Why would Milt threaten to let you go? You're the backbone of that station."

Brooke appreciated Camryn's loyalty.

"Wait a minute," Camryn said. "Does this

have something to do with…?" She hesitated saying the words. "You know."

"Okay." Brooke took a deep breath. "Milt has noticed that I've been letting personal matters get in the way of my performance at WJQC. He thinks it's a much bigger deal than it is, but—"

"Oh, Brooke, how many times did I warn you about using company time to find Edward?"

"And how many times did I tell you I wasn't going to give up my search for our brother?" Brooke's heart raced as it did every time she had to defend her efforts to find their sibling. "I'm so close, Cammie. I can feel it. Gabe has some good leads."

"I'm sure he told you he did," Camryn said. "Brooke, this is getting serious now. You've got to give up this obsession. Edward is a speck of sand in a ten-mile beach. You're never going to find him. And now you might lose your job."

"Thanks, Cam. I called you for sympathy, and I get the same old lecture. It's possible that Milt's bluffing, anyway."

"Deep down, Brooke, you called me for advice, and I've just given it to you, for the hundredth time. And by the way, how are you fixed for money? I worry about those payments to Gabe."

Yeah, and so do I. "I'm fine," Brooke said. "I just pulled into the parking lot. I've got a news show to produce before Mr. Legs starts pestering me for my unrivaled expertise."

"Mr. Legs?" Camryn repeated. "What does that mean?"

Brooke pictured Jeremy in all his six feet, three inches of manly glory. "Nothing," she said. "It was just something Cissy noticed. Has nothing to do with, well, anything."

"Sure, of course it doesn't," Camryn said with a mischievous tone in her voice. "Let me know how it goes today with Mr. Legs."

The sisters always ended their calls the same way. "I love you," Brooke said. "Though I can't imagine why."

"Love you, too, and I can think of a thousand reasons why."

Brooke was smiling when she swiped her ID in front of the scanner at the employees' entrance.

CHAPTER THREE

THE FIRST PERSON Brooke ran into when she went inside the station was Jeremy Crockett. He was coming out of the executive lounge, and looked fresh, eager and neatly pressed. His hands were wrapped around a coffee mug. He smiled at her. "Just the lady I want to see," he said.

"Well, here I am."

"Milt says you and I are going to be spending some time together while you teach me the ropes of news broadcasting. A lot of my training will be hands-on, so you'll see me around the station looking over shoulders, yours especially, and asking questions. But for the nuts and bolts, Milt says you've offered to tutor me."

"Oh, yes, I did, didn't I?" She almost choked on the word *offer*. More like had to agree.

His eyes narrowed. "Do you have a problem with us working together?"

Watch yourself, Brooke, she thought, masking her true feelings with a smile. *Milt made it clear that Jeremy is supposed to assume you volunteered for this assignment.* "Of course not. We'll just have to find time that we can both devote to this endeavor."

"I have time I can devote today," Jeremy said. "You name the hour."

Already he was pressuring her. She hadn't even entered her office yet. "Mornings are always hectic," she said. "Some afternoons aren't much better. We probably should arrange to meet outside of the office. Since we both have to eat, why don't you meet me at Pickler's Pub around the corner at twelve thirty and we'll get started."

"Sounds good. See you then." Jeremy scurried off as if he had decisions to make and other employees to badger. She wouldn't have been surprised if he was secretly heading off to his new office to sharpen pencils. What else would he be doing his first official day on the job? But he was eager, and that was commendable.

By lunchtime, Brooke learned she had been terribly wrong about Jeremy Crockett.

As usual, she dove right into her work, selecting stories for the news show, assigning her research team to verify facts and then turning the summary thumbnails over to the writers, who would write and proof the stories and transform them into edge-of-the-seat masterpieces. In practically every department she went to, she saw Jeremy doing exactly what he'd promised to do—he was looking over shoulders and asking questions...when he could get a word in edgewise, in the busy, stressful atmosphere of a crack news team.

Shortly before Brooke was getting ready to head to the pub, Cissy burst into her office. "Go to lunch with me today," she said. "My treat."

Cissy asked Brooke to lunch two or three times a week, so the invitation wasn't unusual. But today, the enthusiasm for a club sandwich was over-the-top. Cissy was almost breathless.

"I can't," Brooke said. "I've already made arrangements."

"Break them, okay? I have to talk to you."

Cissy was nothing if not persistent. "Talk to me now," she said, glancing at her watch. "I have a few minutes."

Cissy sat in the chair by Brooke's desk. "Okay, but I doubt a few minutes is enough time."

"Cissy, take a deep breath. What's wrong? You seem upset about something."

"You remember the football guy who came to the station yesterday?"

Brooke nodded.

"Have you heard?"

"Heard what? That he's going to work here?"

"Work here?" Cissy's voice rose. "If that's all you think he's going to do, then you haven't heard the whole story. You know how we've all been wondering who will take over for Fred?"

Brooke nodded, though she hadn't been wondering at all. No matter who was chosen to take over the news desk, her work wouldn't change. At least that's what she'd thought before Milt gave her an extra duty.

"I'm glad you're sitting down, Brooke," Cissy said. "That Crockett guy is supposed to become the face of WJQC. Milt Cramer hired him to take over for Armitage. A jock!

What could he possibly know about delivering the news?"

"Well, I guess Milt has the power to do what he wants. He runs the station."

Cissy huffed. "You're taking this rather calmly." She leaned forward. "You knew about this already, didn't you?"

"I heard yesterday."

"And you didn't tell me? I had to hear from a camera operator! I thought we were friends."

Brooke wasn't sure how she would describe her relationship with Cissy, but *friend* probably wasn't at the top of the list. Yes, Cissy was close to Brooke's age of thirty-two, but somehow there seemed to be a decade of maturity between the two women. Whenever Cissy wanted to say something, she was either too excited to get the words out, or, as in the case today, too upset to take a deep breath. In Cissy's world, everything that happened was either the "best ever" or the "worst possible."

"I didn't see a reason to tell you," Brooke said. "It's Milt's place to spread the news to the staff."

"Do you realize what this means? That guy, that Jeremy, will probably do such a half-baked job that he'll ruin the station. And he'll make tons more work for the rest of us who have to cover for his mistakes. We'll probably have to keep our copy down to two-syllable words so he can pronounce them."

Brooke folded her hands on her desk. Poor Jeremy. Brooke wasn't thrilled with the prospect of teaching him but she didn't think he deserved to fail before trying. "Cissy, your comments are extremely prejudicial. Just because the guy was an athlete does not mean he isn't capable of doing other things. Besides, yesterday you trailed after him like a puppy."

"That was before I knew! You're not seeing the big picture, Brooke. Even if the guy manages to string a few sentences together, he's ruined the chances for advancement for people at this station who had hopes of taking over for Fred."

Brooke hadn't heard of anyone with such lofty dreams. "And who would that be?" she asked. "Jim would never leave the weather map. And Dirk loves doing on-location stories. He'd never want to be stuck in the building."

Cissy's breathing became erratic. "I can't

believe you haven't noticed, Brooke. I'm talking about myself…or you! One of the two of us should have gotten a crack at the opening. I mean, look at you. You're gorgeous. You should be on camera."

"Except for the fact that I don't want to be," Brooke said.

"Then I should be. I'm a seasoned professional. I know almost as much about how to deliver the news as you do. And you are the best."

Sometimes Cissy was a little overzealous with her flattery.

"That's quite a conclusion to jump to, Cissy, considering I've never delivered the news."

"You would be the best," Cissy insisted, as if Brooke hadn't spoken. "I would be great, too. I've studied diction and body language." Cissy's voice wavered, and her eyes grew misty. Brooke reached for the box of tissues on the corner of her desk.

"I wanted that job, Brooke. I've dreamed about it. I've prepared for it. It's not fair that I didn't get a chance to audition for it. If you had gotten the job, I could have been your first assistant until you retired. If I'd gotten it, you would have been my producer. We would have been a team, the best one ever." She sniffed loudly. "Now it's all ruined."

Cissy was right about one thing. Brooke had never noticed, never even suspected, that the production assistant had the unrealistic goal of becoming a news presenter. Now that she was faced with the situation, Brooke didn't know what to say. To tell Cissy that she didn't have the temperament to be on air, not to mention the experience and demeanor, would only upset her more. Brooke handed her a tissue.

"Look, Cissy, I'm sorry your dreams for taking over Fred's job aren't going to come true, but that's what they were—dreams. Even if Milt held auditions, dozens, maybe hundreds of people, would have applied. People with on-air experience and credentials. And there is nothing you or I can do about the decision he made to hire Jeremy. He wants the station to go in another direction. He wants Jeremy, with his background and recognizable face, to make waves."

"He wants a pretty-boy jock!" Cissy said.

"Yes, he does." *And I'm the one who has*

to make sure he succeeds. "And again, that's Milt's prerogative."

Cissy sat quietly for a moment while Brooke checked her watch. She was going to be late.

"There is one thing we can hope for," Cissy said.

"What's that?"

"We can hope Jeremy fails. And he will, you know. He'll stumble once too often and Milt will realize what a stupid decision he made. Then I...or you, of course, can move into that spot."

"Cissy, I'm certainly not going to wish for anyone to fail. And I'm going to assume that Jeremy won't." *I hope he doesn't or I could be out on the street...and then I'll never find Edward.*

"You want me to feel like I'm a terrible person, don't you?" Cissy said. "Like I want bad things to happen to one person so good things happen to me?"

That about summed it up. "Of course not. You aren't a terrible person, but you've got to let this go. We work for Milt Cramer. That's the way it is. If we don't like it, we can go somewhere else and find a job. But I'm going to stay right here." *I hope.*

Brooke stood and grabbed her purse. "I've really got to run. You should take a few minutes and then go out there and load that prompter with the best news we've got to offer."

Cissy gave her a look that almost made Brooke cringe. Where had Pollyanna gone all of a sudden?

STILL WEARING HER high heels, Brooke dashed from the station and rounded the corner that would take her to Pickler's. She was already fifteen minutes late, and didn't want to give WJQC's newest hire the impression that being late was acceptable. News wasn't news anymore once everyone had the story. Jeremy should learn that first and foremost.

She had only a few hundred feet to go to the antique stained-glass door to Pickler's when a boy leading a huge German shepherd approached from the opposite direction. Brooke wasn't afraid of dogs, but big, tongue-lolling ones who looked like they were trolling for kisses gave her pause. She glanced down at her beige suit and then looked at the dog's paws. "Hold on to him, kid, okay?"

Apparently the dog thought she was addressing him because he lunged at her, striking her beautiful linen lapels with his front feet. She yelped, jumped away and felt a twinge of real pain when her left foot landed in a sidewalk grate.

"Sorry, lady," the kid said. "He's real friendly. He won't hurt you."

"Won't hurt me? He just about broke my leg!"

The boy tightened his grip on the leash and sped away down the street.

Brooke yanked her heel out of the grate and took a couple of steps. The heels weren't going to work, so she slipped off the left one and tried her best to scrape leaves and who knew what else from the sole. Then, wincing with each step, she very carefully continued to the door.

She entered the pub and stopped abruptly in the doorway. "Oh, for Pete's sake!" Her jaw dropped as she viewed the scene playing out in the busy restaurant. There was Jeremy, looking all cool and collected, pen in hand, signing menus for three waitresses who surrounded his table. Brooke couldn't tell whose smile was the biggest—the ladies fawning over the celebrity star, or the star himself.

He saw her and stood immediately. "My lunch appointment just arrived," he said. "Excuse me, ladies."

He hurried to the door, saw her shoe in her hand, and paw prints on her clothes, and asked, "What happened to you?"

"Nothing," she snapped. "It's fine. I might have twisted my ankle, that's all."

"Or worse," he said. "Here, let me help you."

Before she could argue, he had her arm around his neck and he was supporting her with a strong arm circling her back and his hand on her waist. "Don't put weight on it," he said. "Let me get you to a table."

That was enough to make her feel like a first-class fool. Everyone in the bar was watching. She recognized some of the faces, but refused to respond to the implied questions.

Jeremy settled her at the table and raised her leg to an empty chair between them. "Let me get a look at it," he said.

"So now you're a doctor?"

"No, but I've seen plenty of ankle problems. It's one of the most common injuries on the football field. You can't take a chance. It might be sprained or worse."

"It's not sprained," she insisted. "I twisted it. I'll walk it off in a few minutes."

She hoped he didn't recognize her grimace for what it was—an expression of shooting pain.

"You can never be too sure. An ankle injury, left untreated, can give you problems for the rest of your life."

"I have no intention of letting this one do any such thing," she said.

He smiled. "Your intentions are to be admired, Brooke, but your ankle may not feel the same." He placed his hand on her ankle and pressed an area by the bone.

"Ouch. Don't do that."

He moved his thumb to an area close to the first one. "Does that hurt?"

She did everything she could to keep from crying out. Of course it hurt. She twisted it. "No. It's fine."

"Better or worse than the first area?"

"Better, I guess."

"Good. You have obviously sprained it, but I don't think there is a rupture. You can check with an orthopedist, but I think he'd agree with me. A few days, maybe a couple of weeks, and you'll be fine."

"Couple of weeks! I don't have a couple of weeks."

"The healing of an injury has its own schedule."

"Don't call this an injury!"

As if he hadn't heard her, he said, "Let's start the healing process right away." He stood and called over one of the waitresses. "Can you bring me some ice and a cotton cloth of some kind?"

"Sure, Jeremy."

She returned with the requested items. Jeremy draped the cloth over Brooke's ankle. "Never put an ice pack directly on the skin," he said. "Can cause frostbite, and you don't want that." He gently placed the ice over the cloth. "Leave that alone for fifteen minutes, then take it off for fifteen. You'll need an ankle brace, too."

She speared him with a stare of disbelief. "There's no way—"

"Brooke, look at your ankle. It's already turning black-and-blue, and it's starting to swell. You can't pretend this didn't happen. If you'd rather not have the first lesson, I can take you back to the station."

"Are you kidding? I'm starving. I've been thinking about a Philly cheesesteak all morning. If I have to give you a lesson in order to sink my teeth into one, I'll do it."

He smiled again. "Philly cheesesteak, eh? That does sound good. Even in Charleston, I'll bet the cook can grill up a great one. This is a sports bar, after all."

She looked around as if seeing Pickler's for the first time. "Oh, right. All the TV stations mounted to the wall. I never noticed that sporting events were on each one."

"You never noticed?"

"That's why all the waitresses were ogling you like you were handing out hundred-dollar bills." Brooke wanted to bite back the words as soon as she'd said them. She sounded petulant and childish. What did she care if the waitresses were eyeing Jeremy?

"They just recognized me from the Wild-cats roster. They're football fans. I would think they'd have to be to work here."

"Speaking of work," Brooke said. *Stop with the petty tone*, she said to herself. *You wouldn't be acting like this if your ankle didn't hurt so badly.*

"Look, I don't believe for one second that Milt hired me for my newscasting ability," Jeremy said. "I understand he wants a recognizable facc on the news, and I happened to be the one that answered the call. But you and I both know that to Milt, I'm supposed to be the answer to failing ratings. That's a lot on my shoulders, so I've got tons to learn."

Brooke adjusted the cold pack on her ankle and settled in her chair. "Then let's get started. Can you possibly persuade one of the servers to come back over here and take our order?"

"I'm sure that can be arranged."

Brooke couldn't help wondering what it must be like to deliver a slight nod in some-one's direction and have that person rush to do your bidding. Brooke didn't believe that she was "gorgeous," like Cissy proclaimed, but she wasn't hard to look at, either. She had long blond hair, bright blue eyes and admirable facial features that someone in her mysterious genealogy was responsible for. But no waiter had ever stumbled over his own two feet to answer her call.

"Two Philly cheesesteaks," Jeremy said. "With fries and iced tea." He waited for Brooke to nod her agreement, then said, "I'd like to get something straight before we begin."

SHE TOOK AN iPad from her purse and powered it on. Then she stopped and looked over at him. "What's the problem?"

"It's not a problem exactly." Except that it was to him. Since he'd met Brooke yesterday, he couldn't ignore an attitude coming from her. He wondered if Milt had somehow pushed her into helping him. "Are you okay with explaining the workings of WJQC to me?"

"Of course. Why would you ask me that question?"

"I guess you could say I've been experiencing this gut instinct, like maybe coddling me through this process isn't what you'd like to be doing. You're okay with our arrangement?"

"I just told you I was."

He released a breath he'd been holding. He had no reason other than that iffy feeling to think she wasn't telling the truth. Unfortunately, his instincts had failed him too many times. "I hope so." He smiled. "I'm pinning a lot on this job. I want to succeed. I closed on a house in Hidden Oaks about a year ago and moved my kids in with me. It could be a bit of a problem if you and I aren't on the same page and I'd have to uproot them again when Milt decides he made a mistake."

"First of all, Milt rarely admits to making a mistake," Brooke said.

"He could conclude that I'm a poor study. I guess what I'm saying is I appreciate your taking me on. I promise to be a good student."

"Great. So tell the kids to leave their suitcases in storage," she said. "How many Crock-etts are there?"

"Just myself, one daughter, one son." He swallowed. "Their mother died last…" He paused. "Anyway, I managed to secure custody, which was something of a trial since their mother and I never married. The kids lived with their grandparents while I tied up a few loose ends…like retiring from professional football." Geez, he'd made the last few months sound like a breeze, when the reality was it had been one problem after another. He hoped he was now getting better at this parenting thing.

She set down the iPad and gave him her full attention. "Your kids can't have a football player for a father?"

"They could, I suppose, but I don't want them to. Like Milt told you yesterday, my position has been wide receiver on the Carolina Wildcats football team." He paused again, watching for some sign of recognition in her eyes. "I'm guessing you don't know what that position is?"

"We've established that I don't know much about football," she said. "A wide receiver catches the ball when the quarterback throws it, right?"

"He's supposed to, yeah. But while injuries are a possibility for every guy on the field, the wide receiver seems to get more hits than anyone else. He's usually standing in an open field waiting for the ball with about three heavy guys from the other side itching to take him down—by any means necessary."

"So have you ever been seriously injured?"

He chuckled. No one had ever asked him that before. Wildcats fans already knew, and everyone else with any knowledge of the game just assumed. "Two broken ribs, a broken ankle and multiple dislocated shoulders. Nothing too serious, thank goodness."

"So you're afraid of more injuries now that you have your children?" she asked.

He almost resented the question. Afraid? He wasn't comfortable with that word describing himself. But she asked it so guilelessly that he answered with total honesty. "Afraid for myself? No. A football player learns quickly that cowardice doesn't work. Afraid for my kids to be without a father while he's recuperating? Yeah, that's my fear. That's not fair to them. Besides, I'm thirty-four. Didn't start my pro career until I was twenty-four because I was finishing my master's degree. I've started to notice my joints beginning to give out. All in all, it's time to do something else."

Her eyes widened. "A master's degree?"

He nodded.

"What in?"

"Business management."

"Oh."

She seemed surprised and almost disappointed. What did she think? Milt Cramer had hired a flunk-out to fill this position? There was a lot about this industry he didn't know, like firsthand experience, but there was some he did.

"So…" He got out his phone, which contained the notes he'd been taking this morning and the initial questions he wanted to ask her. "Since we've gotten the uncomfortable stuff out of the way, let's hit the books."

She placed long, graceful fingers over the iPad. For a moment, he was fascinated by those hands. Still, he couldn't help noticing the wince when she adjusted her position on her chair.

"You okay?"

"Sure. Why don't you ask your first question."

FOR BROOKE, FORTY-FIVE minutes passed quickly. She had expected her patience to be tested with every question. She had planned to tolerate Jeremy Crockett as best she could. But she ended up finding him smart, quick to learn and, perhaps best of all, extremely congenial. Maybe he was used to charming everyone he met, but she couldn't deny that he had charmed her a bit, as well. She resented the heck out of the deal she'd had to make to educate him. She didn't want to like him. But the reality of him increasing her workload seemed to fade in the light of his enthusiasm to pick her brain.

"We probably should get back to work," he said. "That's enough for today. I don't want to take advantage of you, and you need to rest that ankle."

The ankle again. She'd almost forgotten about it. But Jeremy hadn't. He'd checked his watch often and removed and replaced the ice pack. "You've seen the hectic nature of the newsroom," she said. "Resting an ankle is on the list of low priorities. Besides, it's much better now."

She tried to stand, sucked in a deep breath and realized that walking back to the station wouldn't be easy.

"We'll get you back," Jeremy said. "You can

hang on to me, and I'll support your weight. Do we pass a drugstore on the way? You need that ankle brace."

"No, we don't, but I have an Ace bandage at home. That should do the trick."

"It will help. Let me take your bag. You don't need to be carrying extra weight."

Thankfully, Pickler's had cleared out and only a few late diners would see her hobbling out the door. And hobble she did. She wouldn't have made it back to WJQC without Jeremy's help. He was amazingly solid and strong, supporting her every step until she hardly put any pressure on the ankle. When he deposited her at her desk, she thanked him for helping her.

"My pleasure," he said. "I can help you with exercises to speed the recovery of that ankle when you're ready. Like I said, I've seen a lot of ankle injuries."

"I'm sure it will be better by tomorrow," she said. "It's Saturday and I won't be running around the newsroom."

"Speaking of tomorrow, would you have time to meet with me again? I don't imagine we'll have much success working in the building, so I was thinking we could find a quieter place. Would you mind if I came to your place for an hour or so?"

She thought for a moment. His suggestion seemed like a big step away from a business relationship, but she couldn't argue with his logic. They would accomplish much more in her condo.

"Sure." She gave her address to him. "If you need directions..."

"I'll find it. How about one o'clock? Can I bring lunch?"

"You treated today. I think I can whip up a salad if that's okay."

"Perfect."

"Fine. See you then."

"Stay off that ankle. No dance clubs for you tonight."

If he only knew. She'd given up the club scene since she'd been paying Gabe. Now she frequented the free venues in Charleston, like the art gallery and historical museum. She'd discovered there was much to admire about these places.

She wanted to resent Jeremy and the intrusion and threat he'd brought into her life. But so far he just seemed like a decent guy, although he was in way over his head with this new position and depending on her to ensure his success. She was well aware that neither of them could fail at this mission. Jeremy had risked everything by quitting football and pursuing this new line of work with his kids dependent upon him. And Brooke could flat-out lose her job.

She hoped he'd learned a lot while getting that master's degree. Maybe he had. It didn't hurt to know the basics of business, even in a television studio. She'd gone pretty far with just a bachelor's degree in English. But she didn't have a couple of kids to raise.

Not counting his education and charm, Jeremy was still a jock—good at knocking obstacles out of his way and focusing on a ball flying through the air, but maybe not skilled in handling people and getting them to do what he wanted. Would he crack under the pressure of deadlines and technical glitches? Despite his fame, would he fail to relate to an audience hungry for intelligent, concise news delivered by a professional? And would Milt blame her if he did? Probably so.

Brooke loved WJQC. She'd threatened Milt

with finding another job, but the truth was, she couldn't imagine starting over somewhere else after a decade. If turning Jeremy Crockett into the best anchorman in the country would guarantee her job security, then that's what she would do. As she scanned the messages on her desk, she mentally bid farewell to her weekends.

Maybe she'd made a pact with the devil, but Jeremy wasn't the devil. Milt was, and he was willing to take advantage of both of them.

CHAPTER FOUR

JEREMY ARRIVED AT Brooke's condo the next day precisely when he said he would, at one o'clock in the afternoon. Despite the ongoing pain in her ankle, Brooke had showered, dressed herself in a T-shirt and matching sweats and styled her hair into a careless top-knot she liked but would definitely not have pleased her mother. Linda had called her this morning. Brooke told her about the celebrity who'd been hired at WJQC and Linda immediately went to tell her husband.

"Craig is beside himself, honey," Linda had said. "He wants you to invite this Mr. Crockett to the house. Can you do that? Daddy would be so pleased."

Okay, so Jeremy Crockett was a big deal, but Brooke refused to primp for him today. She simply wanted him to take her seriously, as seriously as she took herself. She needed him to listen to her every word. A few minutes before he was due to arrive she went to her small kitchen and prepared a salad and iced tea.

"Nice neighborhood," he said when he entered her condominium, which was furnished with Federal antiques.

His smile was warm and genuine. She wondered if he knew anything about antiques.

"The Battery is only a few blocks away," he said.

"I like it," she said. "The Battery is actually six blocks—a good brisk walk." She paused, realizing that her ankle would have to heal before she took that walk again. "This condo is small but enough space for me and my shoes." She loved the city's beautiful historic district, and many people felt that the neighborhood surrounding the iconic Battery, which dated back to the Civil War, was Charleston's finest area.

She noticed Jeremy's careful appraisal of her treasured belongings—her lady's desk, mahogany chairs and comfy floral-print sofa. Including the heavy damask drapes, Brooke had chosen everything for the condominium to fit in with the historical ambience. She loved the classic style and coziness of her apartment.

"Have a seat on the sofa," she said.

"I was hoping you'd say that. I can't see myself on any of the other delicate chairs in this room."

She smiled. While he'd been looking at her furniture, she'd been looking at him. He wore jeans and a solid blue oxford shirt, perfect for a late-spring Charleston day. Something pleasant and piney drifted toward her, a subtle, woodsy aftershave.

Jeremy set his tablet on an end table and took a seat at the end of the sofa. She hobbled to the other end and sat. His eyes narrowed as they stayed fixed on her. "How's the ankle today?"

"Better than yesterday, I would say. But I don't have any marathons in my future for a while."

He smiled. "Mind if I take a look?"

As if he hadn't examined her ankle enough the day before. But she pulled up the elastic cuff of her sweatpants to show him the damage. He lifted her leg and settled the ankle on his knee. Then he gingerly and very gently rubbed the bruised flesh.

"It is a bit better," he said. "The swelling is down. You've been icing it."

"Yes, doctor," she teased. "Following orders."

"That makes a difference. You should have full use of it in a week. Before I leave, I'll show you the most preliminary exercises to regain strength."

"I'd appreciate that," she said and lowered her leg to the floor. "Shall we get started? As promised, I made a salad. I left it on the counter in the kitchen and, honestly, it would be easier if you went and picked up the bowls yourself."

"Sure." He stood and entered the kitchen.

"There's a tray next to the backsplash," she said. "And tea in the fridge."

She heard the refrigerator door open. "Sweet or unsweet?" he asked.

"Unsweet, thanks."

He returned, set the tray on the coffee table and the drinks on coasters.

"It must have been an inconvenience for you to come here on a Saturday," she said. "Your children aren't in school."

"Believe me, they'll make me pay for abandoning them when I get home. I promised them a movie and ice cream. Right now my housekeeper is staying with them."

"Must be nice to have help," Brooke said.

"Finding Marta has made this whole transition a lot easier for me. She agreed to live in and has done more than just keep the house in order and watch the kids. She knows all about hanging pictures and buying the right colored towels. I could probably live with magazine photos on the walls and burlap in the bathroom."

Brooke laughed. She found his appreciation of his housekeeper a nice aspect of his personality. "Where do you want to start today?" she asked him. "This is officially day one of newsroom training, since I sort of spoiled yesterday's session by tripping over my own feet."

"You're the expert," he said. "I'll follow your lead."

"Okay. I think we should start by acquainting you with the city of Charleston."

He nodded, then took a bite of salad. "This is good."

"Glad you like it. Now...basically a good newsperson is always aware of the demographics of the city he broadcasts to. What do you know about Charleston?"

He swallowed, drank some tea and thought a moment. He was taking a while to answer, prompting her to think he didn't know much. She hadn't intended to embarrass him, but he was going to have to be an expert on the city she loved.

He cleared his throat and rattled off many up-to-date statistics about the city and its population.

Pretty good. He'd done some research. "How does all that affect a news broadcast?"

He settled back against the sofa, crossed his legs and finally looked relaxed. "You take New York or Los Angeles, for instance," he began. "For Charlestonians, greater emphasis should probably be placed on state and local stories."

He was absolutely right. WJQC had always tried to fill their five o'clock reporting with stories that would interest folks from South Carolina, leaving a skirmish in the Ukraine to the eleven o'clock news team.

When Brooke challenged Jeremy about the significance of these various details and their relevance to reporting, he had ready answers.

"You've done your homework," she told him.

"I try to. Through the last years, though,

my homework has been memorizing passing plays for the Wildcats. This is, excuse the cliché, a very different ball game."

They went on to discuss the city's neighborhoods, political leanings, school districts and more. When Brooke next looked at her clock, the salad bowl was empty and an hour and a half had passed. If she'd thought that Jeremy Crockett was going to prove himself to be a dumb jock, she was wrong.

After another hour, Brooke sighed at a natural break in their conversation. "That's probably enough for today," she said.

"It's almost four o'clock," he said. "Hope I haven't tired you out." He tapped his tablet on his knee. "I've got a lot of good notes here."

"You did great," she said. "I'm really impressed."

"Maybe you should hold that praise until after another session, but I'm glad you think that." He stood and looked down at her. "I am serious about helping you rehab that ankle," he said. "I'd be glad to give you some pointers that have proven to work."

Her face flushed warm. "I appreciate that," she said. "But if I have to, I could hire a physical therapist, and, well…" She didn't know how to finish the sentence without sounding like a prude…or worse, like someone who might actually enjoy his help.

"It's okay," he said, letting her off the hook. "Keep it in mind. I've helped lots of guys with rehab in the past, guys with injuries similar to yours."

Lots of *guys*. No, this would never work. She couldn't possibly let Jeremy get close to her. He'd already surprised her with his knowledge and enthusiasm for the city. She already liked him, and that wasn't part of her plan. She just wanted to make him camera-ready, earn her bonus, maintain her job and get back to looking for Edward. If she liked Jeremy too much, her emotions might throw her off her goal, and that couldn't happen.

"I suppose we'll have to see how Monday plays out," she said. "Maybe we can get in an hour or so then."

"I'd like to get into the technical stuff, like camera operation."

She smiled, finding it easy to do. "Oh, you will. That's always fun."

She followed him to the door, where he

stopped and placed his large hand on her shoulder. "Is there anything I can do for you before I leave? Get you a drink or a blanket?"

"I don't need a thing." Why did he have to be so darn nice?

He left her condo, and without thinking, she raised her own hand to her shoulder, feeling the warmth of where his hand had been on her T-shirt. Just one day ago, she had gone to work resenting everything about Jeremy Crockett and the time he would take away from what she really cared about. But today, after one foot massage, and learning more about the man he truly was...well, she didn't resent him quite so much.

AS JEREMY WALKED to his car parked along Queen Street by Brooke's condominium, Lynette's words echoed in his mind. *I don't need your help, Jeremy. I have my own money. I'm self-sufficient. That doesn't mean I don't love you and the children we've created, but I don't want to marry you.*

Those words pounded in his memory and ached in his heart. His most earnest proposals to Lynette had been after the births of their two children. Aside from pledging his devotion to her, he'd tried to convince her that they needed to be a family—unified parents to their two children. Sure, he could provide for them married or not, but he wanted more. He wanted Lynette's respect, enough that she would want to make it official between them. Enough that his kids would look up to him and ask his advice every day, not just once in a while. He supposed he was trying to make up for the lousy job his own father had done— nevertheless, being a strong, capable family man was important to him in every sense.

Both times he'd poured out his heart to her, Lynette had smiled and kissed him and explained that she wanted the best for their kids, as well. But that didn't mean she had to be married to their father. They could be in love and remain faithful to each other without a license.

True. But still, Jeremy had a deep-rooted desire to take care of everything and everyone. He'd transferred that desire to other players on the football team. He'd even tried to take care of Brooke and make her ankle better. He wanted to take care of his kids so they didn't want for anything. He wanted them to be happy and well-adjusted, especially about the tragedy in their lives. At this point, he feared he might be failing. Meanwhile, Lynette had resisted every attempt he made to do what he believed was the right thing. Some men were takers. Some were givers. He definitely wanted to be one of the latter group.

Jeremy opened his car door and settled into the driver's seat. He stared out the windshield at a picture-perfect spring afternoon. "What is wrong with you, Crockett?" he said aloud.

How else was he to explain an almost overwhelming urge to help Brooke Montgomery? She had a sprained ankle, that's all, but he knew how to make her better. He was the team player all the other guys came to for encouragement and advice, even after they'd seen the qualified team doctors. He'd helped them. But Brooke didn't seem to want him to do anything like that for her.

"Don't do this, Jeremy," he said as he started the car. "Don't think that every wounded creature needs your help. Some people get along just fine without the supposed Crockett magic touch. You've made a new start with a new job in a new town in a new house with two people who definitely do need you. Your kids. They need you for shelter and food, help with their homework and love. That should be enough." He pulled away from the curb, but he couldn't deny an overwhelming urge that it would have been nice if Brooke had needed him just a little.

"Forget stray cats and wounded birds," he said, recalling his childhood instincts to help every creature that mewed or couldn't fly. "For a guy who played hard and gave as good as he got on the football field, you can be quite a sap in real life."

But he couldn't rationalize Brooke in his mind. She was giving up her time and her knowledge to help him succeed. He was supposed to believe that she was just that self-sacrificing a team player. She had no ulterior motive, and for that he was grateful. But Jeremy wasn't the kind of guy to take without giving back. And he usually wasn't satisfied until he'd given back more than one hundred percent.

CHAPTER FIVE

BROOKE AND JEREMY had another good session for an hour on Monday. Tuesday was nonstop because WJQC and every other station was waiting for breaking news from the White House. Writers were waiting anxiously and fact checkers were kept on hold. When Brooke got the latest news on the air by five, she breathed a sigh of relief.

On Wednesday, she and Jeremy settled down in the break room to discuss media law. Jeremy already knew some of the more exacting details of what is allowed on air and what can get a news station in a heap of trouble. He explained that when he'd first heard from Milt Cramer, he'd done a bit of cramming about television news. So he wasn't completely ignorant about what Brooke wanted him to know. His eagerness to learn reminded Brooke of her own efforts when she started at the station.

His positive attitude was just one facet of Jeremy Crockett. He was smart, adaptable and had more common sense than almost everyone she knew. But she still couldn't shake the feeling that he wouldn't make it in this business. And that feeling scared her half to death. Was he not worried if he failed? He probably had enough money saved from his playing days to exist for years. If Milt carried through with his threat, Brooke couldn't stay afloat for two months. If Jeremy had a flaw, it was that he didn't realize what a tough business this was.

He continued to ask her about her ankle, which was improving every day. "I'm almost to the point that I can wear something more stylish to work than a bedroom slipper," she said to him.

"Just don't push it," he said. "Besides, that's a great-looking slipper."

Sometimes Brooke just wanted to forget the lessons and sit back with Jeremy and talk about anything else. But she didn't let her thoughts stray very often. She was going to have to push him pretty hard or Milt would put them both out on the street. Jeremy with a contract that had been bought out, and Brooke with a paltry severance package.

So Brooke kept coaxing him back on track. At the same time she encouraged his efforts, he seemed determined to encourage her. "You really know this stuff, Brooke," he said. "I'm so thankful you agreed to help me."

She kept a smile plastered on her face and bit back the truth. Ha! Agreed? Not hardly. Self-preservation was more like it. "You're welcome. Now let's get back to learning about these libel cases."

WHEN BROOKE ARRIVED home on Wednesday, she had a message from Gabe on her landline. She hoped he wasn't asking for more money. She'd just managed to put six hundred dollars into his checking account, and at this point she wanted to see results.

She dialed his number. "Gabe, it's Brooke. Any news?"

"Nothing definite. I'm checking some things out tomorrow and Friday. And just maybe I've got a good lead. I've uncovered a file about a kid who seems to be Edward's age. He has a rap sheet as long as my arm, and the funny thing is, his name is listed differently for almost every crime."

"That's strange. How can you be certain of who he really is?"

"I can't. That's the problem. But his name changes are not the weirdest thing. I found a couple of pictures, too, mostly mug shots. In one, he's got coal-black hair. In another he's a bleached blond. Seems this kid was a master at deception…and obtaining false IDs."

If Gabe was describing her half brother, Brooke was definitely not impressed with the life he'd led as a teenager, but she reminded herself that Edward had grown up not wanted by his mother and, probably, the foster system. "Okay, and what do you think? Is it worth pursuing? How are we going to find him?"

"His juvenile record trail grew cold when he would have turned about sixteen," Gabe said. "The last known reference to him was in a record of him appearing before a judge in juvie court. He was accused of stealing a car and was sentenced to six months in detention. His name was listed as Jerry Miller with about a half-dozen aliases attached. Can't find anything after that."

"So what makes you suspect this guy is my half brother?"

"Instinct, I guess," Gabe admitted. "Plus a few clues are there. He's the right age. His crimes occurred mostly in South Carolina, and the judge who tried him was a Carolina judge."

Not much to go on, but maybe more than Gabe had presented in the past. For some reason, she thought she should trust the investigator's instincts.

"Do you think he suddenly became a law-abiding citizen?" Brooke asked.

"Ha! I sincerely doubt it. Kids with that long a record usually don't turn honorable citizen over night. He probably spent more than six months in juvie for misbehaving, got out eventually and upped his crime game. My guess is he spent a few good years in prison under one of his assumed names. Or he made up a new one."

"You don't make this guy sound like a brother I should look forward to meeting."

"Yeah, I know, but it's your call. It's a decent lead, but if this man turns out to be Edward, you may not want to know him."

Brooke seriously doubted that conclusion. Even if Edward needed help, wasn't she willing to step in and do that? And what if he was a good citizen, having corrected his bad behavior? Then all her work and money would have been worth it. Either way, he was her brother.

"What is your plan to find him?" Brooke figured whatever the plan was, it would cost her more money, so she would listen intently to his response.

"I'm going to try to track down the judge that sentenced him in juvenile court. That was nearly twenty years ago. The judge could be anywhere. He could be dead."

Brooke sighed. "And if you do find someone who could have been this judge on this particular date, what are the chances he'd remember a car thief from almost two decades ago?"

"Depends on how many car thieves he's tried in his career. But you're right. His memory could be foggy by now."

The chances weren't good, either for Gabe finding this boy from twenty years ago, or of her taking on the task of rehabilitating a possible hardened criminal in her life if he really was Edward. Brooke accepted that fact, just like she'd had to bolster her spirits with almost every conversation she'd had with Gabe. He always told her that any decision was "her call," and she always convinced herself that this time might produce the results she dreamed of.

"Do you want me to try to locate the judge?" Gabe asked her. "It might turn out to be another wild-goose chase, but you never know. If I find the guy, who will be thirty-five by now, I'll want to interview him face-to-face, so travel time and expenses will be involved."

Of course. No surprise there. "How much?"

"Fifteen hundred ought to cover it. That's a bargain price, Brooke, because I'll be working on other cases at the same time. If I had to charge you for continuous duty, I'd have to have more than fifteen hundred."

That was a higher amount than she'd ever given Gabe at one time. She could possibly check her bank balance and scrape together some of that amount, but it would make a serious dent in her savings. And what if Milt decided to let her go if she failed with Jeremy? She would definitely regret giving that money to Gabe.

But this lead was all Gabe had, and Brooke just couldn't let it go. Maybe this time...

"Okay. I can get the money, but Gabe, if this doesn't work out, I'll have to rethink the whole search. My sister's been telling me for months that I'm wasting my time and money. Maybe she's right."

"Maybe she is, but this is your thing, not hers, and finding this guy seems to be awfully important to you. My advice is you do what's best for you."

She had to trust someone, and Brooke truly did trust Gabe. He'd always been straight with her, and his fees were in line with research she had done on the cost of hiring a PI. Yes, she trusted him, but she couldn't go on financing this investigation forever. Not now when she wasn't even sure what her income would be.

"I don't want to know each little trip you make or conversation you have," she said. "Just call me when you have something positive to share."

"That's the way you want it?"

"Yes." For the last few months, all Brooke

had gotten from Gabe were failure reports. He was doing his job and keeping her updated, but she didn't want to know every time he hit a loose end. Hope was all she had.

"Good luck, Gabe. I'll talk to you when you know something."

Brooke hung up the phone and went to look out her window. "Oh, Edward, where are you?" She resisted the urge to cry. *In prison? We haven't found a match. Are you even alive? We haven't found a death record. Do you even have a memory of your mother having twin babies? And if I do find you, will you turn me away?*

Brooke considered that Camryn was right. Her need to find Edward had turned into an obsession. It had started innocently enough with Brooke's desire to find their real mother, who had rejected them the day they'd located her. And then she'd learned of a brother, and her need to belong, to have true family roots, had taken off and become more and more important to her with each day. The last few months of searching for Edward had seemed like years. The toll on her bank account and her self-confidence was growing steadily.

"I have to stop doing this," she said with firm conviction. "One more try, my brother, and then, unless a miracle happens, I have to stop. But can I? Can I let go of this desire to have you in my life?"

FRIDAY MORNING PROVED to be a relatively light news day. Brooke had made arrangements to meet with Jeremy in the break room for lunch and they'd agreed to have Chinese food delivered. She was looking forward to the appointment, telling herself she couldn't let Jeremy's enthusiasm for WJQC fade. Her willingness to meet with him had nothing to do with the comfort level they had established between them, or the fact that she was just beginning to see qualities in him that she hadn't expected to see.

Brooke was checking her messages midmorning when Cissy opened her office door and popped her head in. Usually staff members knocked when Brooke had her door closed. Cissy did not believe such consideration existed for her. After all, she was "practically Brooke's personal assistant." Brooke waved her in. Maybe some good office gossip would prove interesting today. Cissy always had the latest news.

"Hey, Ciss, what's up?" Brooke said.

"Hi, girlfriend." Cissy's voice had the same familiar singsong quality Brooke had come to associate with her. "Just seeing if you need me to do anything for you. I've finished my proofreading and have a little extra time."

Before Brooke could tell her that she didn't need a thing right now, Cissy changed the subject. "How's your ankle? I see you are walking better."

"Thanks to Jeremy," she said. "He suggested some mild exercises, and I've been doing them off and on every day."

"I guess you like him, right? He has a way of getting into everyone's good graces around here. All I hear are comments about football from the guys and comments about Jeremy's looks from the women."

Brooke smiled. "I agree that the staff seem to like him. Don't you, Cissy?"

"Besides the fact that he took the anchor's job from the rest of us?"

Brooke held her temper. "Cissy, we talked about this."

"I know. But as far as liking Jeremy, I thought I would, but now, not so much."

"Why not? Has Jeremy done anything to upset you?"

"Not that I can talk about," Cissy said.

What did that mean? Brooke wondered. Had Jeremy made an unwanted pass at Cissy? If so, that was a matter for the human resources department. Brooke hoped her first conclusion wasn't true, but why would Cissy's complaint about Jeremy be kept a secret?

"I don't understand what the problem is, Cissy. You were quite taken with Jeremy when you first met him." Brooke hadn't told anyone at WJQC that her own future was wrapped so tightly with Jeremy's. As far as everyone knew, her efforts to help him were just Brooke being the team player Milt wanted her to be.

"I was impressed with him," Cissy said. "He looks like his Carolina Wildcats roster pictures. And that ain't bad. Broad shoulders, narrow hips, a strong face and that thick, light brown hair. But you know the type, Brooke. He's used to the ladies chasing him. Never been married. He's a hot property, and he knows it."

Brooke had never seen a photo of the Wild-cats roster, but she could agree that Jeremy would have taken a good picture. Maybe Cissy's problem with Jeremy was that he *hadn't* made a pass at her. Brooke had never seen him strut his hotness around the office. Sometimes Cissy had good instincts, so Brooke decided to pursue this attitude of hers. "How is he getting along with every-body here workwise?" she asked. "I'm ask-ing about reactions that have nothing to do with football or looks."

"Okay, I guess. At first everyone thought he was this athletic god or something. Now we all realize he's learning his job just like every-one else. He'll never replace you if that's what you're thinking," Cissy said.

"I wasn't thinking that. Jeremy doesn't want to be a producer. He was hired to take over for Fred in a few weeks. Milt just thought he should know as much about the station and the news business as possible."

"He's lucky he's had you to help him," Cissy said. She took a seat in front of Brooke's desk and sighed. "Can I be honest with you, Brooke?"

That was a leading question. "Of course you can. I would hope that you always would be."

Cissy took a long breath. "You and I don't have any secrets, right, Brooke?"

Brooke didn't like to lie outright, so she just waited for Cissy to say more.

"You know that I want Fred Armitage's job. I told you that. And if not me, then you should have it. Bottom line, one of us long-standing, loyal employees should get a crack at that position."

"That's not the direction Milt is going," Brooke explained. "But take your crack. Tell Milt you'd like an audition. As for me, I don't want the job."

"Without your support, I would never get a shot," Cissy said. "If you were behind me, if you talked me up, Milt might take me more seriously."

"Milt has made up his mind, Ciss. But you never know. The only thing I can say is that if you want to approach Milt about the anchor job, go ahead." Brooke knew what he would say, but it wasn't her place to completely squash Cissy's dreams.

"Oh, I don't know. I really thought you would go after that job. You have all the qualifications. Looks, intelligence, confidence. And you've been here over ten years." Cissy leaned over Brooke's desk. "Tell me the truth. Aren't you just a little upset that Milt completely passed you over for this plum position? Deep down, don't you think he should have asked you if you wanted the job?"

Truly, Brooke hadn't been upset. Now that Cissy mentioned it, however, a small niggle of doubt suddenly crept into her mind. Why hadn't Milt offered her the job, or at least an opportunity to compete for it? Why hadn't he at least looked for a replacement among his staff? "No, I'm not upset," she said, without her usual conviction. "I'm happy on my side of the camera. Let someone else be in the spotlight."

"But you'd be great," Cissy said. "Certainly better than a washed-up sports guy. You'd have a classy, polished delivery. Haven't you ever thought about it?"

In all honesty, no one could stand in a control room for ten years without at least imagining what it would be like to be on the other side. There had been times when Fred had messed up or blown a line and Brooke had told herself that she could have done it so much better. She believed, and still did, that a celebrity spotlight, even for a news anchor, was tempting stuff. Before she considered the consequences of her answer, she said, "Well, I suppose a time or two..."

"You have! Oh, my God, Brooke, you'd be amazing!"

Oh, no—Brooke had punched a hole in a dam of enthusiasm that might never be contained. "Calm down, Cissy. That's never going to happen."

"Okay, I get it. You don't want to ruin Jeremy's chances since you're helping him. But that doesn't mean I shouldn't want the job." She paused, twisted her hands in her lap. "I'm going to do it, Brooke. I'm going to ask Milt if I could audition. Goodness knows I can use a thirty-thousand bump in my yearly salary. Me as the anchor and you as my producer! Just imagine it, Brooke."

"Do what you think is best, Cissy, but maybe you should let Milt's plan to hire Jeremy play out. I suppose it's okay to think of what you might say to Milt if he changes his mind about Jeremy, but right now approaching him could be employment suicide."

Cissy smiled. Not a sweet, appreciative smile, but a slightly devious, conniving one. "You're right, Brooke. Bide my time. This jock will prove himself soon enough. He'll stumble and fall, and Milt will realize what a stupid idea he had to hire someone with no experience and no news savvy."

"Actually," Brooke said, "Jeremy's a fast..." She never finished her sentence.

Cissy stood. "I'm so glad I talked to you, Brooke. I knew you'd have excellent advice for me."

"Cissy, I'm just talking common sense now. I'm not advising you to do anything. In fact—"

"Sure, I get it." Cissy headed for the door. "Don't worry, I won't tell anyone my feelings. But you and I—" she pointed at Brooke and then pointed at herself, as if they'd created a conspiracy "—we know what a dynamite combination we'd be. And what having a female anchor would do for ratings."

Brooke could only hope that Cissy would

give up her dream. Maybe she would come to appreciate Jeremy's abilities as he became more and more competent. There was no way Milt would put Cissy on camera, and despite Cissy's claims that the two of them would make this great team, Brooke did not want Cissy at the anchor desk. She had to see Jeremy succeed or that dwindling bank balance of hers would only get worse. It might go from black to red.

TYPICAL OF ALMOST any news day, Friday ended up a bit crazy. A fire near the waterfront had crews out with live reports and video. A man threatening to jump from a high-rise building put everyone's nerves on edge. Brooke canceled the meeting for the break room and ended up buying a sandwich from the deli on the first floor. She had been looking forward to Chinese and, well, she had been looking forward to seeing Jeremy. Always in her mind was the fact that he held the key to her future success at WJQC, but there was no denying that other reasons for her interest in him kept growing almost daily.

So at six o'clock, when he suggested he

could pick up a pizza and come over to her place, she readily agreed. Wow, what had happened to the girl who was never home on Friday nights? She knew, of course. Her determination to find Edward and now this added tension of possibly losing her job had changed her. And at the same time, seemed to have affected her telephone, which almost never rang with invitations anymore.

She would get back on track. She could pick up her life where she'd left it. But right now her life was all about two men. Edward and Jeremy. She might never find one, and she might discover that in the eyes of the other, she was no more than a stepping stone to his success. Unfortunately, the possibility of that happening didn't do much to brighten her days. Anyway, pizza sounded good, and when she got home she opened a bottle of wine to let it breathe.

CHAPTER SIX

JEREMY FELT LIKE he'd stepped back in time
whenever he walked Queen Street in Charleston. A few newer mini mansions had been
constructed in the historic district, but most
homes were original Civil War–era masterpieces. He marveled at the old brick facades,
wrought-iron gates, wooden shutters and well-
worn stone steps to welcoming front doors.
Mounting blocks still existed on some proper-
ties, a reminder of gentler times, when ladies
needed a boost to get into a waiting carriage.

This street suited Brooke Montgomery, he
decided. Oh, she was modern and upscale, but
deep inside he sensed a reserve, a soft mint-
julep demeanor and grace that would have
served her well had she lived almost two cen-
turies before. The furnishings in her condo
were evidence that she appreciated quality
old pieces and delicate lace and china. Jeremy couldn't tell a goblet from a jelly jar, but

he admired Brooke for choosing to live among charming and fine antiquities.

As he climbed the narrow, carpeted staircase to the third floor of the Italianate revival building Brooke called home, he experienced the same pleasing tension he'd come to expect when he was to see her. It had been a long time since a woman other than Lynette had sparked his interest. He and Lynette had been together a long time. In fact, he'd spent only one year of his pro-football career basking in the flattery of women who appreciated his football prowess and didn't mind telling him so at every opportunity. Memories of that old life left him feeling grateful for the attention, while at the same time convinced him that he was never meant to be a *player* in terms of romance and relationships.

He'd dated all kinds of women, from glamorous to girl-next-door types, but none of them had made his heart stop, his hands sweat, his knees wobble. Not one until he'd met Lynette in Colorado at a championship party. After that he'd been a one-woman man. And she'd been good to him, ignoring, for the sake of their relationship, all those publicity photos that often made him look like the focus of many beautiful ladies. The only thing Lynette hadn't done for him was marry him.

But she had given him two children, and he was determined to make Cody and Alicia the center of his life now. And if everything went well, starting tonight, maybe he could see himself dating again. He stopped outside Brooke's door, held the pizza box in one hand and struck the brass knocker. He smiled. Yes, maybe he could see himself dating again.

She opened the door and stepped aside to let him enter. "Hi, Jeremy."

His hands didn't exactly sweat, but he thought maybe his knees wobbled a bit. She looked amazing in denim leggings and a soft, thin T-shirt that showed off some terrific curves.

"I don't see the ankle support," he said.

"It needed a break from my complaining, so I gave it some closet time. Actually, I don't think I need it anymore."

She offered him a seat on the sofa. "I have a bottle of wine open. I sometimes have a glass to unwind at night. Can I pour one for you?"

"Sure, I'll have one. Thanks."

She walked into the kitchen, leaving him alone in the living room. He didn't want to sit, as she'd suggested, so he wandered around, looking at a coffee table with carved legs ending in brass animal feet, a large china cabinet filled with treasures and a small writing desk. Her computer was open on the desk, and he couldn't help looking at the screen.

The space was occupied by a simple spreadsheet that appeared to be accounting of some sort. Bank accounts, credit statements, other details that should have been private. One figure drew his attention immediately. It was her bank balance, and he noticed it was alarmingly low.

"You should be more careful," he muttered to himself. "Anyone could come in here and get your bank numbers."

"What did you say?" she called from the kitchen.

"Nothing." He didn't want her to think he'd been prying, though perhaps he had, but he certainly wasn't going to copy down her banking information. He moved to a window and looked at the street below. But he'd seen more than he wanted to. What was going on with her? Anyone who could afford this condo must have a reserve. But what if she didn't? He'd known lots of guys in the sporting field who'd made millions and blown it all within a few years. Not that Brooke would be that careless, but what if she'd had a rough time lately? He shook his head and tried to forget the bank figure he'd seen. It wasn't his business to question her financial stability.

She came into the living room carrying two glasses of red wine. Before coming to him, she stopped next to her desk, set down one glass and immediately slammed the computer cover closed. Her face colored. She cleared her throat. "So what kind of pizza did you bring?"

"Mushroom and pepperoni," he said. "But it occurred to me as I was driving over here that I should be taking you out to dinner for all you're doing for me."

"You brought dinner. That counts. Besides, this is all part of my job these days," she said.

He chuckled, though he would much rather be looking at her over an intimate table for two at a fancy Italian restaurant and not hearing her calling him "her job."

"I think you qualify for the sympathy medal," he said. "If not a badge of courage. Taking an ex-jock under your wing has its challenges."

"You're doing great," she said. "Thankfully you catch on quickly for an ex-jock." They both sat on the sofa and she took a sip of her wine. "I'd planned to talk about time structure in the five o'clock news. You need to learn to prioritize content, be ready in case there's breaking news, which there almost always is."

He would much rather prioritize the next two hours, but she was obviously all business. "Lead on," he said.

Two hours passed quickly. Jeremy found himself laughing at Brooke's stories of newsroom catastrophes. He listened intently when she stressed certain points as being important. He liked her voice. It was both lilting and commanding, and he could picture her in the production room handing out orders and keeping a strict schedule while having her crew eating out of her hand.

She seemed born to operate a newsroom, and he couldn't wait until she was giving him directions from the control booth. Having her voice come through his earpiece would inspire confidence, even more so if he knew he would be seeing her after signing off.

They finished with the two-hour lesson, only Jeremy wasn't in any hurry to leave. He couldn't help wondering what Brooke thought of him. Here he was considering dating for the first time in many years, and he didn't know if she thought of him as more than an obligation. He wanted to reach over and touch her, breathe in her subtle scent. What if he put his arm around her? Would she jerk away or would she settle her head on his shoulder as he hoped? Jeremy had faced three-hundred-pound tacklers with more confidence than he faced this woman.

Marta was watching his kids tonight, but they would be anxiously waiting for him to get home. He'd still have time for a bit of TV and a snack with them. "I've got to get going," he said, putting aside his personal feelings for Brooke. "Not that I want to." *No, I don't want to. I want to stay here with you, but how do I know if you want the same?* "I feel like we've covered a lot of ground tonight. But I have two kids…"

"I understand," she said. "Besides, it's a Friday night. Who wants to spend it learning about time management in the news industry? I really crammed a lot into your head tonight," she continued. "Hope it wasn't too much."

If she only knew that his head was crammed with much more than she realized. "I can handle it," he said. "Look at the raw material you have to work with—a guy whose head has only been filled with offensive patterns for the past ten years."

"Don't sell yourself short. You're doing great. I think you're going to knock Milt's socks off."

"That's a stretch," he said. "Do you watch pro football on TV?"

"Not unless I'm too lazy to reach for the remote." She gave him a coy, almost contrite grin. "Sorry."

"If you did, you'd notice that most sports broadcasters are ex-jocks. I suppose I'm different because I'm more interested in real news, not play-by-play announcing. But all of us ex-athletes have had to find something worthwhile to do after the field lights are turned off."

"Something tells me there is a lot more about you that makes you different from most ex-athletes."

"I hope that's a compliment."

She gave him another one of those coy grins. "Well, we'll just have to see, won't we? So far so good."

His heart gave a surprising kick in his chest. Was she flirting? Or was she just stating a fact? He put his tablet in its case and started toward the door. At the last minute he turned around. She was right behind him.

"Forget something?" she asked.

"No, but I did have an idea."

"What's that?"

Right now the only idea he had was one that had him leaning into her, smelling the floral scent of her hair and getting another close-up look at those tempting curves. He wanted nothing more than to hold her tight and kiss her. Kiss her? Good grief, he hadn't acted on a kissing impulse that hadn't included Lynette in years. And suddenly, with this woman, it was all he could think about. To thank her? Sure, he could explain this phenomenon that way, but it would be a lie. He wanted to do it because she was a woman and he was a man, and his instincts were taking over. He fisted his hand at his side and held his tablet tightly against his chest.

"Jeremy?" She cocked her head to the side and stared at him. "Is something wrong?"

"No." He gave his head a mental shake. "I was just thinking. We deserve a break, don't you think?"

"I don't know. What did you have in mind?"

"How about coming out to my place tomorrow?"

"To Hidden Oaks?"

"Yeah. It's Saturday. The kids are going to a birthday party, and Marta, that's my housekeeper, will stay with them while I come into town to pick you up. We can work for a while if we want to, but out on the patio if it's nice. I have a pool, and it's heated."

She smiled. "Doesn't sound like we'll get much done."

"You'd be surprised what a beautiful day and a little imagination can accomplish." She seemed hesitant so he lightly wrapped his hand around her elbow. She allowed it to happen. "Come on, say you'll come. Have you ever been to Hidden Oaks?"

"No, but I've heard a lot about it."

"Stay as long as you like. When you're ready, I'll take you home, but we may have a couple of kids in the car for the trip back. You do like kids, right?"

"Ah, sure. Kids are great."

"Then you'll come?"

"Why not? I'd love to."

"Great. See you tomorrow." He squeezed her elbow, leaned in and pecked her on the cheek. A friendly gesture, and she didn't take offense. Should he try for more? Maybe tomorrow.

He walked out onto her landing, looked back at the door knocker and smiled. When he'd arrived earlier and knocked on her door, he'd had an idea that tonight could be special, a step forward for a man who felt like laughter had been forgotten lately and breathing had just become a way to stay alive.

WHAT HAVE YOU just agreed to? Brooke asked herself as she carried the pizza plates and wineglasses into the kitchen. "Sure I like kids." She mimicked her own voice. "I love my nieces, but never planned on having any of my own." *Why didn't you tell him that, Brooke? Why didn't you tell him that most kids make you uneasy, and the responsibility of raising any absolutely freaks you out?*

Esther was like an extension of her and Camryn, and someday Gracie would be the same. But that didn't mean that Brooke wanted to be a mother. Camryn had always been the one to bring home strays and mother them. Brooke hadn't been able to take care of the family cat.

But the kids would be at a birthday party tomorrow. Maybe the housekeeper would be around. Or maybe not. Maybe she'd be alone with Jeremy in the warm sun on his patio. Should she take her bathing suit? Well, of course. She couldn't exactly not after he'd told her about the pool. Bathing suits were certainly inappropriate for business associates. But not necessarily for friends. And she and Jeremy were friends, right? At least until Milt's strategy failed and Jeremy discovered she'd let him down.

Only one thing to do. Brooke called Camryn.

"How's everything?" Camryn asked. "Are you home again on a Friday night?"

Camryn had known about Brooke's dating slump. The funny thing was, she felt worse about it than Brooke did. Although tonight Brooke had to admit that it felt good to leave her novel on the nightstand and spend some time with an interesting, not-bad-on-the-eyes fella.

"Yes, I'm home," she said. "But I haven't been alone exactly."

"What is that supposed to mean? You were alone or you weren't?"

"I wasn't."

"So you had company?"

"I guess you could say that. Remember that guy I told you I had to make into a well-rounded news anchor within six weeks to save my job and the station?"

"I remember. As I recall, you called him a charming but probably no-talent ex-football player."

Brooke cringed. "That wasn't very nice."

"No, but I forgave you because this guy sort of had your future in the palm of his hand."

Hmm…an image of Jeremy's strong hands massaging her foot came to mind and made her feel special for a walk-challenged klutz.

"Anything I might have said about him

being a dumb jock, I regret. He's really pretty smart."

"So are you interested in this guy beyond making him a news-broadcast celebrity? Could he be the one?"

"I guess it's a possibility," she said, resisting the urge to shout "Yes, yes, he could be." She sighed. "But nothing will come of it. He has two kids, and I'm not ready for that."

Camryn laughed. "Two kids is nothing. I've suddenly got four. And I should remind you that kids are not little demons who run around the house leaving toys on the stairs on purpose."

"I know that. And Esther is fun. Gracie will be, too, when she's able to go shopping. But you know I don't want kids in my life. I want to someday be producing the news for CNN or ABC."

"So where does this leave you with Mr. Legs, as you used to call him?"

"He invited me to his house in Hidden Oaks tomorrow."

"Whoa, Hidden Oaks? Fancy. What did you say?"

"I said yes. We're going to work on his training."

"That sounds interesting," Camryn said. "What kind of training exactly?"

"You know what training. I'm determined to turn him into the best newscaster in the South. I can't lose sight of the fact that my job depends on how well Jeremy does as an anchor on WJQC. I can't let him derail my goals. I wasn't lucky enough to have the love of my life simply move in right next door like you."

Camryn hooted. "It wasn't all smooth sailing. What romance novel have you been reading now? And he's a vet who works hard and comes home plenty dirty. We wouldn't even get by if I didn't have my egg business and my graphic-design gig with the school system."

"Okay. Sorry, but I want to be at the very top of my field and have everything that goes with it. Being fired by Milt Cramer is not a step in that direction. Hard to believe that after all the years at the station, my job could rest on the shoulders of this one man."

"Very nice shoulders though, I bet," Camryn said.

Brooke smiled. "Indeed they are."

"If Jeremy lives in Hidden Oaks, he must have a big house. Probably a swimming pool and a great yard. And one of those gorgeous gourmet kitchens."

"I don't know, maybe."

"Then just have fun, Brooke. You can do that, can't you? Forget lost people and unfair ultimatums and have fun with the person you're with…and his kids."

"I'll try. Actually, I'll do more than that. I believe I will. Well, maybe not the kids part." Camryn started to say something and Brooke cut her off. "Love you, sis. Though I can't imagine why."

"Love you, too. And I can think of a thousand reasons why."

Brooke disconnected. Camryn's advice, as usual, was easier said than done. Still, she had the rest of the night to think about which bathing suit she'd take, and all that warm sun, and those big, strong, capable hands and very nice shoulders.

CHAPTER SEVEN

"MARTA WANTS TO go visit her sister today," Jeremy said to his two children at breakfast the next morning. "So please behave and don't give her any trouble while I run an errand. I want her to leave for her sister's without feeling like she's been let out of a cage at the zoo."

Cody laughed. "I get to be the tiger."

"You get to be who you are," Jeremy said, "only better."

"Aren't you going to be here?" Alicia asked. "It's Saturday. You're always with us on Saturday."

"I'll be here most of the day," he said. "But I have someplace to go this morning before Marta leaves. And I'll be here after you guys get back from the birthday party." One thing Jeremy had learned quickly about Hidden Oaks was that parties were on the docket almost every weekend. If it wasn't some kid's birthday, then parents were celebrating kindergarten graduation or the adoption of a new pet. "I'll drop you off at the party when I get back."

"Where are you going?" Alicia asked.

"I'm picking up a friend. She's helping me get used to my new job at the television station. Since I need all the help I can get, I figured we'd have a working lunch out by the pool."

Alicia narrowed her eyes. "Is it the lady you talked about the other day? The one named Brooke."

Jeremy had mentioned a lady at the station who'd hurt her ankle. No big deal, he'd thought. Besides, Alicia couldn't remember to carry her backpack up to her room, so why did she all of a sudden remember Brooke's name?

"Yes, it is," Jeremy said.

"But it's not a date?"

"No, Alicia. Remember when we talked the other day? I don't date. I haven't dated in years." He frowned at the truth of that statement. "I wouldn't even know how to date anymore."

Alicia maintained the same serious expression. "Okay. Go get her. What should we do while you're gone?"

Jeremy shook his head. Both kids had a roomful of toys and projects collecting dust in the garage. Surely they could find something to do. But both pairs of eyes stared at him, waiting for an answer.

"You can wrap the presents for Luke. They're on my dresser. The remote dinosaur is from Cody. The swim mask is from you, Alicia. Wrapping paper is in the linen closet, and only use safety scissors to cut the paper."

Those were words he didn't think he'd ever use. But parents had to think of stuff like that and not just assume. He grabbed his wallet off the counter and his keys from the hook by the back door. "Marta, I'm leaving."

"Okay, Mr. C," she called from the laundry room. "See you later."

He got in his huge SUV, the one he'd purchased to give his children breathing room and himself every option available to an auto buyer. Once he left his driveway, he switched on Sirius radio, but didn't tune in to news for this trip. Instead he picked an oldies channel and hummed along to the Beach Boys. He instantly relaxed. A day at the pool, a pretty woman and the Beach Boys. It might very well be a great day.

Brooke was ready when he got to her condo at ten thirty. She had on white shorts and a checkered top that ended at her waist, where she'd tied the material into a knot. She looked comfortable and laid-back, so different from the serious woman who ran the newsroom at WJQC. He liked this Brooke, who seemed ready for a walk in the park or a picnic.

And then, after greeting him, she picked up a folder and said, "I typed up some examples of breaking news from the last few years. You should know what kinds of stories will interrupt the regular broadcast."

He tried to inject enthusiasm into his voice. "Good idea."

"It's interesting to learn what is considered important enough to disturb our pattern," she said. "Of course there's always an important death, or an unexpected act of nature. But—"

"Can we discuss all this later?" he said. "I've got to get back before my housekeeper leaves for the afternoon."

"Your kids still have a party to go to, right?"

she asked. "I don't think your children will be too interested in breaking news."

"Yep. Believe me, the kids won't want to hang around with us."

Jeremy loved the drive to Hidden Oaks. Once he left the city, the four-lane roads curved in a southwesterly direction into some of the most beautiful country he'd ever seen. Bridges crossed expanses of gently rippling rivers and streams. The Lowcountry of South Carolina was home to a multitude of fish, wildlife, crustaceans, insects and sweet Carolina breezes. As far as the eye could see, canals ran through lush, tall green grass, which lived in perfect harmony with the estuaries that sustained the life protected under their glistening surfaces.

Brooke had been quiet during most of the ride, but she had been carefully observing the passing landscape, as well. "It's really naturally beautiful out here," she said when they were nearing his home.

"I remember you said you've never been to this part of the Charleston area before. This housing development is almost four years old."

"I suppose it's odd that I haven't been here,

but as a news producer, my job was to keep everything running smoothly in the production room. I rarely went out on location, and when I did, I was usually still in the city." She smiled at him. "I've been to many places— London, Paris—but I'm starting to think I've missed a lot right here close to Charleston." He could picture her in some of the most romantic cities in the world. He could picture her almost anywhere.

"You must have traveled the coast, gone to vacation spots such as the Grand Strand," he said.

"Sure. I've been up and down the coast. I guess I just never thought there was anything worth seeing in newly developed residential areas." She smiled at him. "I was wrong. You've picked a nice place to live."

He slowed as he approached the tall, wrought-iron gate. He aimed his resident key at a panel next to the sign that read Hidden Oaks. The gate slid to the side with a soft hiss. "Just a few turns and we're there," he said.

"Before we arrive," Brooke said, "did you tell your children that I was coming today?"

"Yes, I told them about you." *At least I told*

them about your ankle. "They're looking forward to meeting you." He recalled his kids' blank stares when he mentioned Brooke.

"I hope so."

So did he.

As he neared the road that would take him to his three-acre property, Jeremy took a minute to observe Brooke's profile. He wondered why she'd never been married. Surely she'd had serious relationships with men. Maybe someday he would ask her about her past, when things settled down at the station and they got to know each other on an even more personal level. All at once, it was vital to Jeremy that he know more about Brooke, and just as important that she would feel comfortable in his home.

The moment Jeremy had initially seen the property he ended up purchasing, he'd believed he'd come home. And he believed he'd chosen the perfect spot for his two children. The scenic reminders of the Lowcountry were just at the end of his lot. When he first walked into his backyard, he'd heard animals rustling in the grass, birds chirping and squirrels complaining at his interruption into their lives. He wanted Brooke to see the beauty of Hidden Oaks. He wanted her to like it here. He didn't know if she would ever come back, but if he had anything to say about it, she would.

She turned toward him and he immediately readjusted his gaze to the road. He turned right into his driveway and drove under a canopy of magnolias and live oaks. Just ahead, his three-thousand-square-foot white Colonial home welcomed him. It wasn't the size of the house that had impressed him. Others in the neighborhood were larger. It was the grace of it. The shiny black shutters and ornate pillars supporting the upper balcony off the bedrooms brought to mind tranquility and a gentle spirit. He smiled at Brooke.

"We're here," he said.

She nodded. "Goodness, how far do you have to go for a loaf of bread?"

Her comment was not what he'd expected, nor what he'd hoped for. But she was a city girl.

BROOKE LOVED BEING in the hustle and bustle of Charleston. She appreciated being able to walk a couple of blocks to the nearest neighborhood market, museum or theater. She looked forward to strolling on a cool evening down to the Battery and studying the tourists. Or hopping the city tram to the closest trendy restaurant, where, until her quest for Edward had taken over her life, she'd meet friends for drinks and local dishes. Here, in the Lowcountry boonies, houses were so far apart that she wondered how any of the residents got to know each other. Brooke knew all of her condo neighbors, spoke to them at the mailboxes or petted their dogs.

Jeremy gave her a piercing stare, making her wonder what she had said to cause such a sudden and confusing reaction. "We have the Fallway Quick Mart just three miles away," he said. "Plus, there is a huge supermarket in the town of Fallway, a five-mile trip, and Marta goes once a week for supplies. I can always stop on my way home if we need anything special."

That was a very specific answer. Brooke feared she had insulted him somehow, and she hadn't meant to. His home and property were beyond elegant. He pulled into the circular drive in front of the house and cut the engine.

Brooke stared out the window at the large structure.

"I suppose you're wondering how far away the nearest movie theater is," Jeremy said.

"No, actually I was just enjoying the view. But what about the children's school? How far away is it?"

"About two miles. They go to a private school, the Amberson Academy. A bus picks them up every morning." He stepped out of the car, shut the door and came around to open the passenger door. "How's the ankle today? Do you need any help?"

"No. The ankle is completely healed." His front door was opened by a middle-aged woman in a skirt and blouse. Her graying hair was neatly styled in a modern bob. She appeared sturdy, efficient and qualified. Brooke concluded she must be Marta.

Jeremy greeted her warmly. "Marta, this is Brooke. She came today to help me with some WJQC matters."

The two women greeted each other.

"Where are the kids?" Jeremy asked.

"I'm not sure at the moment. I've been in

the laundry room folding clothes. Last I saw them, they were in the upstairs playroom."

Jeremy led Brooke into the living room, where his children were seated in a pair of chairs that flanked a brick fireplace. They were quiet, almost studious, and except for their clothes could have been in a portrait of children from some long-ago time.

"Oh, good. You're here," Jeremy said. "I want you to meet Brooke."

Brooke smiled. "Hello, Alicia, Cody. I'm very happy to meet you."

Neither child spoke. They were dressed in jeans and T-shirts, not party clothes, but their garments were dusted with a white substance that looked like flour. The nine-year-old, Alicia, nodded once while her leg kept up a steady swing against the leg of the chair. The boy, six-year-old Cody, lifted his hand in a casual wave.

Jeremy stared at his kids but he didn't seem to notice the flour. "Is that what you're wearing to the party?" he asked them.

Before either child answered, a cry of alarm came from the back of the house, followed by loud footsteps coming closer.

"Marta, what's wrong?" Jeremy asked.

The housekeeper burst into the room. "Come into the kitchen, Mr. C. I've never seen such a mess."

Jeremy's face registered shock and concern. Following Marta's raised arm and pointed finger, he headed out of the living room. Thinking she might be needed, Brooke followed behind him to what was obviously a large gourmet kitchen with no identifiable details at the moment. Most of the wood floor and the tops of the table and counters were covered with assorted food—cereal, flour, sugar. It appeared that someone had just flung boxes of edible contents everywhere. And then poured a bottle of maple syrup over the entire mess.

Jeremy stood dumbfounded. "What happened here?"

"Whatever it was, it happened in the last fifteen minutes. I've only been in the laundry room that long." Marta crossed her arms. "I suggest you ask your children."

"Alicia! Cody!"

Brooke had never heard Jeremy raise his voice. Of course, what father wouldn't be upset at a moment like this, a moment that reinforced Brooke's opinion of children?

The children stood at the kitchen entrance. "What's wrong, Daddy?" Alicia asked in a sweet, little-girl voice.

"Did you do this?" Jeremy demanded, first looking at his daughter and then his son. "Cody?"

"We were going to fix lunch for you and your friend, Daddy," Alicia said. "But we ran out of time and had to get ready for the party. I'm sorry if we left things messy."

"Messy? Alicia, this isn't messy. This is a catastrophe, which will take forever to clean up. And I don't believe for a minute that this is the result of you kids trying to fix a meal. Why would you do this?"

He waited for one of the children to answer, but all he got from both of them were shrugs.

His chest rose and fell. A vein worked in his temple. Then, as if he suddenly remembered Brooke's presence, he spoke in a controlled voice. "Both of you go to your rooms. I will come get you when it's time to clean this up."

When the kids had gone, Jeremy turned to

Marta. "Go on to your sister's," he said. "The kids and I will take care of this."

"I can't leave you with a mess like this," Marta said.

"You absolutely can," he said. "My children are not going to ruin your plans." He carefully walked across the kitchen floor, avoiding the worst of the disaster, and opened a closet that held cleaning supplies.

Marta shrugged. "If you're sure."

"I'll help," Brooke said, shaking her head at the obvious proof of runaway misbehavior. Why would anyone, no matter what age, make such a mess?

"No, you won't," Jeremy said. "You go on out to the pool. I'll bring you some lemonade. The three Crocketts will handle this. And if my kids have to go to a party covered in maple syrup, so be it. If I cancel their plans I'm only going to be hurting myself."

Brooke thought about arguing with him. She was certainly capable of helping out. But his voice was so raw, and his decision so sure, she followed his direction. The patio was sunny and warm. She slipped off her shoes and chose a padded lounge chair. For the next hour she ignored a feeling of guilt that she told herself she really shouldn't be experiencing and tried to block sounds of a frustrated dad and seriously unhappy children.

Poor Jeremy. She didn't know what he expected of this day, but this definitely wasn't it. Nor was it what she had expected. She reminded herself that both children were grieving. Plus, Jeremy had brought someone new into their household. Kids act out when they are disappointed or unsure. She and Camryn certainly had.

She shouldn't have come to Hidden Oaks today. It was turning out to be an increasingly bad decision. She was obviously interrupting a delicate balance between a father and his troubled kids. If she'd had her own car she would have left, but that wasn't an option. She opened her notes and tried to concentrate on what she would tell Jeremy if he still wanted to talk shop. She doubted he would.

Almost an hour later, Brooke was startled by a light tap on her shoulder. She turned abruptly, thinking her visitor was Jeremy. No. Cody stood behind her lounger. The rocket ships on his T-shirt contrasted with the sad look on his face, and Brooke felt an immediate and unfamiliar tug on her heartstrings.

"Hi, there," she said. "How's everything going in the kitchen? Do you guys need any help?"

"We're almost done," Cody said.

"Does your daddy know you came out here?"

"No. I said I was going to the bathroom."

"Oh, dear. We'll have to let him know where you are," Brooke said.

"I didn't lie," Cody insisted. "I think I can make myself go to the bathroom."

"Okay, but still…"

"I thought maybe I could sit with you a minute."

Brooke pulled up her knees to give the boy room on the end of the lounge chair. "Sure. Have a seat."

"What are you doing?"

Brooke had forgotten about the tablet open on her lap. "Just some work. Your daddy and I have some things to go over." She smiled. "Boring stuff really."

She surreptitiously sent Jeremy a text. Cody is on patio with me.

An answering text questioned Cody's motive. Is he okay? Why did he come out there?

Don't know, but he's fine. No prob.

"I guess it was no fun cleaning up that sticky mess," Brooke said. "Are you still going to the party?"

"Yeah. Dad said we could, but we're going to be punished later." He sighed.

"Is something else bothering you, Cody?" Brooke asked.

"I was just thinking that me and Alicia probably shouldn't have made that mess today."

"No, probably not. I'm sure you didn't think about all the extra work it would mean for your dad."

"I didn't. I'm sorry about that." He paused a moment, then said, "I want a dog. If we had a dog, he would have licked it all up."

Brooke smiled. "Dogs are great," she said. "Maybe someday you'll have one."

"Are you mad at me?" Cody asked.

"No, I'm not. But it might be a good idea if

you told your father that you regret making the mess. You are sorry, aren't you?"

He crossed his arms and leaned back against her calves. Unsure what to do, Brooke lightly patted his head.

He didn't speak for a minute until his chest heaved and he peered up at her. "I should tell the truth," he said.

"Always a good idea," Brooke said.

"I'm not sorry."

She looked down at his face, so serious. "You're not?"

"Nope. Alicia and I have to stick together."

She smiled again. "I see."

"What I did was wrong, though, because I think I might like you even if Alicia doesn't. She says we both shouldn't like you."

Brooke understood what had happened in the kitchen. And she understood what was going on in Cody's head now. He didn't want to betray his sister. "How about deciding for yourself if you like me or not? What do you think of that?"

His breathing returned to normal, the sweet, slow breaths of a child who'd gotten something off his chest. "Okay. Yeah, maybe I will like you."

I'm not sorry. His truthful words, spoken in his soft, honest voice, kept repeating in her mind. She remembered times from her own life when she'd wanted to say those exact words. Sometimes being really, truly sorry took a little time.

Brooke gently rubbed his hair, wondering at the silky softness of it. So blond and curly and a bit sticky from his hands. Other than the residue of maple syrup, his hair reminded her of Esther's, and the feeling she got from comforting him felt strangely natural.

CHAPTER EIGHT

A FEW MINUTES later Jeremy came out on the patio. "Time to get ready for the party, champ," he said. "Have you been having a nice talk with Miss Brooke?"

"Yeah, she shared her lemonade."

"Okay." Jeremy parted a few strands of his son's hair. "Maybe you can jump in the shower for a quick shampoo," he said. "You wouldn't want Luke to think you ate before coming over. If I know his mom, there will be lots of food."

Cody bounced up from the lounge and ran toward the house.

Jeremy pulled up a chair and sat next to Brooke. "So what went on out here?"

"Just a few companionable minutes," she said. "He's a sweet boy, Jeremy."

Jeremy grinned. "If you had said that an hour ago, I wouldn't have agreed with you. Now that the hard work is behind us, I guess

I can forgive him." He shook his head. "I'm pretty sure I know who the instigator of this incident was. Alicia's been having a hard time. I should pay more attention to her."

Brooke nodded. "If a kitchen covered in flour and syrup doesn't tell you that, nothing will."

"I don't know what to do, Brooke. I arranged for them to get professional help in Colorado. When we came here, I thought everything was going to be okay. They seemed happy to be with me, didn't talk too much about their mother. Maybe that wasn't good. Today is a wake-up call."

"It hasn't been that long since they lost their mother," Brooke said. "Grieving takes time." She smiled. "Not that I know anything about kids. I'm certainly not qualified to give you advice."

"Don't you want kids of your own someday?" he asked.

She gave him an earnest stare. "Honestly? It's not on my agenda. I know what I'm good at. Running a news production room. Any kid contact I get from my nieces, and that seems to fulfill my nurturing needs."

"Hmm…" Not much of a response. Was he disappointed in her answer? Better to be honest from the start, she thought. Her feelings about children weren't going to change just because she met a man who had two. In fact, what happened today reaffirmed her beliefs, while at the same time she had to admit to feeling sorry for the kids. Tough to lose a person you loved and depended on.

"I'm going to take the kids to the party," Jeremy said. "On the way back, I'll call and order some sub sandwiches. I was going to fix you a nice light lunch, but frankly, I'm sick of the kitchen."

"No problem. Anything will be fine."

Before Jeremy and the kids left, Cody came back to the patio to tell Brooke goodbye. "Thanks for talking to me," he said, his voice controlled and mature.

She called him close and gave him a little hug. "Anytime, Cody," she said. Alicia must have gone out the front door since Brooke didn't see her.

Jeremy had been gone about ten minutes when Brooke's phone rang. As soon as she saw Gabe's name, her heart began to pound.

This could be it, she thought. *He's had the fifteen hundred for a few days now and he's uncovered something.*

"Hello, Gabe."

"Hi, kiddo. How's everything?"

"I hope things are about to get better," she said.

"Maybe a little better. Depends how you look at it."

The tone of his voice caused her heart to sink. *I'm beginning to look at it like I'll never find my brother.* "Tell me what you've found."

"I located the judge who was on the bench the day this Jerry Miller kid I told you about was brought in for attempted car theft."

"Well, that's good news, isn't it?" Brooke asked. "He might remember the boy."

"Yeah, maybe, but the judge's name is William Smith." Gabe chuckled, causing the hairs on Brooke's nape to stand up. How could Gabe find anything to laugh about in this situation?

"Do you know how many judges there are in the United States named William Smith?" he asked.

"No, but I'm assuming you're telling me that there are quite a few."

"Hundreds. In the last twenty years there have been forty William Smiths on the bench in South Carolina alone. Some are still practicing. Some can't be located by a normal search."

And even if he did find the right Judge Smith, Brooke thought, Gabe's instincts were all that was leading him on this chase. The judge might not remember Jerry Miller. And Jerry Miller might not even be Edward. Basically, they knew nothing.

But she had another fifteen hundred invested at this point, so she said, "You are checking these judges out, right?"

"As fast as I can. You ever been in a court system's archives room, kiddo? Pretty dusty and claustrophobic."

Short of being rude and telling Gabe to get back to those dusty rooms, Brooke simply asked, "So why are you calling today?"

"I feel like we're onto something. I can't shake the feeling that this Jerry Miller might be the one. But I can't locate and talk to all these Judge Smiths on my own."

"So get someone to help you," Brooke said.

"Right. That's what I want to do, but the money…"

"Wait a minute." She tried to control her temper. "Are you saying you've gone through fifteen hundred already?"

"I changed my plan when I discovered the judge and put other cases on hold. I've got no other money coming in. I feel so strongly that we're about to locate Edward that I want to focus all my attention on this case."

"I told you I can't keep financing this," Brooke said.

"That's up to you," Gabe said, as he always did. "Either you want to keep going or you don't. Just tell me what to do. But bottom line is I can't live forever on fifteen hundred, and I can't hire someone to help me search without a few hundred more. It's hard to find good help."

You don't have to tell me! Brooke fisted her hands on her lap. Blowing up at Gabe wouldn't help anything. Her eyes began to burn. "Tell me the truth. What are the chances that the Judge Smith we're looking for would even remember Jerry Miller?"

"I think the chances are excellent. I told

you. The kid has aliases and disguises. He ought to stand out in a judge's memory. Your call, Brooke. Believe me, I wish the judge had been named Huckleberry or something like that. Would be a lot easier."

Brooke felt like she was facing forward on the edge of a cliff. If she backed up and took the smartest route to safety, she'd stay alive, but she'd never accomplish her goal. If she took one more step, just one more, she might sail into an abyss, but she at least would know she'd done everything she could for the adventure.

She swallowed, hoped her voice would sound normal. "How much?"

"Five hundred. I already found a guy. He can give me a week for that amount. He's retired and dependable. Just give me the go-ahead, and—"

"Go ahead," she said, softly.

"What?"

"I'll transfer the money on Monday. That's when I get paid. Just so you know, if I give you money to live on, I won't have any to live on myself."

He chuckled again. "Hang in there, Brooke.

Something good is going to happen. I just know it."

She disconnected, sat staring out at the pool for a moment and then let the emotions she'd been holding in check break loose. Her shoulders shook, the tears in her eyes spilled down her cheeks and she sobbed. She hadn't felt so miserable since her sister had lost the last baby to a miscarriage. What the heck was she doing? She could stop this at any time, consider her money lost and start over. Why did she keep throwing good money after bad? Why did this horrible need to find someone who might not even want to be found keep directing her life?

The sobs just kept coming. She buried her face on her knees and cupped her hands over her ears, almost as if the voices in her head were chastising her for being a fool. Those voices were just like Camryn's, just like anyone's with any common sense.

And then a strong hand wrapped around her shoulder and gently squeezed. "Brooke, what's wrong?"

His voice was so low and raspy, a deep baritone of such comfort, that she couldn't have stopped crying if she'd wanted to. And she didn't.

He moved around her and sat where Cody had been earlier. But unlike his son, Jeremy took her in his arms and held her close. He patted her back, stroked her hair. His face nuzzled against her neck. She breathed in the smell of him, a combination of pine and maple syrup, not a reminder of the trials of parenthood, but the rich, warm, don't-ever-let-go aroma of home. At that moment she felt small and needy, incapable of making a decision. And Jeremy, who seemed strong and capable, was holding her as if his embrace could make everything right.

"Why are you crying, honey?" he asked. "What happened?"

SEEING BROOKE LIKE THIS, so vulnerable and sad, brought out all the protective instincts in Jeremy's heart—all the ones he'd wanted to give to Lynette, but she'd refused. He couldn't help himself. When he saw a woman crying and upset, he wanted to wrap her in the strength of his resolve until he could stop the tears and let her know she wasn't alone.

Some people might call him a sap, but Jeremy needed to be needed. That's just the way it was.

But Brooke was a strong, independent woman. He knew she wouldn't appreciate any platitudes that said he'd make it all better. So he just stayed with her and let her cry out whatever was making her heart ache and hoped he touched her in a comforting way.

After a few minutes, she sniffled and made a sound almost like a laugh. "This is so silly," she said. "I'm not a crier. I never cry." She leaned back. He let his arms fall to his sides. "I'm sorry, Jeremy. I'm really embarrassed."

"Don't be," he said. "I've seen folks a lot tougher than you shed a few tears. How about a three-hundred-pound defensive end who's just been cut from the roster? Now that's a sight that would tug at anyone's heartstrings."

"But that's just it," she said. "I consider myself tough, able to accept whatever life throws at me, but this…" Her voice faded on another repressed sob.

"Do you want to tell me about it?" he asked.

"If I did, you would think I'm an idiot. Everyone else does."

"And just who is everyone else?"

"My sister. And my parents would, too, if they knew."

Wow. What was this grown woman hiding that she couldn't tell her parents? He placed his elbows on his knees and clasped his hands. "I promise I won't think you're an idiot. If you don't know by now, let me be clear. You are probably the least idiotic person I've ever known. How many times have I told you how much I appreciate what you're doing for me, how you jumped right in to help me in this new field. I respect your know-how more than I can say. So if I can help you in any way with a problem, nothing would make me feel better than to do that. I owe you, Brooke. I want to help."

"You don't owe me, Jeremy," she said with a curt bitterness that surprised him.

"And even if you did, all I'd want is for you to become the best anchor in the business. You're doing all you can to make that happen."

His mind raced back to the other night in her condo, the spreadsheet he'd inadvertently seen on her computer. He'd concluded, perhaps incorrectly, that she might be having money problems. Maybe she just wasn't a good money manager, like so many pro-sports players he'd seen, who'd acted with complete abandon and thrown a fortune away on cars, houses, vacations. Not that Brooke was like those burned-out athletes, but money problems could happen to anyone.

"I don't know what has made you so upset, but I'm thinking that maybe you're feeling pressured," he said. "Heck, anyone would. You're doing your regular job, helping me. You've taken on extra hours and extra work." He was just saying words when what he wanted to do was get to the bottom of what was troubling her. And he was pretty sure her computer held the clue.

He paused. How could he ask her about money? The question would be a complete invasion of her privacy.

Her eyes widened. She cocked her head a bit to the side and stared at him. "You're not pressuring me, Jeremy. You've been cooperative from the beginning. But there is another matter going on in my life, and I'm embarrassed to tell you."

All at once he was certain that his hunch

was correct, and he decided to go ahead and clear the air. "Brooke, are you having money problems?"

"Why would you think…?" She swallowed, seemed lost in thought, and then said, "Oh, my computer. I was afraid you'd seen what I was working on."

"I didn't mean to," he said. "I shouldn't have, but…"

"Forget it." She attempted a smile. "If I keep flushing funds into the monetary sewer that has taken over my life, everyone will know, anyway. Especially when I start wearing patched overalls to work."

He grinned at her. "You'd look adorable in overalls." He took her hand. "So this is about money? Because if it is, I can help. I have lots of money. Never thought I would, but I do, and it would be my pleasure to give some of it to you."

Her features grew serious. "You are offering to give me money. Absolutely not, Jeremy. I can't take it and you shouldn't be in such a hurry to give away what you've worked hard for." Her eyes grew misty again. "You never know when suddenly you look back and wonder where it all went."

Jeremy had never been a fool with his money. He'd made investments, spent wisely, was always aware that a malicious twist of fate could make him lose it all and send him back to where he'd come from.

He rubbed her knuckles with the pad of his thumb. She leaned in close, rested her head on his shoulder. "Thank you for the offer, but I'll be all right," she said.

"Sure you will," he said. "But I want you to be all right now. Are we talking a bad gambling debt here? Are a couple of goons going to show up and threaten to break your kneecaps?"

She chuckled. "No, nothing like that. I could probably handle a couple of goons."

"Yes, ma'am, you probably could." He slipped his arm around her. She didn't resist. "So what's going on?"

She sat in thoughtful silence. He didn't know if she would tell him about the revealing spreadsheet on her computer or not. Some people just couldn't admit to going into debt.

He hoped she would tell him, though. He liked her. He had the will and power to help her.

His desire to make life better for Brooke wasn't just about that totally impractical protective nature of his. No, this was about Brooke, about doing something for her. This wasn't ego or pride or anything like that. He took a deep breath. "Tell me, Brooke."

"Okay," she finally said. "But you can't lecture me."

He smiled. "Oh, well, shoot, if I can't lecture that takes all the fun out of it."

She laughed against his shoulder. "I figured you'd want to lecture me just to get back for all the lectures I've been giving you lately."

"I promise I won't. We're leaving lectures off the table. Now tell me what's going on. You don't have to, but there are sub sandwiches in the kitchen, and I'd like to see your appetite return before I bring them out."

She inhaled, turned her hand over so he grasped it by entwining his fingers with hers. He felt the tiniest pressure when she squeezed his hand. "First of all, I'm adopted. My twin sister and I were adopted at birth by a wonderful couple who are more than any kid could hope for."

He nodded. "Okay. And then what?"

"Our parents told us as soon as we were old enough to understand, and my sister was never curious about our background. I wish I could have been like her, but I wasn't. My first inclination that I just had to know who I am came in middle school with a stupid genealogy project where we had to trace our family trees. Cammie, my sister, just wrote down all the details about our adoptive parents. I couldn't do that. I left my tree blank. The teacher was nice about it. She even let me skip the assignment, but it got my head spinning. And from then on I became determined to find our mother."

"I can understand that," Jeremy said. "You must have felt like there was this huge hole in your life."

"Yes!" Her eyes opened wide. She squeezed his hand with a steady pressure. "You understand. It's the need to know, to understand where I came from. As good as my life has been with my adoptive parents, I had to make sense of this for myself."

"Sure. I understand. Not everyone needs to know, but you did. How did your parents react to your desire to find your mother?"

"I never told them. Cammie said it would only hurt them, and she was right. So I kept my quest to myself. Besides, I didn't have any means to find my mother. I was just a kid, so I kept the idea in the back of my mind, knowing someday I would look for her."

"And did you?"

"I did, after I got the job at the station and had some money to use for the search. It wasn't easy. My mother had covered her tracks pretty well. And she had agreed to a closed adoption, so I had to spend money and time to find the right person who would bend the rules and give me the information I needed."

Jeremy was suddenly engrossed in her story. It was so real and could have been his own, though he'd taken a different path. But he'd often wondered… "What was it like?" he asked. "Did you meet her face-to-face?"

"Yes. She lives in Myrtle Beach, about midway between me and Cammie. We both went to meet her. Cammie didn't want to, but I talked her into it."

Jeremy hated to ask. He could see the anguish in her eyes. "How did it turn out?"

"She wanted nothing to do with us. She told us to leave, that she had enough on her plate with a lousy job and a sick husband." Brooke swiped at moisture under her eyes. "We would have helped her, Jeremy, but she didn't give us the chance."

"And that's the only time you saw her?"

Brooke nodded. "I will never go back. But there's one other thing…"

He spoke softly. "Tell me."

"She let slip that she had a three-year-old son. She didn't mean to, but she assumed that since we already knew about her, we also knew about Edward. She gave Edward up for adoption at the same time and asked us not to tell him where she was."

This was all starting to make sense to Jeremy. One door to Brooke's past had closed that day, but another had opened. Knowing her as he did now, how could she have ignored this latest clue into her background? "You have a brother," he said.

"A half brother."

"Where is he?"

"I wish I knew. I've been looking for him for months, first on my own, through internet research, then checking halfway houses and prisons. I did all I could on my own."

He could only imagine her pain. She needed so desperately to know where she belonged, to find this one link to her past. "I'm assuming that today you discovered something about Edward, and that's why you were crying." He hoped she hadn't found out that Edward was a criminal or, worse, that he was dead. Her search couldn't end that way.

"It would be nice if I had," she said. "But, no. A while back I hired a private investigator. I trust him. I really do, but I've been paying him significant amounts since he started his search. Every time it seems he's close to finding Edward, something happens and he needs more money."

"And today he needed more money."

She nodded.

Jeremy wished he could talk to this detective. He was fairly good at reading people, and he'd like to know if this guy was leading on

Brooke. He supposed that finding an adopted kid decades after he was given up would be a challenge, but there were a lot of scam artists in the world.

"I told him I'd wire it to his account." Brooke stared at Jeremy with luminescent eyes that told the whole story of the agony of indecision she was going through. "I don't know how long I can keep doing this. I'll be broke when I send the five hundred he needs now. I suppose I'll recover, but it will take time…"

"I'll give you the five hundred," Jeremy said. "For heaven's sake, Brooke, I owe you that much or more for the time you've taken with me. You've been so generous—"

"Quit telling me what a great person I am to help you."

"But you are. Even if Milt weren't paying you I would still be grateful. I wouldn't make it without you on my team."

"First of all, Milt isn't paying me. And I can't take your money," she said. "And I told you before. You don't owe me anything. Milt asked me to help you, and I was…well, okay with the extra assignment. WJQC needs a qualified anchor. All of our futures depend on it. I don't know if Milt told you, but the station's finances aren't great right now. All the people who work there want the five o'clock news hour to boost our ratings, get our advertisers back."

He covered her hand in both of his. He continued, "And I told you before. Money isn't a problem. I can't take on the burdens of the station, but I can certainly help you. I don't want to argue about this. You're taking the money and that's it."

She closed her eyes and released a long, slow breath. When she looked at him again, there was a softness to her features, a level of comfort he was grateful to see. She was going to accept his help.

"I'll pay you back," she said.

"Fine. Pay me back. In twenty years if you want to. If I have anything to say about it, I will know you that long. Professional athletes make absurd amounts of money, so I'm happy to give you a bit of mine."

"I don't know what to say."

"Don't say anything. Now that it's settled, there's something I should tell you."

"What?"

"I was given up for adoption, too, when I was five, so I can relate to your need to know."

"Oh, Jeremy, that is so sad. But look how you turned out. You must have gone to wonderful parents."

His answering laugh was cynical. She had no idea how wrong she was. "I never was adopted, Brooke. I stayed in the foster system for a few years until my mother came and picked me up again. I think she thought we could pull each other up by the bootstraps. But that didn't happen. We only brought each other down until I went to college at eighteen."

"But how did you turn your life around? How did you end up in college?"

"Simple. I could catch a football, and I reveled in the challenge to be the best at it. And for that, I was given a full ride to Bellingsworth College. Don't know where I'd be today if I'd been a klutz on the football field."

She gave him a warm smile. "I love that story. Not the beginning of it, but the end, when you discovered yourself and worked hard to succeed. Maybe something like that happened to Edward, too."

"Maybe it did. I hope you find out."

"Jeremy, the fact that you're even listening to me gives me hope. My sister tells me all the time to leave Edward in the past. I suppose she's right, but our lives have gone in such different directions. Camryn's hasn't always been easy, but now she has everything she deserves, and I feel like everything I desire is always just out of reach."

"Well, now you have me, and I'm on your side. Maybe I can help you find Edward. Because of my background, I have some contacts. What is his full name?"

"That's a problem," she said. "He has used different aliases. Every time he was caught doing something wrong, he seemed to adopt a different demeanor. The investigator is trying to locate him now under the name Jerry Miller, who was last sentenced by a juvenile-court judge named William Smith. Not exactly a stand-out name."

"It's a challenge," Jeremy said. "But let's be hopeful. I won't leave you alone with this, Brooke. You can count on me."

Her shoulders relaxed. Her gaze caught and

held his. "You don't know what this means to me."

"I think I do." He leaned forward, cupped her face with both his hands and kissed the top of her forehead, just like he kissed his kids at the bus stop. Only this was different. This gesture made his heart stop. When he drew back, he kept his hands on each side of her face. He stroked her cheeks with his thumbs and looked into her eyes. Her skin was moist from the tears, but was soft and silky.

And then she leaned just slightly toward him, but it was enough for him to know that she was feeling something, too. He hoped it wasn't just gratitude. He hoped she felt just a bit of what his senses were telling him now. This woman, so tough and competent, was also warm and vulnerable. Very gently he pulled her face to his, ready to let go of her if she gave the first sign that she wasn't ready for what every nerve in his body was signaling for him to do.

She didn't pull back. She closed her eyes and touched her lips with the tip of her tongue— a beautiful, sweet invitation. He pressed his lips to hers and savored the salty, citrusy taste of her mouth, her tongue. He slipped his hand to the back of her head and held her still while his mouth moved over hers. He didn't know, but thought perhaps the kiss lasted almost a minute. But when he drew back, he felt that he'd only just started.

She took a slow, deep breath. Her eyelids fluttered open.

"What are you doing to me, Jeremy?" she said.

"I hope I'm making you feel better, Brooke."

She touched her lips to his again, a brief, sweet reminder of what they'd just shared. "I would say that is a challenge you've successfully met," she said.

CHAPTER NINE

Two HOURS LATER Jeremy and Brooke were in his SUV driving back to Charleston. There had been no more discussion of her brother, but a check for five hundred dollars was tucked safely into her purse.

She hadn't wanted to take the money. It was wrong to take money from anyone, especially someone who wasn't family. But Jeremy had been so insistent, almost as if she would be doing him a favor by taking it.

"Look, Brooke," he'd said. "I like you. I like helping people if I can. Just keep the money. I don't need it and you do."

Hard to argue with logic like that. And she would pay him back—every cent.

So with his two kids in the backseat watching a video and soft country music on the radio, Brooke sat quietly, occasionally stealing a glance at the man who had not only saved her from temporary financial ruin, but had also provided moral support. Whenever their gazes met, he smiled at her. She felt comforted and appreciative. And remembering the kiss, she felt so much more than that. She had dated lots of men. She enjoyed going out, having fun. But Jeremy was different. Fun? Yes. And kind and smart and interesting. Which is why her feelings were suddenly different, too.

"So," he began when they were about halfway to her condo, "have you told Milt anything about what you're trying to accomplish? Does he know about Edward?"

He knows I'm stealing time from work and have been for months. And he has told me that I'm as good as gone from WJQC if I don't make a success of you. "No. Finding Edward is such a personal matter. I don't know if Milt would understand."

"Kind of a shame," Jeremy said. "Milt seems like a nice enough guy, one who cares about his employees. He'd probably understand, even give you some time off with pay if you confided in him."

Brooke felt her face begin to flush, the curse of all blondes when faced with anxiety. Jeremy was so wrong about Milt. He was fiercely protective of WJQC, but he expected one hundred percent effort and loyalty. "I don't want to tell him," she said, "and you can't, either. No one at work knows anything about this, and I want to keep it that way. It's enough that I blubbered all over your nice shirt today."

"Hey, no problem. It's not my story to tell. I just thought if you had a bit of support from Milt, you might be able to find Edward sooner."

She huffed, remembering Milt's exact words about the time she was stealing from WJQC. And later, warning her not to tell Jeremy anything about their "special arrangement." And now she was insisting that Jeremy keep her secret, as well. There were too many secrets associated with WJQC, and Brooke feared that one of them would blow up in their faces.

"Milt is a company man above all else," she explained to Jeremy. "If an employee has a problem, he does not offer a warm-and-fuzzy shoulder to cry on. We all do our jobs, and what happens when we walk out the station door at the end of the day is our problem."

Thinking she needed to state her case even

more firmly, she added, "So, please, Jeremy, no matter how helpful you think Milt might be, do *not* mention this to him."

"I understand, Brooke. This is between you and me, and that's fine. I hope you feel like you can come to me if you hit any more road-blocks. Remember, I've been where Edward has been—probably alone, confused and in trouble. I know if I had a sister as determined as you are to find me, I'd sure as heck want to be found."

She lightly touched his arm. "Thanks. If I ever do find Edward, I hope he feels like you do. That's my biggest fear. After searching all this time, spending all this money, I'll find him and he'll brush me off, just like my mother did."

He gave her a supportive grin. "One step at a time, Brooke. Don't get ahead of yourself."

She sighed. "It was a nice day, Jeremy. We probably should have done a little work. I had planned on going over budgetary concerns."

He laughed. "Thinking about where our conversation ultimately led, I'm pretty sure I would have been bored out of my mind if we ended up discussing budgets. Save it for Monday?"

Her face warmed again. They were on the same wavelength. Her mind had returned several times to that moment on the lounger when he'd held her, whispered comforting words to her, kissed her. Oh, my, yes, kissed her. Possibly the best kiss she'd ever experienced. And definitely a kiss she'd like to repeat.

Remember the mantra, Brooke, she thought to herself. *One step at a time. You're less than two weeks into this project of Milt's, and you've only got four to go. Make a success of Jeremy first and then just maybe you'll be able to keep your condo, pay him back the five hundred and find Edward. Jeremy's kisses, if you're lucky, can come later. If he doesn't ultimately wow the viewing audience in Charleston, then he's very likely out, you're out and everything else unravels.*

"Hey, Brooke," Cody called from the backseat.

She turned to see his face. "What is it, Cody?"

"These Minions are so funny. You should see what they're doing."

"I wish I could. Maybe I can borrow your video sometime."

"Sure." He settled back and continued watching.

Brooke was glad she'd told him to call her by her first name, circumventing the Southern manners of his father. She felt a kinship with Cody that was strangely satisfying. But Alicia, that was another story. The girl had sat sullenly for the last half hour, not speaking to anyone.

JEREMY WAS LUCKY to find a parking place right in front of Brooke's condo. After giving strict instructions to his kids to stay in the car, he walked Brooke to the entrance of her building.

"I'd like to take you to your door, but…" He glanced at the street.

"No problem," she said, taking his hand. "Thank you for everything today."

"You're welcome." He leaned in and kissed her on her lips. A quick but meaningful meeting of lips that he hoped would convince her of his desire to help in any way possible. She smiled, opened her door and went inside.

When he returned to his car, Alicia was in the front seat.

"Glad you came up to join me," he said. "I haven't heard much about the party. How'd it go?"

She gave him a look that pulled at his heart-strings as much as it tested his patience. "Why the stink eye?" he asked as they drove off. "Are you hoping I change my mind about punishing you guys for that kitchen mess?"

"No. I know you're going to punish us."

He smiled. "Does a weeklong grounding seem fair?"

"Sure. Do what you want," she said. "In case you can't tell, I'm mad at you."

"And I was mad at you. So we're even, though I don't think I'll ever get the scent of maple syrup off of me."

"I don't want to talk about the stupid kitchen."

"Okay. So tell me, what's on your mind?"

Her big blue eyes seemed to lash out at him from across the car's console. "I saw you kiss her!"

Jeremy had hoped an ornamental tree in front of Brooke's condo would hide that few seconds of activity. But apparently not. "I did, Ally. I like her," he said, willing her to understand.

"You used to kiss Mommy," Alicia said. "Only Mommy."

"I don't like kissing," Cody announced from the backseat.

"Point taken, buddy." He paused, catching Cody's smile in the rearview mirror.

"Ally," he began again. "I know you miss Mommy. I do, too. I will always miss her, but she's been gone for a while now."

"I haven't stopped loving Mommy," Alicia said, her tone anxious, her words rushed. "But I guess you have."

"No, I haven't. Not at all. I will always love your mother. My memories of her are special to me, but Mommy isn't here anymore. We have to learn what that means, understand what that means. Meanwhile, we are still here, and Mommy would want us to have happy lives." He gave her a serious look. "Aren't you happy sometimes, Ally? At least part of the time?"

What if she answered no, that she was never happy? Then he hadn't listened enough, hadn't comforted her enough. He'd let her down, and that wasn't an option.

Alicia shrugged and didn't look at him. "Sometimes. Maybe. I just don't think you need somebody new. Cody and I are here."

Cody leaned forward and frowned at his sister. "Hey, leave me out of this. I like Brooke."

Alicia shot the stink eye to the backseat. "You like everybody."

"No, I don't."

Alicia crossed her arms.

"Okay, Ally," Jeremy said. "It's possible that I may want to find someone new that I like and that both of you kids like, too. I'm not saying that Brooke is that person, but hopefully sometime a special woman will come into my life and make me feel like your mother did. Can't you understand that?"

Alicia huffed.

Jeremy tried not to smile. "Sweetheart, you and your brother make me feel like I'm the luckiest guy in the world. I have two wonderful children that I adore, and you make me feel like I want to be the best father I can be to both of you. But that's not the same as the feeling I had for your mother. And the feeling I wouldn't mind having again with another woman."

"By kissing her?"

"Yes. That's part of it."

Alicia stared at her lap. "I don't like it, and I don't like her. We don't need her in our family."

"Brooke is not a part of our family. She's a business associate of mine. She's helping me become a news anchor. I've told you all this."

"Then you don't need to kiss her."

That was true. Jeremy had had many business associates in his life and he didn't kiss them. "Okay, maybe you're right," he said. "But adult relationships start with kissing. It's perfectly normal."

"Well, I don't want you to do it again."

He seemed to be at a crossroads with his daughter. When he stopped for a red light, he turned in his seat and smoothed his hand down Alicia's single dark blond braid. "If I like a woman and want to kiss her, that's my decision. It doesn't—and never will—change how I feel about you and Cody."

"The light's green," she said.

"So it is. I've decided not to enforce grounding until tomorrow. Tonight seems perfect for burgers and arcade games. What do you think?"

"I think yeah!" Cody shouted.

"I'll think about it," Alicia said.

He smiled at her. "Fair enough."

THE NEXT WEEK at WJQC was busier than normal. A string of convenience-store robberies made the residents of Charleston nervous, along with the approach of a nasty, early-season tropical storm. Forecasters warned that the storm could escalate to hurricane strength. That bit of unwelcome news put location crews on the streets for preparation interviews. Fred Armitage vied for camera time with the station's superpretty and competent meteorologist, who discussed pressure and wind speeds until even Brooke thought they were all doomed.

Still, in the midst of all this mayhem, Milt Cramer found time on Friday to call Brooke into his office for a private chat. Yes, Milt found time, since he mostly sat in his office "administrating," while Brooke, with much to do, kept looking at the clock on his wall.

"How's our boy doing?" Milt asked when he'd told Brooke to sit and relax, an order that was impossible to follow.

"Very well," she said. "He's a fast learner, and I can't say enough about the enthusiasm he has for this position. I put him in front of a camera yesterday, just so he could get a feel for what it's like. He did well. It won't be long before I'm giving him a real test. If I'm right, he should do fine as an anchor."

"Great, but will he be ready in three weeks?"

"I hope so," Brooke said. "This week has been nuts, as you know. I haven't had time to give him much coaching." The truth was, she hadn't coached him much at all since Friday, a week ago. Saturday had drifted quite easily into a fun afternoon touring around Charleston, and this week Brooke had been swamped.

"You're right," Milt said. "It's time we put Jeremy in front of a camera and lights for a proper test and see how he does. What about Wednesday of next week? I'll have a sample script made up for him."

"That might be a bit early," Brooke responded. "I haven't covered more than the basics on voice inflection and mannerisms. We've been concentrating on all other aspects of news production."

"Then get to it!" Milt said. "Time's running out. You know how much I've invested in this ex-jock. When I hired him, I knew it was a risk, but one I was willing to take because I had the top producer in the business to train him."

"Yes, I'm aware of all that, and I'm doing my best."

Milt smiled, but it was a calculated quirk of his lips that made Brooke uneasy. "If you succeed with Jeremy, you'll be able to write your own ticket in this business. Not to mention making me look good for taking a chance on an unproven commodity."

So now Jeremy was "a commodity"? Milt made his new anchor sound like a stock option. "Actually, Milt," she said, "I was already pleased with the ticket I have with this station."

"Then prove it. Have you stopped using WJQC time to mess around with whatever personal matter has been stealing your focus from your job?"

Brooke nodded. She didn't want to verbalize her feelings about Edward, nor did she want to tell Milt that she had no intention of giving up on her "personal matter."

"Okay, then, we're agreed. Jeremy will have a camera test on Wednesday."

"I suppose so."

"And quit giving so much airtime to that redheaded goddess who does the weather. That stupid storm won't be any more than a rain event. More real news, Brooke. Keep our focus where it should be. What we need now is a scoop, something that will wake this city and make it take notice of WJQC."

"Yes, sir."

"Thanks for stopping by, Brooke," he said.

She wanted to grind her teeth. She certainly hadn't "stopped by." She'd been summoned.

"Next year I see you and I working together with the fluidity of a Swiss watch, with Jeremy Crockett at the news desk. Don't disappoint me. When WJQC takes all the awards at the Silver Medallion banquet next year, I want you at the table."

Which I won't be at, if Jeremy fails, Brooke thought. She rose from the extremely uncomfortable chair Milt had offered her and went back to a different kind of intensity in the newsroom. At least this kind of pressure was like oxygen to her brain. She thrived on it. But would she be able to make Jeremy camera-perfect by Wednesday?

While contemplating the seriousness of her meeting with Milt, Brooke was startled to feel a tug on her elbow when she reached her office. She spun around. "Jeremy, you startled me."

"Oh, sorry. That's the last emotion I was hoping to elicit. Can I come in your office with you?"

"Sure, but I don't have time for coaching right now."

"Good, because I'm not interested in coaching, either."

He followed her inside, then shut the door behind them. "What a week, eh? So much news, so little time."

"That's the truth." She busied herself with messages on her desk mostly to avoid direct eye contact with Jeremy. She didn't need to forget her priorities right now, and one look at those deep brown eyes... Well...

"Any news on the Edward situation?"

"No, not yet."

"I've put a few feelers out," Jeremy said. "Maybe one of them will turn up something."

She shuffled papers.

"The kids have a sitter tonight. Marta has agreed to stay in. Since I've barely seen you this week, how about dinner tonight?"

She finally looked up at him. "Oh, dear. I can't tonight. Like you said, 'so much news.' After tonight's broadcast, I'm going to the local office of NADA to check on the hurricane predictions."

"Okay. Lunch tomorrow maybe?" he asked.

"I'd love to meet with you tomorrow," she said, thinking to use the opportunity to prepare Jeremy for his camera test. "But not for lunch. We can meet here and go over some specifics regarding camera presentation. Maybe we can order sandwiches from the deli downstairs."

Brooke was uncomfortable with the disappointed look on his face. It had been a while since a man was sincerely disappointed in not being able to see her. She'd been missing this, she realized. But she simply couldn't do it, not until Jeremy had passed every test to become Milt's golden boy. She'd been thinking about Saturday with Jeremy every day, reliving his kiss, remembering how they hadn't done anything to prepare Jeremy for the future and that she hadn't cared. Being with him outside of the studio was threatening to make her forget the prize.

She was still a news producer, and her job meant everything to her. But she might have to decide to leave WJQC and find a new position—the last thing she wanted.

Jeremy smiled, but it seemed forced. "Okay, you're the boss. If all I can get with you this weekend is a working lunch, I'll take it."

"Great. I plan on getting a lot done. Meet you here about ten? I'll bring coffee."

He nodded and headed for her office door. Brooke sighed when he walked out. She'd resisted every urge to accept his invitations, but she really should congratulate herself. She was doing this for Jeremy as much as for herself. The man had given up a lucrative career with the Wildcats to give this news thing a try, and she wanted him to be successful. He'd started a new life with his kids, and he deserved to achieve what he wanted every bit as much as she did.

The only difference was Jeremy would probably land on his feet no matter what happened. Brooke might have to start over from the ground up if he failed. "Keep it strictly business, Brooke," she said to herself. "Maybe when this is all over, there will be time for more. Only three weeks to go."

Unfortunately, her thoughts went back again to Saturday, a warm sun, strong arms making her feel better and an unforgettable kiss.

CHAPTER TEN

BY WEDNESDAY, SITUATIONS had calmed down in the newsroom. The tropical storm, which never developed into a hurricane, was hovering a hundred miles off the coast. The convenience-store robber had been captured, and Charlestonians were looking forward to Founder's Day festivities set for the end of June.

Location shoots were focused on costume shops and folks hunting for authentic Colonial attire for the parade.

With time available in the broadcast studio, and encouraged by Jeremy's recent reading in front of a camera, Brooke set up a true test screening of Jeremy's talents as an anchor. She loaded Milt's test script into the prompter and called Jeremy to sit at Fred Armitage's desk. He arrived in a suit and tie, appropriate attire for an anchor. Brooke admired his dedication to get the details right, almost as much as she admired the way he looked in a suit.

Cissy stuck by Brooke's side, as if the test couldn't possibly go off without her assistance. "What is he going to read?" she asked Brooke.

"Milt included a variety of stories," Brooke said. "There's one about dogs being mistreated in Copington Acres, and one about a police raid on a suspected drug operation on the south side. For a lighter look at the news, and to create balance, I loaded a story about neighbors helping neighbors, specifically a volunteer project to fix up the home of a World War Two vet."

"Okay," Cissy said. "That should provide a wide range of delivery options. I can't wait to see how he does."

Cissy was practically rubbing her hands together like a cartoon villain. "Don't you have somewhere you need to be?" Brooke asked her.

"And miss this? No way. Besides, you might need help."

Brooke couldn't help thinking that the production assistant truly wanted Jeremy to bomb badly.

Brooke gave Jeremy last-minute instructions, hoping that he would be good, but knew this was his first time in front of a rolling camera. She didn't expect a miracle.

"Jeremy, take the anchor's chair and position yourself a bit forward so you're closer to the camera. Make sure you feel comfortable in Fred's chair. Remember what I told you about looking as if you've just walked into the viewers' living room."

He did as she instructed. Looking at him from the control room, Brooke's first thought was that the camera would love him. Light brown, perfectly groomed hair, square shoulders, a handsome face with enough imperfections to make him identifiable, and dimples. Brooke stared at the indentations in Jeremy's cheeks, just slightly larger than dimples. Why hadn't she noticed them before? They were a prominent feature of his face and would make him appear as if he could be everyone's little brother.

"How are you feeling, Jeremy?" she asked through the microphone attached to the earpiece at the side of Jeremy's head. She wished she could be in the broadcast room with him, but he might as well experience directions from the news producer the way they would be delivered if this was an actual broadcast. She hoped he would be helped by seeing her through the glass divider.

"I'm great," he said. "Ready to give this a try."

"Okay. No surprises this time. No breaking news or interruption of what would be an actual news report, though this will be considerably shorter. I probably won't be giving you any direction at all. Just read the prompter to the best of your ability. Keep your focus on the camera with the red dot lit. And, Jeremy, remember what I told you. People are watching you from their living rooms. Make them believe they invited you in."

"Got it," he said.

Brooke instructed Cissy to hit the recorder. "Okay, in ten." She cued the WJQC news report music and graphics, and counted down, while initiating the prompter. "Five, four, three, two, one."

Jeremy's voice was strong but not as confident as she'd hoped when he said, "Good evening. I'm Jeremy Crockett with the news of the day." There was the slightest quiver in his delivery, but she could work on that.

He delivered all three stories with very little change in his voice modulation. He reported on the home-improvement project with the same inflection that he used to tell about the drug raid. He didn't make a mistake in pronunciation. He didn't skip any important details. He kept up with the prompter with only a minimum of noticeable pauses—again, an easy fix. But he didn't alter his delivery style. He even smiled while talking about the drug raid. Brooke blamed herself for over-emphasizing the living-room-guest angle.

When the five-minute trial was over, Brooke ordered the cameras to stop, opened her mic and said, "That was great, Jeremy. Take a few minutes to wind down, and I'll talk to you later."

She shut down her microphone, thankfully moments before Cissy's giggling filled the production room.

"What are you laughing about?" Brooke asked.

Cissy tried to contain her laughter. "Good grief, Brooke, he stunk. He's stiff as a board."

"Well, what did you expect? He's never been in front of a working camera."

"He's been here three weeks," Cissy said. "Hasn't he learned anything?"

"Of course he has! He's been like a sponge, soaking up everything I've told him about WJQC."

Cissy sputtered, "Maybe you should have spent more time on camera presence, girlfriend. This guy is never going to make it as our new anchor."

Brooke tried to rein in her anger. "Give him a chance, Ciss. This is new to him. Remember when Fred first started? He could have put the audience to sleep."

"And yet…" Cissy laughed again. "He was much more exciting than Mr. Legs over there." Cissy placed her hand on Brooke's shoulder. "This isn't your fault, Brooke. I know you've been trying with him, but he just doesn't have what it takes, and I doubt he ever will."

"That's going too far, Cissy. There's still time left to work with Jeremy, and I'm confident I can improve his camera presence…"

Cissy's features grew more serious. "What are you so upset about, Brooke? This could work to our advantage. I want Jeremy to fail, don't you? We talked about this."

"No. You talked about it. I want Jeremy to succeed."

"But you and I both deserve shots at that anchor position. Don't you want it if I can't have it?"

"No, Cissy, I don't."

"And you don't think I deserve a shot?"

"This has nothing to do with what you deserve, Cissy. Jeremy is Milt's choice. He expects me to make him camera-perfect. Milt wants Jeremy to improve our ratings."

"And after that performance, you think he will?"

Brooke felt her temper flare and the temperature rising in her cheeks. "I don't know! What I do know is that my job depends on turning Jeremy into—" She stopped abruptly. "Never mind."

Cissy stared hard at Brooke's eyes. "Into what? What does your job depend on, Brooke?"

"Nothing. Forget I said anything."

"Oh, no. Something's going on. Are you saying that you won't have a job here if you don't make Legs into Super Anchor? Milt will fire you?"

Brooke's shoulders slumped. She wished she could take back the words. "I don't know. Maybe." Oh, dear, she'd said very little, but yet too much.

"If that's true, then you should be mad as hell," Cissy said. "It's up to you and me to open Milt's eyes. He can't get away with that. Does Jeremy know about this?"

"No, he doesn't, and you can't say anything. Not a word to anyone, Cissy. Promise me."

"Oh, I won't say anything, but it's time word got out around WJQC that the anchor position is not a sure thing. Milt will see for himself that Jeremy isn't going to make it, and that will open the door to you or me."

"I plan to talk to Milt before he views this tape," Brooke said. "I'm not done with helping Jeremy. And I'm going to do everything I can to see that he is WJQC's anchor."

Suddenly those words meant more than just the fulfillment of an ultimatum. Brooke truly believed them.

"You're wasting your time," Cissy said. "I'm putting my money on you or me being the next WJQC anchor. And if you are half as smart as I think you are, you'll jump on this horse with me and ride all the way to the five o'clock news."

One more word from Cissy, and Brooke feared she would scream. She looked out at the broadcast room where Jeremy had been pacing. "I've got to go talk to him," she said. "Remember, what we discussed is just between you and me."

"Of course. But I have your best interests at heart even if you don't. Sometimes it takes a friend to make you realize your true potential." Cissy headed for the door. "The guy may be gorgeous, but for our purposes at WJQC, he's a loser. Deep down you know that."

JEREMY STOPPED PACING the minute he saw Brooke enter the studio. All smiles, he came over to her. "Well, how was it? For a first-timer, not bad, right?"

He seemed like a boy, wanting to be praised for hitting a home run. Brooke simply couldn't crush that enthusiasm. Besides, Cissy's opinion was so one-sided and self-motivated.

"Not bad," she echoed.

"I'm sure you have a few comments," he said. "I never expected to be perfect my first time in front of a camera."

She plastered a smile on her face. "Well, yes, I do have a few suggestions."

"Great." He took her elbow and led her to a quiet corner of the room. "It's almost time for the news," he said. "I'll wait until you're finished and then why don't we go out for a drink and we can talk about ways I might improve my performance. What do you say?"

What could she say? She had to tell him the truth and maybe over a drink would be the best way. They would both be relaxed. "Sure. Meet you at Pickler's at six thirty?"

"Pickler's it is. See you there."

He left the studio, and Brooke watched the production crew set up for Fred's newscast. She smiled at Fred as he approached the news desk, a makeup artist trailing after him. Fred always asked the makeup artist to make him look ten years younger. Brooke had learned long ago that he wasn't joking around. Over the time she'd known him, Fred had acquired quite a vanity streak. She sighed, thinking maybe the best way out of this mess was to convince Fred the station couldn't live without him and he should cancel his retirement. If she said that, Fred would be the only person Brooke was going to flatter tonight.

After the broadcast Brooke walked over to Pickler's. Jeremy was seated by the door under a soft overhead light. Her knees went a bit weak. He'd abandoned his tie, unbuttoned his sports coat and loosened the collar of his shirt. This man would certainly not have to make special requests of the makeup artist.

He stood and pulled a chair out for her. "How'd it go tonight?"

"Fine. Slow news day. Fred even got to report on a cat rescued from a sewer drain."

Jeremy chuckled. "What can I get you from the bar?"

"Just a red wine, please. I managed to get over here without spraining anything, but I still have to drive home."

"If you had sprained anything, I would have been happy to drive you home," he said and headed to the bar.

And I would have been happy to let you, she thought. Ten days had passed since The Kiss, and while Brooke's memories of the event hadn't faded, she definitely wanted to see if what her senses remembered was the real thing. There was only one way to test that, so she shook her head. "Not tonight, Brooke. And maybe after this meeting, never again."

He returned to the table, placed a wineglass in front of her and poured from the decanter. He pulled his chair around the table and sat close to her. He had chosen an intimate spot in the bar, away from the thinning happy-hour crowd. It was quiet, nice...romantic, even.

She lifted her glass. "Thanks."

"I know we have to talk about my performance," he said, "but can I bend your ear about another matter first?"

"Of course you can." She felt a wave of relief. Maybe the glass of wine would steady her nerves or at least give her courage.

"I want to talk about my daughter, Alicia."

"Oh, okay." If he only knew, she was probably the least qualified person to talk about children, but thanks to her association with her ten-year-old niece, she did know a bit about girls. They liked to pick out their own clothes, watch movies, eat ice cream. Somehow she doubted that this conversation was going to follow those parameters.

"I've wanted to have you out to the house again," Jeremy began. "But I realize the last time you were with my kids, Ally didn't do anything to make you feel comfortable."

Jeremy frowned. "Usually Ally is happy to meet new people, but I guess you can understand that the last year has not been easy for her."

"I understand completely."

"She wasn't herself on that ride back from Hidden Oaks," Jeremy explained. "Ordinarily she's talkative and a curious kid, always asking questions. All that has changed since her mother... Cody seems to have found a balance while Ally is still struggling."

"Getting over such a loss takes time, Jeremy."

"I know. But I'm running out of ways to reach her, to help with her grieving. I'm watching my sweet little girl become more and more withdrawn."

Brooke wished she could think of something to say that wasn't a platitude, but again, she hadn't experienced the kind of loss that

Alicia and Cody had. Though sometimes she felt that not knowing about Edward was something like a loss.

Jeremy took a deep breath and let it go. "I can't let Ally's sadness take over her life. And it is. Her grades are suffering. She's moody. She's obstinate. You saw firsthand with that display in the kitchen."

Brooke tapped her finger on her wineglass. "Maybe you should take her to see someone. A therapist. We did a story on family counselors in Charleston. We have a number of really good ones."

"I'll look into that, first thing. She saw a therapist in Colorado," Jeremy said. "We—her grandparents and I—thought she was okay, but now I'm not so sure."

"I'm sorry to hear that," Brooke said. "And I feel badly for both of you. Is there anything I can do to help?" She hesitated to say more, feeling she was out of her depth.

He took a long swallow of his drink. Maybe he needed courage, too. "I was hoping that you could talk to her. I know Ally hasn't been over the moon around you, but she needs a strong female in her life… It's what she's been missing and I can't give that to her."

"But Alicia hasn't shown that she wants me for a friend, Jeremy. I'm likely the last person she wants to confide in."

"I know, and I realize that what I'm asking is a huge imposition."

"No, it isn't, and I would love to help, but I'm hesitant because Alicia is so negative toward me."

"The truth is she resents you, as if you're trying to take her mother's place. But if she got to know you better…"

"That's a tough one," Brooke said. "I would never do that. Take her mother's place."

"I know it," Jeremy said. "But Ally's emotions are all over the place and she sees things differently than we do. And if you and I are going to continue to hang out with each other—"

"Are you talking about a relationship? Maybe now isn't the right time to be thinking about that. Ally is still adjusting and we've only known each other a few weeks."

"If you don't want to see me again on a personal level, then just tell me. But if you do, I'm asking you to maybe spend some time with my daughter. Just give it a try. Once she sees how smart and kind you are… It's not like her to form an opinion about someone so quickly."

"And show that I'm not a threat to her mother's memory?"

"Yes, that, too."

She drummed her fingers on the table. "Gee, Jeremy, you're not asking a lot."

"I know it's a lot, Brooke." He covered her arm with his palm. "But you are the first woman besides Lynette in years that I've felt any connection with. And I felt it from the first time I saw you bustling around the newsroom with your hair all…" He wiggled his fingers around his own head. "I'd like to see if this might work between us. What about you?"

Yes. I would like very much to give this a try. But not now. Not when nearly everything that means something in my life depends on how you succeed. Not when you have a troubled daughter, and I don't know the first thing about how to untrouble her. Not when my heart is beating so fast right now that I feel I might run a marathon in a minute.

"It would mean so much to me," Jeremy added.

Brooke thought about all the reasons she should avoid approaching Alicia, but Jeremy's last words got to her. She said, "Maybe I could speak to Ally, Jeremy. But don't get your hopes up. I've never had kids." *Never wanted any.* "With the exception of my nieces, they are alien beings to me."

He leaned in, kissed her lightly on the lips. "Thank you. So after we stay here and have dinner tonight, you'll come out to the house again soon?"

"We're having dinner?"

He laughed. "I guess I sprung that on you. Believe me, when I was contemplating how I would approach you with my feelings, I wasn't the least bit hungry. Now…" He brushed a lock of her hair off her shoulder. "Now I could eat a twelve-ounce steak, no problem."

He called over a waiter and asked for two menus. "Of course, all this newfound confidence of mine could be squashed with your critique of how I did in front of the camera." His smile told her he didn't think it would be bad news.

DINNER WAS ENJOYABLE and relaxing. Jeremy couldn't remember the last time an hour had gone by so quickly. Yes, Brooke's critique of his performance was still the reason for this meeting, but so far the atmosphere had been comfortable. He hoped when Brooke started talking about his on-camera experience, she would be positive.

In the meantime, he told Brooke about his past, his relationship with his mother and how he admired his sister, Phyllis.

No matter where they ended up, Jeremy and Phyllis called and talked for hours, and visited at least two or three times a year. Jeremy told Brooke how smart Phyllis was, but that she hadn't had the good fortune he'd found by playing football in high school. Jeremy went to Bellingsworth on a full ride. Phyllis took six years to get through college by working and attending night school. He was so proud of her and would do anything to help her now. But she didn't need his help. She was married, with a solid career as a technical writer.

Brooke listened attentively.

"Sounds like you have a great bond with your sister," she said. "I can't imagine my life without Camryn in it. We're very different, but it's the bond that counts, and we have that. She's my sister, my confidante, my best friend."

"I would love to meet her sometime," Jeremy said.

"Cammie and her husband live in the extreme Lowcountry and raise chickens and children. I bet you guys would get along."

Strangely, the mood shifted, and a wave of tension rose up between them. "Brooke, is something wrong?" he asked. "We still haven't talked about the camera test."

When she spoke, she sounded so intense. "Then let's get to it," she said, motioning for the waiter to bring the check. "Thank you for dinner."

Jeremy left cash on the table and stood. "I'll walk you to your car," he said. "I'm sensing maybe this restaurant isn't the best place for us to go over my performance today."

"No. Maybe it isn't."

They walked out of the restaurant and headed toward the station. Suddenly, he was unnaturally nervous. "So, do you want to come out to the house tomorrow or on the weekend?" he asked.

She walked slowly, forcing him to rein in his energy and follow her lead. "Let's decide about that after we talk."

Now he was uncertain. He'd thought he'd done well enough, so well that he'd opened up to her about Ally and his family. Maybe she'd just been "sympathy listening" or avoiding the real issue. "Give it to me straight, Brooke. Was I awful? Didn't feel that way when I was talking to the camera."

"No, of course you weren't awful, but there might be room for improvement."

"Did I stumble over any words, mispronounce some key elements of a story? In other words, did I sound like a dumb jock with delusions of grandeur?"

"No, nothing like that," she said.

Okay. That was good. He'd taken a few English classes in college, and he thought he had a solid grasp of language and grammar.

"Probably the most significant thing I noticed…" she began.

They reached the parking garage. He held

the door so she could precede him inside. She kept walking, not missing a step.

"I found you to be a bit stiff," she said.

"Stiff?" he echoed. "Well, that's a problem."

"Yes, sort of. You need to relax, treat the camera like an old friend that connects you to all those new friends you're going to be making in Charleston." She stopped, turned to face him. "Actually, I think your delivery is my fault. I've put so much pressure on you. And I haven't given you enough information about how to address the camera."

"Obviously, we need to work on that," he said. "I'm sure Milt won't want a robot at the news desk."

"No," she agreed. "He's going to want to see a calm, confident professional."

"And do you think I can be that?"

She didn't answer right away, and he felt his temples throb. He must have been horrible, and she didn't know how to tell him.

"I think you can be," she said. "But you need to loosen up, talk *to* the camera, not *at* the camera. We have more than two weeks to go, so no reason to panic."

"Panic? I wasn't even considering panicking. But now that you brought it up…"

She leaned against her car door. He stood in front of her. "Anything else?" he asked.

"Not now."

Not now? Then when, and what?

"It's enough for us to work on your delivery. Why don't you think about things you do for enjoyment, things that make you happy and calm. Things you'd like to do. If you think about those things before the red light comes on the camera, maybe you will automatically relax."

He rubbed the nape of his neck. He'd signed a contract with WJQC, but he supposed if he really stunk, Milt could buy him out. He thought of his kids, coming all the way from Denver. He thought about the house he'd bought in Hidden Oaks. These had all been positive steps for Jeremy, but if he had to give them up and move somewhere else and start over, he could do it. He could find another job, and he had plenty of money that would last for a while. And surely he wasn't just a dumb jock.

Brooke reached out, took his hand. "Jeremy,

I didn't mean to upset you. We've had such a lovely evening."

"Yeah, the calm before the storm."

She smiled. "Delivering on camera is difficult. It's my job to put you at ease. And I will. I promise."

Her face was so serious, so determined. In a way, he was sorry he'd put so much pressure on her. She almost acted like his success was a measure of her own importance. Crazy. She was the most dedicated professional he'd ever met. He'd wondered what was in this tutoring gig for her and decided she was just that committed to her job, and the station. "Sure, Brooke. It's all going to be fine."

She maintained a grip on his hand as if she was transferring her knowledge into his palm. "Yes, it will," she said, but for the first time he wasn't totally convinced.

He leaned in toward her. Okay, if things didn't work out for him here, he would move on, but he didn't want his failure to feel like hers. Maybe he would never be better than he'd been during his test, but he didn't want her to bear the blame. "Let's not talk about this any more tonight," he said. "We have time." He placed his hand on her nape.

She swallowed. "Okay."

His lips met hers. He kissed her with a gentle pressure that soon had her responding as if she'd been thinking the same thing. A dimly lit parking garage. They were the only two people there. He was doing what he'd been thinking of doing for over a week now. The kiss intensified.

When he drew back, he smiled at her. "To be perfectly honest, Brooke, that just happens to be one of the things I really enjoy doing. Maybe I need to remember holding on to you before that red light comes on. So if you want me to be a really good broadcaster, then maybe we should practice."

She smiled, too. "I'll consider it. I'd like to help any way I can."

She got in her car and he walked to his. She'd just given him bad news about his chances at WJQC, but so what? Being a failure at WJQC wasn't the end of the world for anyone.

CHAPTER ELEVEN

ON SATURDAY, FOR the first time since she'd met Jeremy, Brooke drove herself out to Hidden Oaks. Jeremy had insisted he come to pick her up, but she had said, "That's silly. I'm perfectly capable of driving a half hour."

She wasn't able to take in the countryside, as she had during her last trip into the Lowcountry residential area, but she saw enough today to wonder at the beauty of it all. Magnolias were beginning to blossom. Spanish moss hung like fairy's wings from the old oak trees. The South in early June was a beautiful place to be.

Brooke enjoyed the drive, although there was no way she could imagine ever moving into this remote rural area. She liked being able to walk a couple of blocks to get a deli sandwich or a soda. The closest movie theater was three blocks away from her condo. Some of the city's best hotels were also within walking distance, and Brooke often strolled by them and just took in the old charm that was her home city. For sure, lots of land, open spaces and warm, humid air were nice for a person with children, but not for Brooke Montgomery. She was all about the city, and couldn't foresee giving up the conveniences she'd grown used to. Not even for... She stopped the thought before it fully formed. As much as she'd come to admire and like Jeremy, there was no way either one of them would consider a relationship. There were just too many obstacles between them.

Thinking of Jeremy's children, Brooke experienced a moment of anxiety when she pulled into the circular drive in front of his house. She wasn't concerned about Cody. They had made inroads into a comfortable relationship the last time she'd been here. But Alicia. That was another story. She'd pretty much given her word to Jeremy that she would try to communicate with the girl, which explained why Brooke had been up until the wee hours last night studying experts' advice on grieving children and how to help them. Not that any of it would work. Hopefully, Alicia would give her a chance to try what she'd learned.

Jeremy came out his front door when she turned off the engine of her car. If he was upset about her critique on Wednesday, he hid it well. He wore a cotton shirt with a print of various Lowcounty trees on it and beige shorts that fit him just right. Brooke sighed. Whether in a suit or casual outfits, Jeremy could wear clothes.

He smiled as she got out of her car in a lemon-print sundress and yellow sandals. She walked around her car and he gave her a quick kiss on the lips. Was this going to be the usual way of greeting each other? She wondered. If so, she didn't believe she'd complain.

"You look great," he said. "Did you bring your swimsuit?"

"No, I did not," she said. "We are working today, remember?"

"I remember, but the kids are here, so I'm doing double duty as anchor trainee and daddy-man. Hope that's okay."

"We'll make it work. We can get a lot done if you've planned activities for the kids." She looked across the expansive front yard and off to the side of the wraparound porch. She didn't see any children. "Where are they?"

"Upstairs changing into their bathing suits.

I've already given them lunch and told them they could swim while we worked on the patio. Have you eaten?"

She checked her watch. Eleven o'clock. "No, but that's okay. I'm not particularly hungry."

"No worries," he said. "Marta left fruit, cheese and crackers for us before she went off to do some shopping. I don't think we'll starve. Can I get you a glass of wine?"

"At eleven in the morning?" She laughed. "I think I'll pass. But iced tea would be great."

He walked her to his front door and through the entryway and great room to a sunny area with floor-to-ceiling windows. The last time she'd been here, she hadn't seen much more of the house than the kitchen, which had been a disaster.

"You can go on out," Jeremy said. "I'll bring the tea."

She sat at a patio table and opened her iPad where she'd typed up her notes from Wednesday. She and Jeremy simply had to buckle down today.

"Hi, Brooke," a voice hollered from the door to a cabana bathroom. Cody came outside, a towel over his arm and swim rings on his small biceps.

"Hey, Cody. Good to see you again."

She must have been staring at the safety rings on his arms because he squeezed one and said, "I'm not going to need these much longer. I never learned how to swim in Colorado, but Marta takes me for lessons once a week now."

She smiled. "Where'd you swim in Colorado?"

"At the Y. But Mom didn't take me much. She said it was always too cold. I like it here better."

"I'm glad you do," Brooke said. "South Carolina is a great place to do outdoor things."

"I'm going to get in the pool now. I want to get the whale raft before Ally takes it."

"Okay."

He started down the steps. "Will you watch me? Daddy says somebody has to do that for now when I'm little."

"No problem."

Cody was a ray of sunshine with his curly blond hair, slightly sunburned cheeks and dolphin-covered swim trunks. He seemed to be adjusting to the loss of his mother, but

Brooke's heart still ached for the emotions he must be dealing with inside.

The cabana door slammed shut a second time, and Alicia came outside. Only three years older than Cody, she could have been a model in a Macy's magazine. Her pink bikini with matching half skirt tied around her waist and round sunglasses with pink lenses seemed to be the latest fashion. Her flip-flops, decorated with imitation colored stones, slapped against her feet as she walked by Brooke without speaking. Her dark blond hair was tied in a ponytail.

"Hi, Alicia," Brooke said.

The girl stopped, turned around. "Oh, hi. I'm getting in the pool. Daddy will want you to watch us until he comes out. I think it's silly—"

"He's out," Jeremy said, walking to the table with a tray in his hand. He placed a glass in front of Brooke and then another in front of an empty chair, which he soon filled. "Be careful, you two," he said to his kids. "No roughhousing."

"I noticed Ally spoke to you this time," Jeremy said to Brooke. "That's an improvement."

Brooke didn't respond. She doubted Alicia would have spoken if Brooke hadn't first. But, okay, it was an improvement.

"You didn't say anything to her about me talking to her, did you?" Brooke asked. She didn't want Alicia to be on pins and needles thinking she was going to get a lecture.

"No. That has to be a spontaneous thing when you think the time is right. I trust your judgment."

If only you were putting your trust in anyone but me. Brooke adjusted the iPad so both she and Jeremy could see it. "Shall we start?"

THE TOP OF the iPad screen didn't alarm Jeremy much. *Comments for Jeremy.* That could mean anything—good or bad. But the first comment shocked him into preparing himself for what was to come.

"Flat voice?" he said. "You thought my voice was flat?"

"Well, yes, for the purposes of WJQC, at least. Another station might feel differently."

She was doing her best to deliver a crushing critique under a sheen of politeness.

"Brooke, a flat voice is a flat voice, no matter what microphone picks it up." He shook his head. "I always considered myself the locker-room cheerleader for the Wildcats, saying things like 'come on guys, more effort' or 'put your heart into it.' A guy can't say stuff like that with a flat voice."

"I'm sure you were great at building enthusiasm for a football team," she said. "But speaking in front of a still camera with a bright red light is a lot different." She sighed—sighed, as if she was pulling on reserves from deep within to broach this subject.

"Let me try to explain it this way," she said. "Years ago, voice training for TV was a fairly simple activity. Men were told to use a low, masculine timbre throughout the broadcast. Women were told to always sound like they were in their kitchens explaining how to cook." She smiled. "Thank goodness those days are over."

"Yeah. Now we're supposed to weep and wail and grind our teeth," Jeremy said.

"No, of course not. Newscasting took a different turn when popular anchors managed to deliver news, good and bad, as if they were sitting in a chair next to the listener. And they did it by eye contact, honest presentation and trust building. They eliminated the monotone of their predecessors and became...well, human."

"And after one test, I've suddenly moved us all back to the subhuman age."

She cocked her head to the side and narrowed her eyes at him. "Am I going to have to deal with this childish sarcasm for the rest of the afternoon?"

Okay, she was right to be upset. But he'd thought he had nailed that test. And the dinner and drinks afterward. "All right, I get it," he said. "So what do I have to do to correct my faults?"

"One simple solution is to record your conversations. When you are talking to your kids, for example, set your phone to Record and play it back when you're alone. That's probably about as honest as you're going to get in dealing with people on a face-to-face basis."

"You mean I should talk to the viewing audience like I talk to my kids?"

"No, not exactly. You're taking me too literally. But you should try to establish that kind of intimacy."

"I don't know. I can try. What else?"

She scrolled down her iPad screen. "Recognize that the human voice has peaks and valleys. It's supposed to. A voice inflection can change in the middle of a sentence to become more listener friendly. Vary your sentences. We try to do that for the anchor before the material is loaded into the prompter, but you can eventually learn to play around with our writing to make it more comfortable for you. A short sentence every now and then is a good tactic if you want to hold someone's attention."

This all made sense and turned his ideas of broadcasting upside down. He'd thought the idea was to deliver the news as blandly as possible. "Just the facts, ma'am," as one TV police sergeant from the 50s used to say.

"But don't be maudlin. Show some emotion but not too much. The reason people still remember Cronkite's reporting of the death of John Kennedy was because he showed more true emotion than he ever had before. And rightly so. The situation called for it."

He glanced over the pool, taking in the bobbing heads of his children. All was right in that world. "So what should I do? Practice? And how does a person practice to be a newscaster?"

"It's training," she said. "I'm sure you understand that. You trained to be a wide receiver. Work on making your script voice sound like your ad-lib voice. Keep your words simple. Use words like *traffic tie-up* instead of *transportational gridlock*."

"I would never say *transportational gridlock* in my lifetime," he said.

She laughed. "Yes, but you get the point."

"So it's like those people who need to walk ten thousand steps a day wearing a monitor from the time they get up. I have to have a microphone ready every time I plan to say more than a few words."

"Can't hurt. Talk, talk, talk, and then listen. How many times did you catch a football before you were drafted by a professional team?"

He shrugged. Not all that many times, actually. Maybe he was just a dumb jock. Maybe his talents were destined to be centered on what his body could do and not his brain.

"And one other thing—don't ever smile during a serious story."

"Okay. I'll try to remember that," he said. "Don't give up on me, teach."

Her smile was warm when she said, "Not a chance."

"Hey, Dad!" Cody's voice drew Jeremy's attention away from the mesmerizing blue of Brooke's eyes in the sunlight.

"What is it, Cody?"

"Why don't you get in and swim with us?"

He looked at Brooke. "Do you mind? I think I may have some stress to work off. Wanna come?"

"Go ahead. I'm perfectly happy in the sun."

He stood, unbuttoned his shirt and chucked it on his lawn chair. Thinking about a dive from the deep end, he walked to the diving board. And he was aware, every step of the way, that Brooke's attention was fixed right where he wanted it—on the body that could catch a football, not the man who could deliver the news. That made him feel a bit better, but he'd still like to be the man who could be both brawn and brain for Brooke.

BROOKE STAYED BY the pool until the Crocketts got out, dripping and panting. "That was so fun," Cody said.

"You bet it was," Jeremy said. "Won't be long before you can take me in laps."

Cody snapped off his arm wings. "Gotta

get rid of these stupid things first." He tossed the wings to a chair and came over to Brooke. "Did you watch us?"

"I did. Looked like you were having fun." She looked around for Alicia. The girl was not on the patio. She'd obviously gone inside without stopping to talk.

"I need a snack," Cody said. "Dad, will you get something for me and Brooke?"

"Sure will. I promised Brooke some lunch and I don't want her to think I'm not going to keep my word."

Jeremy dried off and hung his towel over the back of a chair. "I'll be right back," he said. "You guys will be okay?"

"We'll be fine," Brooke said.

Cody sat across from her. "Did you have a pool when you were little?" he asked.

"No, I didn't, but I lived pretty close to some great beaches on the Carolina coast. My parents would take us almost every Sunday if the weather was nice."

The next hour went quickly with Brooke, Jeremy and Cody munching on fruit and cheese and chatting about Cody's school and his successes in soccer. If someone had sauntered onto the patio, they might have thought they were witnessing a perfectly happy, typical family gathering. Only in this case, the missing person made the whole thing far from typical.

"I should be getting back to Charleston," Brooke said.

"I can't interest you in a movie and pizza later?"

"It's tempting, but no." Brooke didn't think she could add much to a Crockett family outing, especially when one family member didn't like her interference in their lives. An opportunity to talk to Alicia hadn't evolved naturally, so Brooke would wait until she had another chance to engage the girl. Besides, Brooke needed some time, as much as Jeremy did, to process everything she'd told him today. She didn't want him to become discouraged. The last thing she needed was for Jeremy to quit. She just simply wanted him to be great, for his sake as well as hers. Was that too much to ask? According to Cissy, he didn't have a chance.

Brooke went into the house to use the bathroom. She passed a small, classically decorated room, Jeremy's office perhaps, since the furnishings were dark and masculine. She almost walked by before seeing Alicia at the desk. Brooke stopped, considered her options and then went inside, armed with the lessons she'd learned from her reading the night before and her desire to help Jeremy with this troubled child.

Alicia looked up but didn't speak.

"Hi," Brooke said. "Since I saw you here I thought I'd say a quick goodbye. It's been a lovely day, don't you think?"

"I suppose."

Brooke interpreted the kidspeak as "it was until you got here."

Colored pencils littered the desktop, and Alicia was coloring an intricate design of flowers and small animals. "Wow, that looks hard. Coloring was never like that when I was a kid."

Alicia continued filling in the tiny spaces without looking at Brooke. "We use pencils now. Nobody uses crayons anymore."

"In any case, it's quite a work of art." Brooke tried to think of something to say that might initiate a conversation with Alicia. Unfortunately, nothing came to mind that didn't sound rehearsed. "Well, goodbye," she said.

"Goodbye."

She started to leave when she noticed a photograph on the desk. It was a picture of a very pretty woman about Brooke's age. Her hair was dark blond like Alicia's, and though she couldn't tell for sure, Brooke was certain her eyes were the same soft blue.

"That is a beautiful woman. Is it a picture of your mother?" she asked.

Alicia nodded.

"She's lovely."

"Yeah."

"You look like her."

"That's what Daddy says."

Encouraged by the responses, however short, Brooke probed a bit deeper. "I'm sure you miss her so much."

"Yeah."

"I'm very sorry that she died. Mothers are very special, and I'm certain your mother loved you and Cody a lot."

Alicia's eyes became tiny slits. Her lips turned down. "How would you know that? You never even met her."

"You're right," Brooke said. "I guess I must have gotten that impression from what your

father told me." She tried to remember something concrete from her research last night but
she found herself floundering."

"She did, though."

Brooke paused, leaned in toward the desk
and the small voice that had reached out to
her. "She did?"

"She did love us."

Brooke nodded. "It's not fair that you lost
your mother, Alicia. I wish I knew the right
words to say. To make things better for you."

"Daddy says that, too. But he can't do anything about it."

"He would like to. Your daddy wants you to
be happy, but he understands that sometimes
you just can't be."

The child picked up a colored pencil and
pressed hard on the page. The tip of the pencil
snapped off. "Now look what you made me do!"

"We can fix it. Doesn't your dad have a
pencil sharpener in here?"

Alicia pointed to a bookcase where an elec-
tric sharpener sat on a low shelf.

Brooke extended her hand for the pencil.
"May I?"

Alicia gave her the pencil and Brooke sharpened it to a fine point. "Look. Good as new."

Alicia continued with her coloring as if nothing had happened, as if Brooke was no longer there.

"I would like to learn to color like that," Brooke said. "Maybe you can teach me."

Alicia looked up at her. "You don't need a teacher to color. You just have to stay in the lines."

Brooke took the initiative of pulling up a chair to the desk and sitting down. "What else do you like to do, Alicia?"

Another shrug. "I don't know. Stuff."

Brooke took a deep breath. "Would it be okay if you and I did some stuff together sometime? Whatever you want. You can pick the activity."

Alicia stopped coloring. Was she weighing up her offer? "Maybe."

It was a start, and Brooke allowed herself to feel encouraged. "I enjoyed seeing the picture of your mother, Alicia. Any time you want to talk some more, I would love to listen."

No response, but Brooke was pleased with what had happened so far. It felt as if a door had opened. Maybe Alicia would walk through. "I have to go now," Brooke said, pushing the chair back. "I hope I see you again soon. Have a good week at school."

The girl raised her head and looked into Brooke's eyes. "Thanks for fixing the pencil."

Wow. Brooke smiled, but secretly, she wanted to cheer.

Brooke said goodbye to Jeremy and Cody, who were both back at the pool. Jeremy offered to walk her to her car, but she told him to stay with his son.

She suddenly felt drained from two of the most difficult conversations she'd ever had in her life. First, she'd had to tell Jeremy that he had a lot of work to do. Second, she spoke to a grieving child who made her own heart ache. She didn't know which conversation was hardest, but as she got in her car and headed back to Charleston, she felt as though she'd made some inroads with both Crocketts today.

And the odd thing was, she truly wished she could help both of them, and not just because her job depended on it.

THAT NIGHT ON the phone, Brooke confided in her sister. "Come on, Cammie, you're the child expert. How can I reach this kid?"

"It's tough, Brooke. Everyone grieves differently. I never had to comfort Esther over the loss of a human in her life, but I remember what it was like when those wild boars massacred our chickens."

Brooke remembered, too. That incident, which took place in the middle of a stark, cold night, had sent her sister to the hospital, where her pregnancy was monitored and normalized. A few weeks later, Camryn had delivered a fine, healthy baby girl, but it had been touch and go for a while.

"Okay, so how did you reach Esther when she learned about the chicks?"

"I let her talk, Brooke. And I let her know that despite how awful that night was, we would go on. I do remember reading something once that might be helpful."

"What? Anything," Brooke said.

"Well, don't dance around the fact that someone is dead. Don't use euphemisms for death. A child who's nine knows that death does not mean the person is just going to stay asleep forever. Dead is dead. We all die. Our job as the adults is to help the child cope, not sugarcoat the truth."

"Okay. That sounds wise."

"And make the child feel safe," Camryn added. "A death in the family can cause enormous anxiety and fear. Help the child know that she is safe and will always be cared for. That might be more a job for her father, but it can't hurt for you to second the notion."

This was good advice and much easier to grasp when told in Camryn's simple, honest way. "Anything else?" Brooke asked.

"If I think of anything else, I'll call you. But, Brooke?"

"What?"

"Why is this so important to you?"

"I don't know." Brooke answered so quickly and without thought that she felt her head spin. Of course she knew. She cared for Jeremy, and she cared for a little girl who would rather destroy an entire kitchen than reveal her true emotions.

"I bet you do know," Camryn said. "I bet the woman who always said she didn't want to have children, that she couldn't cope with them, has just found that her heart has a soft spot for the little creatures. And perhaps their father."

"You always sound like such a romantic," Brooke said. "I guess that's why I love you."

"You've got romance in your soul, too, sister. And compassion and a heart that's almost too big to fit in your chest. And truthfully, I know these emotions scare you to death."

No way was Brooke going to continue this conversation. If she let Camryn expound on her idea, they could go on talking for the rest of the night. "Kiss Esther and Grace for me, okay?"

"I will. And Brooke, good luck with this. The most important thing I can tell you is to be yourself. You're a good person, you know? I expect to hear how it's going."

Brooke wouldn't know how it's going for two days. She had no plans to see Jeremy on Sunday and the next day was the beginning of a new week. How much time she would have with Jeremy was, as always, anybody's guess.

CHAPTER TWELVE

MILT CRAMER BREEZED by Brooke's office door midmorning on Tuesday. With no greeting, he simply said, "Brooke, I need to see you in my office now." And he kept walking.

Brooke abandoned the news stories her team had selected in the production meeting that morning. She'd get back to them later. She hustled to Milt's office.

Milt sat behind his desk, his hands folded on top. He leaned back in his chair. "Sit down, Brooke. We have to talk."

She sat, but not comfortably, with her feet flat on the floor, her knees feeling stiff. "Is something wrong?"

"I would like to think not, but I'm afraid so," he said. "I hear our boy did that broadcast test on Wednesday. Is that so?"

So that's what this was about. Brooke relaxed. She could easily defend Jeremy's first attempt in front of the camera. Many others, she knew, had done a lot worse and had still ended up being successful. "He did, yes," she said. "You and I talked about giving him time in front of a camera. Actually, I thought Wednesday might be a bit early, and—"

"How do you think he did?"

"Not bad. But he isn't quite ready yet. With a little coaching he'll be up to the task."

"You're skirting the truth, Brooke," Milt said. "He was lousy!"

Brooke tamped down a spike of anger. He hadn't seen Jeremy's performance. How could he judge? "That's not so, Milt. Jeremy wasn't perfect, but he was okay. Quite good, actually."

"No. He wasn't. Even that ditzy girl with the pink hair who follows you around all the time…what's her name? Chrissy? Missy?"

"Cissy."

"Yeah, her. She said Jeremy looked like a cardboard cutout sitting at the desk. And his voice sounded flat as a pancake."

"This was his first attempt at working in front of a camera," she said.

"He's been here three weeks. He's watched Fred. He's shadowed everyone in this building. You gave him practice camera time once before. And that's not even counting that he's been in front of cameras his whole football career."

"That's not the same," Brooke argued. "Speaking to a reporter about a sports game can't compare to delivering the news to a general audience."

"Still, he should be a pro. I thought he was when I signed him to a contract. He was confident enough then. 'I can do it, Milt,' he said to me. 'This is the chance I need.' I believed him, and then, just to make sure he was camera ready and picture-perfect, I set him up with you to round out the rough edges. Turns out the guy is all rough edges, and maybe you can't fix him."

"Milt, you're jumping to conclusions."

"Am I? Do you have any idea how much money is involved with that contract?"

Brooke remembered Jeremy telling her that he'd taken a pay cut from pro football to serve as anchor for WJQC, but now probably wasn't the time to say that. "I assume it's a considerable amount," she said.

"You're darn right it is, and I counted on

you to make him an anchor—not just any anchor. The best one in the Charleston area."

"Don't read too much into what Cissy told you. She doesn't have experience in judging what makes a good anchor. I'm telling you that Jeremy shows all the signs of a competent reporter. We still have time before you want to introduce him to the Charleston audience."

"Only a couple of weeks. Jeremy is supposed to take over for Fred on June twenty-fourth." Milt placed his elbows on his desktop and leaned forward. "You knew what this deal means to me, Brooke. And what it means to you and everyone at this station. I'm starting to wonder if you've been putting all your effort into this. Or if you're still wrapped up in whatever personal thing is going on in your life."

"I'm putting every spare moment into this," she said. "And as for my personal issues, they aren't your concern. They never were. I haven't brought my problems into work since you warned me about it."

"Good to know, Brooke. We've always been a team, you and me. And I've counted on you for this. I had to get you to recognize the importance of hiring Jeremy for this job."

"We're a team? You said you'd fire me."

"I say a lot of things. And it's still a possibility. We have a board of directors at WJQC. I have to answer to them. They've been wanting Armitage out for months, and I've stalled them because Fred has been here so long. Thank goodness Fred announced his retirement before my hind end was up to the fire. Crockett was my ace in the hole. He was going to save the station, make the board happy, wow the listening audience. If he doesn't, Brooke, I'm going to look like a fool."

"You're not going to look like a fool," Brooke said, hoping it was true. "Jeremy will be ready."

"Then you're going to have to up your game," Milt said. "Missy got that tape from the production room and brought it to me."

Brooke felt her jaw drop. "She what?"

"Her critique was pretty accurate. He stunk, and I can't help thinking that you weren't even going to show it to me."

He was right. She wasn't going to. Not until Jeremy had practiced a lot more and they'd made another, better test that Milt could compare it with. *Oh, Cissy. Why did you do that?*

"You've got to get this right, Brooke. A lot is riding on Jeremy's success."

As if Brooke didn't already know that. Her job was riding on it. Jeremy's new house, his lifestyle, his promises to his kids. Yes, there was a lot riding on this venture.

"And you've got to show a little patience. Give me the time you promised me, Milt," she said. "Jeremy won't disappoint. He'll practice. I'll arrange more practice sessions. We'll review. He'll be ready."

"Okay," Milt said. "But as long as we're testing this guy, let's see how he does on the interview circuit. He's got to be able to talk to people face-to-face. I want him to interview the chief financial officer for Charleston on Wednesday. That's tomorrow. I've already set up the appointment, and I had to cross hell and high water to get it. Davis has been keeping his head in the sand lately."

This was not good news. It was rumored that the CFO was skimming funds from the top bids of contractors. Nothing had been proven yet, but a cloud of suspicion was hanging heavily over the entire department's head. "With regard to what?" she asked.

"With regard to the funds being misused on the city bridge projects. I want to know what this guy, Davis, is up to. The citizens of Charleston deserve to know. There will be an election soon, and Davis has hinted that he'll be running for mayor."

Oh, great, investigative reporting of the most difficult kind. Milt wanted Jeremy to flex his muscles in front of the city's second most important official and get answers? Brooke didn't know if Jeremy was up to the task. And besides, the assignment was not fair. Jeremy wasn't hired to be an investigative reporter. He was hired to be the front man, the face of WJQC. "I'd rather you wouldn't send Jeremy on this assignment," she said.

"I'm sure you do, but I want to see if he's got the right stuff to handle a tough interview. If he has it, then nothing around here should stop him. I'll send you and Jeremy and a cameraman to city hall tomorrow," Milt continued. "Let's see what Jeremy can discover. I hope it's the lead story for Fred that night."

Brooke didn't see a way out of this latest

demand. Milt needed to find confidence in his choice for anchor some way, and now he'd decided to test Jeremy's prowess at digging deep into Charleston politics. Well, maybe this could work, she thought. If Jeremy proved himself at city hall, maybe the poor performance on tape would be forgotten.

"I'll expect you to provide Jeremy with thought-provoking questions," Milt said. "And prepare him to face off with the CFO if it comes down to that. Let him know he can't pussyfoot around with his questions. Good grief, Brooke, the man was the toughest offensive end in professional football for years. Surely he can handle a schmuck like Davis."

"I'm certain he can," Brooke said. "I'll have him ready tomorrow." Tomorrow? Talk about pressure!

"See that you do. If you and Jeremy can break this story, our ratings will go way up."

Brooke left Milt's office with a mix of emotions. This could be the assignment that would endear Jeremy to Milt for a long time and secure all their futures. Especially if Jeremy ended up with a scoop none of the other stations had. But Jeremy would have to play true hardball at the CFO's office. He'd have to ask leading questions and provoke Davis into giving answers.

He could do it, she told herself. Jeremy's rough-and-tumble background was just what was needed to get the truth from a politician who might be skimming funds. Jeremy would be direct and forceful. This would be a piece of cake for a man whose gut instinct was to do the right thing. Wouldn't it?

JEREMY HAD BEEN busy all day listening to various reporters on WJQC. He practiced his own voice modulation and tried to implement the techniques Brooke had given him. Once he felt more confident about his progress, he would concentrate on camera operation, sound systems and technical glitches that happen no matter how much care is taken to avoid them. He finally caught up with Brooke early in the afternoon when he walked by her office.

"Hello, gorgeous lady," he said, stepping inside.

Brooke laughed and played with the tousled blond hair that waved around her shoulders.

Okay, she didn't look as put together as usual, but the word *gorgeous* still applied.

"You've got to be kidding," she said. "Have you had as busy a day as I've had? If so, you look much better than I do."

"Not possible. But yeah, I've had a busy day." He parked himself on the edge of her desk and frowned down at the pile of papers still on her blotter. "Let's get out of here and go to Pickler's for a drink."

"I'd love to," she said, "but give me a few minutes to clean this up. You go on over and I'll meet you there."

He stood and headed for the door. "See you there." Walking the couple of blocks to the pub, Jeremy was aware of the warmth in his heart and an outlook on life that had taken a decidedly upward turn. Maybe he was being corny, but Brooke Montgomery was making him a happy man. He might even have burst into song if he didn't think he'd frighten everyone on the street.

A little more than three weeks. That's as long as he'd known Brooke, but every day he felt he'd gotten closer to her, and every day he'd begun to think of a future with her.

Sure, they had some problems to overcome. She was a city girl. He loved his life in the Lowcountry hammock. He had kids, and he still wasn't quite sure how Brooke felt about that, but Cody had become one of her biggest fans, and Alicia would come around. And he still had to convince Brooke that the woman he'd been with for so many years was now gone, and he was ready to start over. Jeremy was confident he had some skills he could use to prove himself to Brooke, ones she didn't seem to mind. Another reason to smile.

In fact, just thinking of kissing Brooke, holding her in his arms, made a silly grin seem appropriate. *Who would have thought it, Crockett?* he thought to himself. *That you could fall so hard so fast.* But he had. Or he was. Or he soon would. Whatever the path, he was ready to take it.

Jeremy took their usual table in the bar, next to the window, and waited for Brooke to come. She walked in after about a half hour. They'd have to order their drinks right away. Jeremy had promised Marta he'd be home in time for her to catch a seven-thirty movie.

When the waitress brought their drinks,

Brooke took a sip and suddenly turned serious.

"Something on your mind?" he asked her.

"Yes, there is. I had a meeting with Milt today."

"Not bad news, I hope."

"No, not bad. But he wants you to spread your anchor wings a bit and venture into new territory."

Jeremy frowned. Was Milt thinking of moving him to another area of production? Had Milt seen that tape that, according to Brooke, was less than satisfactory? "What kind of new territory?"

"He wants you to get the experience of handling an interview—actually an investigative-reporting assignment."

Jeremy relaxed. That was okay. He'd witnessed lots of interviews in his playing days. He'd been interviewed more times than he could remember. Some of those interviews still pained him since they'd involved some bonehead mistakes he'd made on the field. He could manage this new idea of Milt's. "So who do I get to interview?" he asked Brooke.

She told him about some rumors flying

around city hall, the possibility of money mismanagement. "I know that Fred will be reporting this story," she said. "But Milt wants you to know how a serious news item like this makes it to air. He thinks you'll be perfect in a match with Kirby Davis, the city's chief financial officer. I'll prepare questions for you, and we'll have a cameraman present."

"I don't know much about the CFO," Jeremy said. "Just that his name is Davis, and he's eyeing the mayor's office."

"That's true," Brooke said. "But some people believe he's become the most powerful man in Charleston. People who hold the purse strings often are."

"Do you know if the rumors about him are true?"

"I don't, but Milt seems to think they are, and he's excited about a matchup between you and Davis. He wants you to flex your muscles on this one, Jeremy. Pull out all the stops."

Somewhere in his core, a tingle began and it spread to his suddenly pounding heart. This was real news. This was finding it, uncovering it, leading it in the right direction. He was suddenly jacked about the whole idea. Imagine him exposing an ethical problem in the mayor's office.

He agreed immediately and even told Brooke he would be looking forward to the next afternoon.

"That's great," she said, obviously relieved that he reacted the way he had. Did she think he'd turn down an opportunity this great? That ladder to the anchor's desk, which had seemed to reach the clouds, was now just a bit shorter.

"And afterward I hope you'll go out with me to Hidden Oaks," he said. "It's pizza-and-board-game night at my house. Cody wants you to come. Not as much as I do, but a lot."

"That's sweet. But what about Alicia?"

"She didn't object," Jeremy said. "Let's take our victories when we can get them."

He paid the bill and walked Brooke to her car. The long, lingering kiss in the garage was the capper on an already great day.

CHAPTER THIRTEEN

No one in the station seemed to know about the big interview scheduled for Wednesday afternoon. Milt had obviously wanted to keep his scoop private…from everyone. But Jeremy and Brooke were ready. When they met Kirby Davis, they would lead with some general questions and then move in with the ones that should get to the bottom of whatever corruption was going on in the city center.

Jeremy arrived in a spectacular dark blue suit that fit him perfectly. His white shirt and red-and-blue tie gave him an all-American look that would do well on camera. Plus, he told Brooke he'd been practicing his voice modulation.

As time approached for the small crew of three to leave for city hall, Cissy swept into Brooke's office. "What's going on?" she asked, her antennae focused, as usual, on any hints of private maneuvering.

"Nothing," Brooke replied, glancing at her watch. "Today has been as blessedly quiet as possible."

Cissy shook her head, narrowed her eyes. "Okay. So why is Legs dressed to kill? Why is your desk clean at two thirty in the afternoon? Why has Milt kept to his office all day?"

"I can't answer all your questions, Cissy, but as for me, I have an appointment this afternoon and have to leave early. And regarding Jeremy, maybe he just wants to look more the part of an anchor, so he's dressing up a bit."

Cissy sputtered an uncomplimentary laugh. "As if a new set of clothes will help. He still stinks on camera."

Brooke had had it with Cissy's constant demeaning of Jeremy's efforts. "Speaking of that," she said. "I didn't appreciate you showing the tape to Milt."

Cissy pretended a wounded expression. "It wasn't a secret, was it? I mean, everything Jeremy does reflects on all of us. Milt should know where his golden boy stands as an anchor for WJQC."

"He knows," Brooke said. "And your going

to him in private with that tape only undercut Jeremy's attempts to do a good job. He was still untrained and raw on that tape. It was just to be a learning tool."

Cissy cupped her hand over her mouth and stared hard at Brooke before she said, "Something's going on with you, Brooke. I thought we agreed that one of us should be WJQC's new anchor? Have you completely forgotten about that?"

"We never did agree, Cissy. I'm happy as producer."

"Well, I'm not happy as a lowly copywriter, and I still believe that auditions should have been open to all long-standing employees at the station." She plopped into a chair even though Brooke was clearly giving signs that she had to leave. "I don't kid myself, Brooke," she said. "I know you would make a better anchor than I would. You deserve it. You know more. You've been here longer. I appreciate the ethics of working up the ladder."

Brooke sighed. "Being here isn't the main qualification for anchor, Cissy. I could have been here fifty years, but it wouldn't mean that I would connect with the viewing audience."

"Of course you would," Cissy insisted. "I know you don't like it when I flatter you—"

No, I don't.

"—but we're friends. And hey, look in a mirror. That blond hair, those intense, honest blue eyes, that figure meant for a marble statue." Cissy chuckled. "Why, the good ol' boys in Charleston would be missing their early-bird dinners just to see the five o'clock news. And I'd be right beside you on the road to the top."

"Stop it, Cissy," Brooke said. "Jeremy is going to be our anchor. Deal with it."

Cissy shook her head. "Seems like I want what's good for you even if you don't. Who knows where we—I mean *you*—could end up if you used WJQC as a stepping stone. You could go on to any of the big cable networks. Let me tell you—" she stopped long enough to take a breath "—I wouldn't turn down a chance to be famous."

"Good, then go be famous. I just don't see it happening at WJQC." Brooke stood, grabbed her briefcase and jacket. "I've got to leave now. I'll see you tomorrow."

"Okay. Hope your appointment isn't anything serious. Are you going to a doctor?"

Brooke did a quick ten count in her head. "No, I'm fine. This has nothing to do with doctors. Please close my office door when you leave."

She hurried past Jeremy's office, stuck her head inside and said, "Leave a few minutes after me. I'll meet you in the garage."

He smiled. "Why? Are we being stalked?"

"Something like that."

NERVES FINALLY CAUGHT UP with Jeremy on the ride to city hall. Despite playing pro football for a decade, he wasn't a confrontational person on any other level. But he'd always thought of himself as a moral one, and if deeds in the city center needed to be exposed, he wasn't opposed to being the one to do it.

"Last check," Brooke said as they pulled into the city hall's parking garage. "You have your questions?"

"You know I do. I have a little cheat sheet, and besides, I've memorized them. Start with the friendly stuff first and then go in for the hit." He hoped the smile he gave her was full of confidence. "By the time we get to the nitty-gritty, Mr. Davis and I should be good buddies."

The cameraman chose a parking spot and got out to retrieve his equipment from the trunk. "This is it," Brooke said. "You're not nervous?"

Well, yeah, he was, but he said, "No. I'm fine. Quit worrying. Anyone would think Milt was grading *you* on this performance and not me."

She gave him a strange look. "Don't be silly. Why would Milt care about anyone but you?"

Jeremy shrugged and held the car door for her. The trio took the elevator to the third floor, where they were scheduled to meet with Kirby Davis. The room they entered was sparsely furnished with a couple of desks, a few straight-back chairs and some professional lighting. A typical interview room.

An efficient-looking middle-aged woman sat at a desk right inside the door. "You must be the WJQC crew," she said. "We're expecting you. Mr. Davis will be in shortly.

He knows you're coming." Nodding to the cameraman, she said, "Why don't you set up? You're welcome to use any of our lights. Naturally, we want our personnel to look their best, and our lights are very flattering. Also, we generally use a backdrop of the cityscape for filming."

Jeremy glanced at the large photograph of downtown Charleston on the wall. Viewers might think they were filming in front of a picture window, when really the photo captured the outside world. Smoke and mirrors, and air-conditioned comfort, he thought. Whatever worked.

The cameraman carried two chairs and placed them in front of the mural. "You'll be here, Jeremy," he said. "The mayor will sit opposite. We've always figured there was a position of power in being on the right side."

"Anything you say, Nate."

"We're ready," Nate told the woman at the desk. She picked up a phone and punched in a couple of numbers. A few minutes later a tall, formidable-looking man came into the room. His gray hair was neatly groomed. His face was tanned, as if he'd spent time in the sun. The three-piece suit he wore was stylish. However, from the expression on his face, it seemed like he was uncomfortable, and Jeremy felt a sudden pang of sympathy. Interviews could be difficult for some people, but if this guy was longing to be mayor, he'd better get used to them.

And then the man came closer, and Jeremy's heart slammed against his chest. It couldn't be. There was no mistaking the wrinkles around the eyes, the cool gray of his gaze, the firm set of his lips. This man, the second-most powerful guy in Charleston, was as familiar to Jeremy as he'd wished his own father had been.

"Tug? Is that you?" Jeremy said, his voice breathless, his words a hoarse whisper.

The man stared at Jeremy. "Crockett! I don't believe what I'm seeing." Davis shook Jeremy's hand and brought him in for a hug. "Hot dang, son, aren't you a sight for these sore eyes."

Jeremy stepped back. "What's going on, Tug? What are you doing in city hall?" And then he remembered Tug's last name. Davis. No one at U of Bellingsworth had known him as anything other than Tug. "Get out of here, Tug. You're the chief financial officer?"

Davis grinned. "Guilty as charged. Duly sworn in." He smoothed his hands down his lapels. "Who woulda thought it, eh, boy? Looks like my accounting degree finally paid off."

Certainly, Jeremy would never have thought he'd see Tug in such a position. He hadn't seen Coach Tug Davis since his senior year at Bellingsworth. Back then, the two men had been as close as two fleas on a dog's ear. In fact, Tug had gotten Jeremy his shot with the Wildcats, a deal that had paid off big-time. Tug and Jeremy had shared a bond that was legendary at Bellingsworth. No kid could have asked for a better offensive coach, and Tug swore no coach could have asked for a better protégé than Jeremy Crockett. The gratitude Jeremy had always felt for Tug was endless.

"Where have you been?" Jeremy asked his mentor. "I heard you left Bellingsworth after that first losing year. That had to be eight, nine years ago. Rumors were you tried to get a position in the Midwest, but I never knew where you went." Jeremy suddenly felt guilty.

He should have kept track of Tug. He'd meant to, but life… Well, no excuses. "Did you keep coaching?"

"Nah. Truthfully, I had a bit of trouble finding something. But it was probably time to move on." Tug chuckled. "Getting gray and getting old. Not a good combination."

"So now you're a big deal here in Charleston. Incredible."

Putting his hand on Jeremy's arm, Tug led him to the pair of chairs set up for the interview. "Not so strange, really. I've always gotten along with people, always wanted them to do their best and been willing to help. Look at you and me…"

Jeremy sat in the chair Nate had picked out for him. "You and I are a special case, that's for sure. But politics? How did that happen?"

Tug briefly explained how he moved to Charleston six years before and got involved in local politics. "My wife wanted to live here to be near her sister, so here we are. Got a nice house in the historic district. I ran for a few local offices and finally hit the big time when this mayor got elected." Tug sat back in his chair and sighed. "You're looking at a happy man, a lucky man, Jeremy. Now tell me about you. Why did you quit the pros?"

Jeremy summarized the last two years of his life as quickly as he could. "After Lynette died, I had to raise my kids. Got them both living with me now and a house in Hidden Oaks. And hopefully a career in broadcasting."

"Woo-hoo, Hidden Oaks," Tug said.

"It's nice there." Mentioning his career brought Jeremy's focus back where it should be—on the upcoming interview. He looked across the room where Brooke was watching, waiting. She motioned in a get-on-with-it gesture. Since Jeremy figured she hadn't heard anything of his conversation with Tug, she couldn't know what a momentous occasion this was.

"That's my news producer over there," Jeremy said. "I think she wants us to get started."

"All right then. Let's talk," Tug agreed. "Imagine you as a TV personality, though I'm not surprised. I always figured you'd succeed at whatever you tried in life."

"That makes one of us," Jeremy said. "Truth is, when I met you, I was wild and undisciplined. I didn't have much hope in succeeding at anything."

Jeremy took out his notes, though he didn't think he'd need them now. This was Tug. Good ol' Tug. One of the best men Jeremy had ever known. If anyone would be honest in politics, it was "Tug" Davis. There probably wouldn't even be a story here. He smiled to himself. He'd never known Tug's real name was Kirby. Jeremy relaxed. He'd ask a few leading questions, anyway, and get Tug on the air. Might help the guy's chances to be elected mayor someday. It was the least he could do for his former mentor.

The interview went as expected for the first ten minutes. Tug talked about his rise to his current position, his plans for the city, specifically the refurbishing of old bridges across the Yaloosee River. "Some of those bridges are approaching sixty years old," he said. "We've got contractors lined up to begin work on them. Gonna use cement to look like the old limestone compounds they used two hundred years ago. I don't want to spare any expense to beautify this city and keep it historically accurate."

For the first time since sitting down with Tug, Jeremy experienced a moment of unease. Tug's plans for the city were lofty, extravagant even. "I'm surprised there's enough money in the budget to accomplish all these projects," he finally said.

Tug gave him a conspiratorial kind of smile. "Always a means to find money, son. Just gotta look in the right places."

Jeremy glanced at Brooke, who'd moved close enough to hear the interview. She gave him a wide-eyed go-ahead look as if to say this was his chance to get to the meaty questions about budgets and bids and accountability. Jeremy tucked his notes into his jacket pocket and folded his hands on his lap. If only to convince himself that Tug was an honest man, a good man, he had to at least ask him some hard-ball questions. But they wouldn't come from his prepared notes. They would come from his heart. He asked the cameraman to pause shooting.

"Tug," he began, "I've got to tell you something."

"Yeah? What's that?"

"There are rumors going around about your office."

"What kind of rumors?"

Jeremy tried to phrase his concern without an accusatory tone. "The usual ones, Tug. Contractors, city projects, special favors. You know the kind of thing I'm talking about. That's why I'm here today. The evidence we dug up is pretty sound, and my job was to get you to slip up and admit to possible wrongdoing. Of course, now that I'm sitting face-to-face with you, I don't want to believe any of it."

"Are you calling me a crook, Jeremy? Are you saying I'm playing with the city's money?"

"No, that's a little harsh."

"And it's all nonsense. I've got accountants breathing down my back. I work in a building full of lawyers. I couldn't get away with anything—"

"I'm not accusing Tug Davis of being a crook," Jeremy said. "I've only been in this town a little over a year. I studied the hierarchy of Charleston politics, but no way did I ever imagine you would be part of it. I guess, when it comes right down to it, I'm asking if the *CFO,* this new guy I'm just meeting, could be liable in any wrongdoing."

Tug's cheeks reddened. He turned to Nate. "Don't turn that camera back on," he said. "Interview's over."

And all at once, Jeremy knew. His old friend, the man he'd most admired in his life, the man he'd trusted, was hiding something and it was big. Jeremy looked at Nate, who had a puzzled look on his face. "Do as he says," Jeremy said softly.

Brooke came closer. "Why did we stop?"

Jeremy held up a hand. Turning back to Tug, he said, "You can tell me what's going on or you can send me away with no story. It's up to you. But someone else will follow in my footsteps and ask the questions I didn't ask you today. You can't avoid interviews forever, Tug."

"You should go now, Jeremy," Tug said without looking in Jeremy's eyes.

Jeremy nodded. "I'd like to help you, Tug. If you've got yourself in some kind of trouble…"

"We've got nothing more to say to each other," Tug responded. "Let's leave our memories of each other where they belong. In the past."

"Okay." Jeremy started to walk away. Before he reached the door, Tug came up behind him and grabbed his arm.

"Follow me over here," Tug said, indicating a quiet corner of the room.

Jeremy followed him. Brooke and Nate kept their distance.

"Let's talk," Tug said, "Just like the old days. Back then we could tell each other anything."

"That's true. I'm listening."

"Things got tough for me after Bellingsworth," Tug said. "I wasn't exactly fired but I resigned under pressure. I couldn't find a job in football. My wife had some medical problems, and I didn't have insurance. Wiped out all our savings."

Excuses before the admission. Jeremy didn't like the sound of this. "Go on."

"Turns out I was a natural at politics. Had just enough notoriety to make my coaching career work for me. The ladder to this office wasn't hard to climb. But I was still in the hole financially. Costs a lot to get the attention of the right people."

"I'm sure it does," Jeremy said. "So you never recovered? And you're in trouble now?"

"Don't judge me, Jeremy. My wife and kids and I went through a couple of lean years..."

Like most people, Jeremy thought. *Like I did from birth to the age of eighteen.*

"When I was appointed CFO, my wife had her heart set on this fine old house near the Battery. Then my daughter got engaged and wanted a big wedding. I started calling in favors. It's not hard to get people to cooperate when you're in a position of power."

"So this is all about trade-offs, bartering?" If so, maybe Tug wasn't all that dishonest. Jeremy supposed a lot of local big shots had similar dealings. *You scratch my back, I'll scratch yours.* Wasn't right, but possibly this story could have a satisfactory ending.

"At first, yeah," Tug said. "But I needed cash. Judith wanted to renovate the house. She joined some clubs in town, and our social obligations increased. And that dang wedding." Tug shook his head. "Whew! And already there's talk of trouble in my kid's marriage."

He chuckled. "Be careful what you spend your money on, son."

"How much have you taken?" Jeremy asked.

"It's not bad. And I'm going to pay back every cent. I swear. Once I'm over this rough patch…"

Jeremy rubbed the back of his neck. This was the man he owed his life to, and he was no different from every legendary crook in local politics through the years. Skim off the top, swear you'll pay it back and hope you don't get caught.

"I know you're disappointed in me, Jeremy," Tug said. "I can see it in your eyes. It breaks my heart to see it. It all happened so fast. A little here, a little there. But I'm going to make it right."

Jeremy exhaled. "Before the story breaks, Tug? Are you going to make it right before this is on the five o'clock news?"

Tug wrapped Jeremy's arm in a strong grip. "You can't do this story, Jeremy. Everything I've told you is off the record. No cameras. For everything we meant to each other…"

Jeremy wrenched his arm free. He looked

at Brooke, whose expression was one of impatience, curiosity and even dread. She had no idea what he and Tug had been talking about. But she wasn't happy.

"I'm glad it was you who came today," Tug said. "You believe me, don't you? I'm going to pay back every dime. Just don't run this story, son. It'll be the end of me. I'll never be able to hold my head up in this town again."

Tug's eyes were desperate. They filled with tears. He swallowed hard, then said, "Please, Jeremy, for old time's sake."

"You're just borrowing time," Jeremy said. "The story will come out. If not by me, then someone else."

"I'll figure something out by then," Tug said. "Time is what I need. Don't betray me, son. Not after all we went through together. When I met you, you barely had a clean change of clothes. Remember?"

Jeremy's mind flashed back to those awful weeks after he graduated high school. He was wild, drinking, driving "borrowed" fast cars, dodging responsibility, looking for his next thrill every day. And then this guy, Tug Davis from U of Bellingsworth, showed up at his house, a plain-spoken, simple man who painted a dream for Jeremy right in his mother's two-room flat. Tug offered him a chance, a future, a college education and a stepping stone to pro ball.

And Jeremy knew he couldn't be the one to bring him down now. "I've got to go," he said. "I won't run the story, but that doesn't mean someone else won't."

"I know." Tug grasped both of Jeremy's shoulders. "Thank you, son. I'll figure it out."

Jeremy turned away from his mentor and strode across the room. When he met up with Brooke, she tried to stop him. "What's happening?" she said. "What went wrong?"

"There's not going to be any interview," he said. "We're going." Without pausing, he left the room, with all its flattering lights and mural of a beautiful town on the wall. All fake, just like the man he'd spent the last hour with.

CHAPTER FOURTEEN

"JEREMY, WOULD YOU please stop!" Her heels clicked on the laminate floor of the office building, sounding loud to her ears, but apparently not affecting Jeremy.

He kept walking—down the corridor and out the front door of city hall—before he finally stopped for a breath. Brooke reached him and took his arm. "What happened?" she asked again.

He turned around, locked his gaze with hers. His lips were thin, his eyes narrowed. He was breathing heavily. Something had gone horribly wrong, and Brooke didn't like being in the dark.

He stared down at her hand on his arm. She wasn't about to let go of him. "Jeremy, what's going on? You have to tell me."

"This wasn't the story for me," he said at last.

"What are you talking about? We prepared. We had all your questions ready. For the most part, this interview would have been a piece of cake." He didn't speak. She didn't avert her gaze from his face.

Nate came up behind them, his equipment in his portable bag. "I'll meet you at the car," he said.

"Yes, we'll be at the car soon," she told him. Then she turned to face Jeremy. "Why did you do that? It looked to me like everything was going well. When they say to turn off the camera, you know you've struck gold, and that's just what Davis did. You should have kept filming."

"Do you have any idea who Kirby Davis is...or was?" He smirked. "No, of course you don't."

She ignored his biting comment. "He's the chief financial officer of Charleston, the man who was going to cement your relationship with Milt if you had done a halfway decent job today. But I saw him hug you. So I'm assuming he's someone from your past. At least someone you know."

"Oh, I know him all right. The man who is now CFO was the offensive coach at Bellingsworth when I went there. He recruited me from high school, convinced me that I could succeed in college ball. He was my mentor for four years, Brooke. So yeah, I know him. And I owe him, for bringing me up from the miserable life I was living, for making me believe I could be something, for straightening me out when I really needed it."

"I'm not sure I understand," Brooke said, although she was beginning to follow Jeremy's explanation as a sort of idol worship. "Isn't it his job to recruit talented players? Wasn't he just doing what he was paid for? You're the one who starred on the football field."

"Don't you get it?" Jeremy said. "I wouldn't even have been on a football field without Tug."

"Tug was his nickname?"

"That's what we all called him. Even the newspapers."

"Well, so what? His influence on you doesn't have anything to do with who he is today, which is very likely a crooked politician." Jeremy jerked away from her, stared into the distance. She guessed she'd crossed a sacred line of his.

"You're wrong," he said. "It has everything

to do with who I am today." Jeremy drew in a long breath, finally turned and looked at her. "Someday I'll give you the details of where I came from, who Jeremy Crockett really is. But for now just understand that I felt I was lucky just to have a bed to sleep in. My mother and I moved nearly every time the rent was due. Sometimes we slept in our car."

"I'm sorry," Brooke said. "But, Jeremy, that's all in the past. It's not who you are now."

"Oh, yeah, well when I meet up with someone who changed my life as much as Tug did, I'm reminded of that kid from rural North Carolina who can't ever forget the people who took him out of that life and forced him to make something of himself."

"But you were the one with the talent," Brooke said. "If Tug hadn't noticed you, someone else would have."

"You don't get it, Brooke," he said. "You don't know how football coaches and recruiters work. In four years I went to four high schools. Each time I played football, but I was never in one school long enough to get noticed. Except Tug noticed me, one of the few college coaches who did. And he talked me into going to Bellingsworth. Got me the money, a place to live, my meals, everything. I'd still be back in Lockhaven, North Carolina, mowing lawns if it weren't for Tug."

"Okay, so you owed him a debt. I get that," Brooke said. "But what happened today has nothing to do with football. More than ten years have passed since you graduated from Bellingsworth. You went on to become this big star, and I would think that's enough payback for any coach. How many coaches can strut around saying they mentored the great Jeremy Crockett?"

"Stop it, Brooke. You don't get how important this is to me."

She backed away. Something in his eyes told her that she was completely excluded from this part of Jeremy's life and the decision he'd just made that might ruin his career at WJQC. His past, his college years, his obligation to a man who had taken a dark path in the last ten years. No, she didn't get it. "What did you talk about after the interview? Did Davis admit to anything?" she asked him.

Jeremy looked away. His face flushed, and Brooke knew she'd hit on the truth.

"It doesn't matter because we talked off the record, and I'm not doing the story."

"Of course it matters. The man is cheating the citizens of Charleston, the people you are going to be reporting to every night of your life. The people you expect to trust you and your words."

He didn't speak so she tried another approach. "You do realize that Milt is going to be furious?"

Jeremy nodded, his anger seeming to subside at the very real consequences of his actions. "I'll talk to Milt."

"And tell him what?" Brooke challenged. "That the biggest crook in our government is an old friend to whom you are beholden, and you just didn't have the heart to expose him? How do you think that is going to go over, Jeremy? Do you think Milt will just say 'Oh, well, that's okay then.' Because he won't. Milt Cramer is a newsman. He would turn in his own mother if she was stealing from anyone."

"I don't know what I'm going to tell him," Jeremy said. "I have to figure it out. But I'm not reneging on my word to Tug. Someone else might get this story…"

"Someone else will!" Brooke practically shouted at him. "And it won't be you, and it won't be WJQC. We had our shot at this, and you let sentimentality dictate your behavior. That's not being a newsman, Jeremy. That's blowing everything we've worked for. Milt will tell you that, too."

"So maybe I'm not a newsman," Jeremy said. "But here's what I don't get, Brooke. What's your stake in this? Why are you getting so upset over one story? I kind of thought by now that I meant more to you than that. What do you do, live, sleep and drink the news? There's more to life than that."

What was her stake in this? If he only knew. But she'd sworn to Milt that she wouldn't tell him and, anyway, now that she'd been keeping the truth hidden for so long, she didn't know how to reveal everything now. She straightened her spine, took a deep breath and said, "Yeah? Well, this is your dream, not mine. I was just helping you to live it. But maybe I've made a mistake."

He wouldn't look at her. He simply mumbled, "Maybe you have."

"I'm going to the car," she said. "Are you com—"

"You go ahead," he said. "I'll take a cab."

"Fine." She hurried away from him and stood by the car until Nate had loaded his equipment. They drove off, neither of them speaking for several minutes.

"What the heck happened back there?" Nate finally said.

"Jeremy knew Kirby Davis from years back. He didn't want to expose him." Even when Brooke related the last few minutes so simply to Nate, her anger spiked again.

"Wow, Milt is going to blow a gasket," Nate said. "He told me to make sure everything was working just right and keep the camera on Davis as much as possible. I think he really wanted to see the guy sweat."

"Oh, I think Davis has plenty of sweating ahead of him," Brooke said. "But it won't be WJQC who gets the scoop."

"I probably shouldn't say anything…"

"What, Nate? You can't not tell me now. What have you heard?"

"Just that Milt isn't as confident in Crockett as he thought he'd be. I was working the camera when Jeremy did that test the other day. It wasn't pretty, Brooke. You're going to have to give him more camera time than those few tests you've already arranged."

"If Milt doesn't fire him first," she said.

Nate shook his head. "One thing I know about Milt is that he doesn't like anyone to think he made a mistake, and this would be a big one if things don't turn around."

Brooke cringed just thinking about the possible shake-up at the station once Milt heard about the fiasco at city hall. Jeremy would be gone. She would be gone. Who would fill that anchor's chair if that happened? And who would produce the news? She couldn't help reminding herself of that old adage No One is Indispensable. She just wished it wouldn't apply to her.

Brooke had loved her job since the first day she'd walked into the station as a copywriter. She'd moved quickly up the ladder, and had been producing for almost ten years now. Every day presented new challenges, tough decisions, last-minute revisions. The job was not without pressure, but Brooke thrived on it. She never understood her sister's decision to move to a small farm and live a peaceful, calm life. Tension fed Brooke's soul. And that wasn't even counting the lifestyle her producer job had provided.

Brooke had a mortgage on a desirable condo in the best part of town. She had nice things that she was grateful for. She worked hard and she vacationed hard, earning her time off honestly. She'd been to many corners of the world, always taking in the sights with a producer's eyes. How much of this life would she have to give up when Milt fired her? She didn't want to think about it. The truth was, she didn't want to give up any of it.

But then Jeremy Crockett walked into the station and everything changed. The smooth-running but less-than-spectacular years of Fred Armitage were coming to an end. A true personality—a local hero—was slated to take Fred's place. Jeremy was meant to shake up the viewing audience with his good looks, reputation and modest demeanor. Brooke had never imagined he couldn't do the job. That he *wouldn't* do the job. He'd been such a quick study, cooperative, willing to learn.

And today, on his first assignment coming from Milt's own desk, Jeremy had blown it.

But in the meantime, Brooke had fallen for the guy. She hadn't meant to, but for the first time in her modern memory, she'd actually placed a man at the top of her list of priorities. A man with kids, no less. A man who lived in the country. And now she was facing not only giving up her life, but also giving up the man who'd made her days at WJQC even better than they'd been.

She looked out the passenger window of the WJQC vehicle. No way was she going to let Nate see the emotions she was feeling now. She'd been so close to having it all—the job, the man, the future. Maybe that had been Brooke's dream, but it was no more credible than Jeremy's dream. They'd both wished for too much.

Brooke ran into Milt the minute she entered the station.

"How'd it go?" he asked her. "I want to see the tape. Did Davis squirm?"

"Not exactly," Brooke said.

"Why? Jeremy didn't get him to talk?"

"Jeremy didn't try," she said.

"Huh? What does that mean?"

"He'll tell you when he gets here," Brooke said. "But there is no interview."

"I made it clear to both of you…" Milt's puffy cheeks were red with anger.

"I'm going home, Milt," Brooke said. "I've got some thinking to do."

"You're darn right you do," Milt said.

She left, went directly home, poured a glass of wine and sat on her balcony looking over the grand old homes of Charleston. She was struggling with a massive case of self-pity, and Brooke Montgomery didn't do self-pity well at all.

After an hour, her phone rang. She picked up, saw Jeremy's cell number. Her heart raced. He was calling to say he'd screwed up. He was going to apologize. Maybe she could get Milt to give them another chance. Maybe he would contact Davis on his own.

"Hello? Jeremy?"

"It's not Daddy," a small female voice said. "It's me, Alicia. I'm using Daddy's phone."

Brooke blinked several times. "Oh, hi," she said. "Is something wrong, Alicia?"

"You were supposed to come here tonight,"

the girl said. "I was waiting for you. I have some pictures to show you. Now Daddy says you're not coming."

"I'm so sorry," Brooke said, trying to think of something that wasn't a tired old phrase like "something came up" or "I'm not feeling well." Instead, she said, "What are the pictures, Alicia? Can you tell me about them at least?"

"They're pictures of my mommy and me. I thought you would like them. You said…"

The child's voice caught on a sob. Brooke had gotten through to her during her last visit, and now she'd let her down. "Describe them to me, sweetheart," Brooke said. "I promise I want to see them, and I will, another time."

"It's okay." Alicia sniffed. Brooke closed her eyes tight. "I have stuff to do now."

They disconnected, and Brooke realized she'd just experienced a first in her life. This was the first time she'd ever made a child cry. And even more remarkable, this was the first time a child had brought tears to her own eyes.

CHAPTER FIFTEEN

JEREMY WENT TO work the next day. When he pulled into the garage, he saw Brooke's car. He was sorry for how they'd parted the evening before. They were both upset and angry, and today was probably too soon to try to make it right. Maybe they never would bridge the distance between them now, but Jeremy hoped they would.

He passed the conference room, where she usually was first thing in the morning, conducting a production meeting to review potential stories for that day's broadcast. The door was closed. He didn't go in. He didn't have a right to be there. Perhaps he didn't have a right to be anywhere in the station. He'd find out soon enough. He continued down the hall to Milt's office.

He knocked on Milt's door.

"Come in." The voice that called out was

gruff, cold, almost as if Milt knew who was on the other side of the door.

Jeremy entered.

"You've got some nerve, Crockett," Milt said. "After that fiasco of yesterday afternoon."

Jeremy swallowed what pride he had left. "I need to explain what happened, Milt."

Milt crossed his arms over his chest and leaned back in his chair. "Make it good, and make it fast."

"Can I sit down?" Jeremy asked.

"Don't bother. You won't be here that long."

Jeremy shifted his weight from one foot to the other. He'd never felt this uncomfortable in anyone's presence. "I don't know how much you heard, but I was put in a tough situation."

"As far as I'm concerned, you were only put in one situation, and it was the one your boss specifically told you to be in. I don't give a darn how tough it was for you, Jeremy. This is the news business, not some sports-bar gathering where you're the big star."

"I know that, sir, and I went to city hall fully prepared to deal with Davis, fully prepared to ask him hard questions."

Milt didn't utter a sound.

"I had no idea that the chief financial officer of Charleston used to be my coach at Bellingsworth. I knew Tug Davis back when I was really struggling. He got me into college, saved my sorry butt from making a complete failure of my life."

Milt leaned forward, rested his elbows on the desktop. "You know what, Jeremy? I don't care. We meet lots of people in this life. Some help us out. Some squash us like bugs. In the end, it's up to each one of us to make the decisions that will help us succeed. In my view, you didn't owe some football coach from a decade ago half as much as you owe the people of Charleston who might vote for him to be mayor."

He narrowed his eyes. "And what exactly did you owe the people? The truth. And what did you give them? Nothing. Not a dang thing. You had your chance yesterday and you blew it, for yourself and for this station. You could have brought in a story that would have made the airwaves sizzle. But what did you do? You played footsie with a washed-up coach who probably wouldn't give you the time of day off a football field."

Jeremy bit his bottom lip to keep his anger

in check. What did Milt Cramer know about Jeremy's past, about his relationship with Tug? "With all due respect, sir, Tug Davis did a lot more for me than give me the time of day. I couldn't be the one to drag him down. I know it'll probably happen, but I couldn't be the one to do it."

He took a breath. "Besides, Milt, you didn't hire me to be a reporter. I was willing to try. Heck, I've been willing to try everything in this station. I've worked cameras, studied budgets, played with lighting and modulated my darn voice until I'm practically hoarse. All that I did to be a good anchor, not an investigative reporter."

"Seems like there's one thing you forgot, Crockett," Milt said. "To be a good anchor, you've got to deliver worthwhile news. And where that news comes from is the responsibility of everyone at WJQC. You let sentiment get in the way of your performance, and sentiment has no place in a newsroom."

A long moment passed during which neither man spoke. Finally Jeremy decided it was time to discuss the bottom line, although he already had a pretty good idea where that line left him. "So what are you going to do, Milt? Are you going to fire me?"

"It's what I should do," Milt said. "There's nobody else on this earth I would let get away with such a flagrant disregard for an order. But the truth is, I'm still thinking about what I'm going to do. You've got me over a barrel, Jeremy."

"What are you talking about? We both know the contract has loopholes that will get either one of us out of the deal. Yeah, it may cost you a bit of money, but—"

"It's not just about the money!" Milt said. "It's my reputation that's on the line here. I talked you up big, Jeremy, to the board of directors, to colleagues, to anyone in the news industry I thought would turn green with envy. And when word gets out that we could have had this story—"

"I don't think it will, Milt," Jeremy said. "I'm absolutely certain Tug won't talk about it."

"Oh, it'll get out. There isn't a hot news story in the city that isn't like water in a sieve. And when it leaks, I'll be ruined." He shook his head. "But it's not just your pitiful performance yesterday. I saw that audition tape. Sorry to be so blunt, Jeremy, but you stink."

Jeremy's deepest instinct was to quit on the spot, turn tail, walk out of WJQC and forget the whole thing. A man could take only so much criticism, and Jeremy had taken enough for ten men. But one thought kept him from following his instincts. Brooke. If he quit now, he would disappoint her, and he'd do almost anything to keep from doing that. "Brooke is working with me," he said. "She has worked her heart out to make me an anchor. You know that. You asked her to tutor me. She volunteered, and it'll kill her if this one incident blows my chances after all she's done."

Milt just stared at him for a long moment. "Right... Brooke," he finally said. "That's another decision I've got to make today."

"What's that supposed to mean?"

"Nothing. Just leave my office, Crockett, will you? I've got a lot of thinking to do."

Jeremy left Milt's office. He didn't know where he would go. Usually he met up with Brooke, scheduled a plan for the day and visited various departments in the building. Today he was lost, with no destination. Today might be his last.

The production meeting was just breaking

up as he went by. Writers and editors filed out of the room. Brooke was the last one to leave, and Jeremy was waiting for her when she came into the hall.

"You speaking to me?" he asked.

"I don't know," she said. "Do you still work here?"

She looked tired, like she hadn't slept well. If so, they had a rotten, sleepless night in common. "It's debatable," he said. "Milt is thinking about it."

She sighed. "Frankly, I don't know what we should be doing. It's time for you to make another audition tape, but maybe we don't need to. If you're not fired, Jeremy, you go on the air a week from Monday. Ten days from now. When do you think Milt will give you his decision?"

"The ball's in his court," Jeremy said. "But I've never had a dressing-down like the one I just got from him in his office. If I was a betting man, I'd put my money on me being in an unemployment line by tomorrow."

She almost smiled. "Milt can be tough. But don't jump to conclusions. He's invested a lot in you, and I'm not just talking money. He's invested his credibility in you, and if there's one thing I know about Milt, he hates to lose face."

Staff members walked by them, and Jeremy felt like he and Brooke were the biggest news of the day. Surely everyone in the building knew about his screwup with Tug. "Can we go somewhere for a cup of coffee?" he asked Brooke.

She checked her watch. "I have a few minutes, but only a few. Let's go to the coffee shop downstairs."

They took the elevator down, then Jeremy ordered two cups of coffee and sat across from her at a small table. The restaurant wasn't crowded.

"You know the worst part of this?" he began.

"I think I have a good idea," she said.

"It's that I disappointed you."

She started to say something, and he held up his hand. "Let me finish. You've put so much effort into helping me. I've told you often enough how grateful I am. I actually think I'm ready to go on the air, and it's all because of you." He shook his head. "I don't know why you took on this assignment. I've wondered about that a hundred times at least. I can't imagine why you thought a banged-up jock would make a good anchor, but I never once thought that you didn't believe I would."

"I do believe it," she said. "I still do. That's what makes this such a difficult situation. If Milt fires you..." She paused, looked down. He waited.

"If Milt fires you," she continued, "it's a darn shame that the people of Charleston won't see the amazing transformation of wide receiver to polished newsman. And that's not all my doing. You've worked hard, too." She took a long sip of her coffee. "So don't give me the credit. I don't deserve it. I just wish you had—"

"I know, and even when I promised Tug I wouldn't bring him down, I was thinking about you, what you expected of me, how you would think differently of me now."

She didn't say anything. She just sat there and turned her coffee cup in her hand.

Finally he said, "Do you, Brooke? Do you think differently of me?"

"As a member of WJQC, I guess I do."

"I'm sorry. And I have to be honest with

you. If I could go back and do yesterday over again, I wouldn't change anything."

She stared at him with wide, luminescent eyes and shook her head. "I know that."

He reached across the table and took her hand. "But what about your thoughts on you and me? Can you get over what I did? Or have I ruined everything?"

"What exactly do you mean by *everything*?"

"Come on, Brooke. You must have noticed that somewhere along this journey we've taken, you've come to mean more to me than your role as private tutor."

She focused on her coffee cup. "I guess I suspected. But I didn't know for sure."

"Well, then, it's time I eliminated all doubt. I've been following you around like a puppy for a month now. I hang on your every word. I make up excuses to see you." He touched her hand with the tip of his index finger. "If that doesn't tell you something, I don't know what would." He cleared his throat. "So will you answer the question? How do you feel about me and, more specifically, about you and me, because if you say you can never forgive me, that will be the worst consequence of my actions."

"Oh, Jeremy."

He smiled. "I'm sorry, Brooke. But that's not an answer."

"I know. I don't have an answer. All I can tell you right now is that I foresee some changes at WJQC in the near future. You might not be the only one facing a major shake-up. It's probably not a good time to think about our relationship."

He knew what she was trying to tell him. She might be called into Milt's office for not getting the new star to do his job. But Jeremy had confidence that Brooke could stand up to Milt and land on her feet. But the biggest shake-up was that he would have to start over again looking for a job. Maybe he wouldn't find one as an anchor. Maybe he would have to follow so many other ex-jocks who went into sports broadcasting. Not that there was anything wrong with that. But he'd had his heart set on the news-anchor position. And he wondered if Brooke would be disappointed in him if he didn't find an assignment.

He held her gaze. "I'm sorry, Brooke, but our relationship is about all I think of these days. I know we have obstacles to overcome.

I live in the country. You like the city. I have two kids who are going through a lot right now."

"How is Alicia?" she asked.

The question startled him. "She's fine, I guess. Why do you ask?"

"No reason. I just think about her sometimes. I hope she's adjusting."

"I think she is. It's just going to take more time. Everyone I've spoken to about it says we have to take each day as it comes and work with it." With all that was going on, he knew he shouldn't ask, but what he felt for Brooke was real.

"Speaking of days, tomorrow is Friday," he said. "Will you go to dinner with me? Just as friends, if that's the way you want it."

She paused before giving him an answer. "Tomorrow may not be such a good idea," she said. "We should wait and see what Milt decides."

"What Milt does won't affect how I feel about you, Brooke. And I hope it won't affect how I hope you feel about me."

"We both need to wait for shoes to fall, Jeremy," she said. "I should get back."

"Okay. I'll walk you to the elevator."

They left the coffee shop, and he pushed the button to call the elevator. When it arrived, he said, "Have you decided to at least try to forgive me for yesterday?"

She smiled. He felt the tension go out of his shoulders. "It's more important that you forgive yourself. Who am I to lay any more blame on your decision? We all have to live with the consequences of our actions."

He smiled back at her. "I'm not sure that's total forgiveness. But I'll take it."

He started to walk away, but she stopped him.

"Jeremy…"

"Yeah?"

"Tell Alicia I said hi, okay?"

"Sure."

"I'd like to see her."

"That can be arranged."

She nodded. "Talk to you tomorrow."

"I'll count on it. But for now, I'm going home. I think this is the first of many days I'll be able to spend quality time with my kids."

CHAPTER SIXTEEN

JEREMY DID LEAVE the building, and by late afternoon, Brooke decided she could no longer avoid a conversation with Milt. She went to his office, and he immediately invited her in.

"So, Milt," she began, "are you going to fire me?"

He gave her a serious stare. "What was your part in that debacle at city hall?"

"I might have been able to alter the course, I guess. I suppose I should have emphasized some important points regarding being a reporter to Jeremy."

"You think?"

"But in all fairness, Milt, I was training him to be an anchor, the one who reports the news after it has been gathered by others on the staff. He had no idea what he would be facing yesterday. Meeting up with his mentor was completely unexpected."

Milt folded his hands over his waistline.

"I heard all that. Doesn't excuse a thing, as I see it."

"I understand that. And to be fair to Jeremy, I don't think he's looking for you to find an excuse. He did what he thought was right. Honestly, I can't find much fault with that."

"He let us all down, Brooke—me especially."

It was time to move on. Brooke prepared herself for Milt's response to her question. "Okay. I know where you stand, Milt. But where do I stand with regard to my job?"

"I'll let you know Monday," Milt said. "I have a lot to consider…whether I'll give Jeremy another on-camera test, whether I'll keep him on staff, though I don't think I can. Channel Seven is promoting their broadcast for tonight saying they have hot news from city hall. You and I both know what they've got. The station manager called me this morning and told me not to miss tonight's show. He ended with laughing about how he'd heard we blew a big story yesterday."

She couldn't argue. That was just the nature of the news industry. When one channel missed an opportunity, word traveled quickly and other news outlets quickly jumped at the chance to get the scoop.

She just wished Milt could see WJQC as a collection of people—good people who worked hard—and not as a reflection of his own ego. She knew he would find it difficult, if not impossible, to live down Jeremy's performance yesterday.

Would firing Jeremy help Milt save face? Probably, but Brooke hoped it wouldn't come to that.

"Okay, Milt," she said. "I'll see you tomorrow."

"Jeremy has sent word that he's taking the day off," Milt said. "Wise decision for him. I'll talk to both of you on Monday." He gave her a coy grin, the type she'd experienced in the past. He liked to keep people on their very uncomfortable toes, but he needed her and she knew it. "Don't lose sleep over this," he added.

She left his office believing she still had her job at the station she loved in the city she adored. But she couldn't deny that something vital was missing.

That night Brooke called her sister. In as

few words as possible, she described the last couple of days.

"Milt won't fire you," Camryn said. "Where would he find anyone half as qualified as you are?"

"That's what I'm hoping," Brooke said. "But the truth is, no one's indispensable."

"He may fire Jeremy, though."

Brooke sighed. "Yes, he might."

"How do you feel about that?"

"Lousy. Jeremy has worked so hard. He's not perfect, but I think he has what it takes to sit in that anchor chair. And he wants it, Cam. And I want it for him. The truly horrible thing is that what he did can be interpreted as a noble gesture. His heart was in the right place."

"Obviously Milt doesn't see it that way."

"No."

"What will you do if Jeremy is fired? Are you prepared to take a stand with WJQC in defense of a coworker?"

This was the first time Brooke had heard that scenario stated so bluntly. What would she do? She and Jeremy had grown close, but other than working at WJQC, Brooke had no options. She didn't have a hefty bank account that would tide her over. What's worse, she'd recently borrowed money from Jeremy. Brooke had bills and obligations and an investigator who kept asking for more.

"Stand up for Jeremy and give up my job? I don't know, Cam. I wish I could say that I would."

"Hmm…still," Camryn mumbled. "Jeremy is more to you than just a coworker?"

"Well, sure. He's a very good friend."

"This is me, Brooke, the one person who knows you better than anyone in the world. The one person who won't judge you no matter what you tell me. I'm not a mind reader, but I haven't missed many clues the last few weeks. Jeremy Crockett is more than a project to you. I've been sitting back and waiting for you to admit your feelings for him. I didn't want to pressure you, but even Reed has noticed how extrapositive I've been lately. Thinking of you falling in love…has put a huge smile on my face that won't go away."

Brooke choked back a sob. "Maybe I do love him. I think about him all the time. When

I'm with him I'm relaxed and happy, and optimistic. Is that love?"

"It's awful darn close," Camryn said. "What about the physical stuff? The kissing? Holding hands, touching because you can't *not* touch him?"

"It's all part of it, Cammie. He's the most wonderful... Well, you know."

"I do. But you have to make up your mind. This is your life."

"I can't follow him out of WJQC in protest, Cam. What if it didn't work out between us? He hasn't asked me to commit to him. And he has kids, for heaven's sake."

Camryn chuckled. "How will you ever survive the terror of children, Brooke?"

"Don't make fun of me," Brooke said.

"I'm sorry, but I'll bet that thoughts of Jeremy and his success at the station, and his kids, have made you almost forget about Edward. And for that I'm grateful."

Brooke leaned back into her comfy sofa cushion. It was true.

"I still want to find him," she said.

"Okay. But one thing at a time. I know you'll do what's right for you."

Brooke heard a click on the phone line. Another call was coming in. She checked the digital screen. *Jeremy.* "I have to go," she said. "I'm getting a call."

"Okay. Keep me posted. I love you. Though I can't imagine why."

"Love you, too. And I can think of a thousand reasons why."

Brooke ended the call with her sister and connected to Jeremy.

"Hello, Jeremy. What's up? Where are you?"

"I'm home with the kids. As for what's up, I just called to say I miss you."

Brooke's heart beat a crazy rhythm she'd never experienced before. She wished she could reach out and touch Jeremy, feel his cheek, lay her hand on his chest. "I miss you, too," she said.

"But I'm not the only one, Brooke. I told Alicia what you said, and she asked me to call you to see if you could find some time to see each other. What's going on?"

"Did she really? I was so worried she was angry with me for not coming to Hidden Oaks yesterday.

"I had spoken to Alicia the other night about her mother. I told her I'd be happy to talk to her again if she wanted to. I thought maybe she needed someone to confide in. Remember? You actually put that thought in my head. I'd like to help her if I can."

"I would be so grateful if you could connect with her. I try, but there always seems to be this wall between us."

"How about Saturday?" Brooke said the words before she'd actually thought about them. All she knew was that she felt an urgency to talk to Alicia, to try to find a way out of her grief and help her overcome it. Despite her doubts that she could do so, Brooke wanted to try.

"What do you have in mind?" Jeremy asked.

"Why don't you come here, just the two of you? There is a hotel nearby that my niece loves. It has a hamburger specialty restaurant and an ice-cream parlor. Probably an ideal place for Alicia and me to talk."

"You know, that's a great idea. A day just for Alicia and me, and then Alicia and you.

I'll make plans for Cody to stay with Marta. I can only see one problem with the plan."

"What's that?"

"You didn't leave time for you and me."

"Maybe we can steal a moment or two."

"Thanks for this, Brooke. I seem to connect with Cody on every level, but I'm lost with Ally. She needs a woman to talk to, and I'm so glad it's you."

"I'm happy to listen. See you here at about eleven if that works for you."

"Okay. See you Saturday, Brooke."

They disconnected. Brooke found the pamphlets she'd left on her nightstand and began reading more about childhood grief. Then she moved on to more details on various recommended websites. As she read, she realized it was necessary to have advice from the experts, but on Saturday she would basically be winging it. Even with a strong foundation of knowledge, she would be experiencing entirely new territory. Face-to-face with Alicia, one-on-one. She prayed she wouldn't blow it.

JEREMY AND HIS daughter arrived just before eleven o'clock on a warm, sunny Saturday morning. Brooke wore a modest, light blue sundress and sandals. She'd fashioned her hair into a ponytail with a narrow blue ribbon. She wanted to look caring and welcoming but wasn't sure if she'd achieved that. At any rate, she figured pantsuits were out.

Alicia looked adorable in capri pants and a halter top in a splashy floral print. Her sneakers were covered in pink sequins. Brooke commented right away on how cool they looked.

"See, Daddy, I told you Brooke would like them," Alicia said.

"And you were right." Jeremy gave Brooke a special smile over his daughter's head. The smiled warmed her to her toes, as did Jeremy's appearance in navy khaki pants and a white button-down shirt. His clothes fit so well, Brooke wondered if even his casual outfits were tailor-made. She doubted it. Jeremy wasn't the type to want custom clothes in his closet.

"I must be the luckiest man in Charleston to be taking you two beautiful ladies out today," he said.

Brooke wanted to kiss him. She saw the

same desire in his eyes. "The hotel is within walking distance," she said. "We'll have time to see the indoor aquarium before lunch."

The short walk to the hotel seemed filled with adventure to Alicia. She appeared to have taken on Brooke's penchant for window-shopping, and the two women gazed at dresses in the stores and guessed at the price tags. Alicia was happy, and Brooke was encouraged. Maybe Alicia's private time with Brooke wasn't the only reason for her contentment today. Maybe it was special attention from her father. Whatever it was, it was working.

After a lunch of hamburgers and French fries, Brooke suggested she and Alicia go for ice cream.

"What will you do, Daddy?" Alicia asked her father.

Brooke held her breath. Maybe Alicia was uncomfortable leaving her father behind.

"I saw a large-screen TV in the lobby," Jeremy said. "There's a college football game on now, so don't worry about me."

"Not football again?" Alicia said.

"Now and always, cupcake. Get used to it." He smiled at Brooke. "Have fun, you two.

Come find me when you're through with whatever it is you girls do on your own."

Brooke found a table for two in the ice-cream parlor. She and Alicia ordered sundaes and waited for them to be delivered.

"This has been a fun day," Alicia said. "I like it when it's just me and Daddy."

"I'm sure he does, too," Brooke said. "And I'm happy that you're having such a good time. To be honest, I wasn't sure you'd accept my invitation today."

Alicia gave her a totally serious pout. "I was mad at you for not coming to our house when you said you would."

"I know. I hope today has helped to make up for that. I had no idea I'd hurt your feelings."

"I wanted to show you some pictures." Alicia took her small purse from her lap and set it on the table. "I brought them today. Daddy said it would be okay."

"I'd like to see them."

Alicia took several photos from her bag and spread them across the table. "What do you think of Mommy?" she asked right away.

"The same thing I thought of her in the picture in your daddy's office. Your mother was a beautiful lady."

"I know." Alicia held up one picture. "This is Mommy and me and Cody on Christmas. We all did the tree together."

Brooke studied the shot. Her breathing became ragged. She and Camryn and their parents always did the tree together.

"And this is all of us in a pumpkin patch. Daddy was supposed to come but he had to play football. I used to get so mad at him when he couldn't come to things."

"But now you're with him all the time," Brooke said. "I don't bet you are still so angry with him."

Alicia looked down at the floor. "I was really mad that day I messed up the kitchen," she said. "Cody and I really weren't fixing food. We were throwing it all around."

"I'm pretty sure your daddy figured that out," Brooke said.

"I was mad, because of you. I thought if Daddy liked you, he wouldn't care so much for me and Cody. I don't want to think about Daddy not being with us."

Brooke took her hand. "Oh, sweetie, you

know that's probably not going to happen. Yes, people have accidents and people die, and it's very sad. But your daddy loves you both so much."

"I know he does, now, but it was hard at first, leaving Colorado and coming here."

"Sure it was, but you shouldn't worry about losing your daddy. He brought you here to be with you all the time. He bought that nice house and hired Marta. He intends to keep you and Cody close and safe."

"I know he's trying," Alicia said. "But I still miss Mommy."

"And that's okay," Brooke said. "You loved your mommy, and it's hard to believe that she's gone. But you have these wonderful pictures and your memories of times you spent together. Nobody can take away your memories, and I would love to hear about any of them you want to talk about. Talking about them helps to keep the memories alive, even if your Mommy isn't."

Alicia slowly gathered the pictures and returned the stack to her bag. "There was this one time…"

Brooke had a good idea that this story

would be the first of many, and she sensed an outpouring of relief from Alicia. Sometimes, the best medicine was knowing someone would listen.

A half hour later, Alicia was laughing. "And Mommy said she was the best ice skater in all of Colorado. So we went out to the lake and we all put on our skates, and Mommy fell almost right away. She didn't hurt herself, but she said something hurt really bad. I think she said it was her pride."

Brooke laughed, too. "I can imagine."

Alicia sighed. "We probably should check on Daddy."

"Okay."

"I'm not sorry you're his friend anymore."

"Thank you. I like being your daddy's friend."

Alicia slurped the last of the ice cream from her soda glass. "Is there something wrong with Daddy?" she suddenly asked.

Brooke sat straight. She hadn't expected a question like this. Was Alicia worried that her daddy might die? "No, I don't think so," she said. "Your father is healthy and strong. Do you think he's ill or doesn't feel well?"

"It's not that. I think if you love someone, and they want to marry you, then you should get married. That's what most people do. But Mommy wouldn't marry him. So there must be something wrong with him."

Brooke could understand how a child might come to such a conclusion. But she didn't know enough about Jeremy and Lynette's relationship to explain why they never married. She knew Jeremy had wanted to marry, but Lynette had never consented.

"Well, let's stop and look at this for a second, Alicia," she finally said. "Do you really believe in your heart that there's something wrong with your daddy that would keep him from getting married?"

"No. I think he's perfect. If he asked you to marry him, would you do it?"

Brooke felt her face flush. Such an honest question required an honest answer, but Brooke didn't have one. "Your daddy would make a wonderful husband, just like he's a wonderful father," she said. "But I've never thought about marrying him myself." That wasn't exactly true, but when she did think about it, she didn't know how to explain her feelings to a child—his child.

"Marriage is a big step," she added. "People usually know each other for a long time before they decide to marry. I believe your father is putting his efforts into being the daddy you and Cody need. And maybe that's enough for now."

Alicia nodded. "But if he does ask you, will you not hurt his feelings?"

Brooke took Alicia's hand. "I would never want to hurt his feelings, sweetheart. Now let's go see if we can peel one man away from a television set."

They found Jeremy in the lobby. He looked up when they came in. "Hello, ladies," he said. "How was the ice cream?"

"It was good," Alicia said. "Can I look in the gift shop?"

"Sure." He gave her a ten-dollar bill. "You can spend it, but get something for your brother, too."

She scurried into the shop and Jeremy held Brooke's hand. "How did it go?"

"It was okay. We talked about her mother, about you. It was an open and honest discussion." Brooke smiled. "She's a sweet girl, Jeremy."

Jeremy glanced through the window of the gift shop, where Alicia was looking at stuffed animals. "I know someone else who's pretty darn sweet," he said. He walked Brooke behind a nearby potted palm. "I think you've forgiven me. I hope I'm right."

"Oh, I've forgiven you." She let her gaze melt into his. "You were doing what you thought was right. That's all anyone can do."

He lowered his head and kissed her, a quick, passionate embrace that left her breathless. "That's what I thought was right just now," he said with a warm smile.

CHAPTER SEVENTEEN

KNOWING MILT ARRIVED at the station most mornings by 7:30 a.m., Brooke got up early on Monday and headed in shortly after sunrise herself. She and Jeremy were to hear their fates, and if she was fired, Brooke had some serious planning to do.

As expected, she found Milt in his office. "May I come in?" she asked from the hallway.

"Of course. You're here early." He motioned to a chair in front of his desk. "Have a seat."

Seeing no point in delaying bad news, she sat and said, "So have you made a decision? Do I have to go look for a job?"

"No," Milt said. "I'm not going to fire you, Brooke. Fact is, I never was going to. It was all a bluff."

"A bluff?" After talking with him last week, she had expected as much, but still, anger pounded in her temples. She couldn't let him get away with this. "So this was all a game to you?"

"Not a game. An effort to get you to concentrate on your job and quit using company time for personal matters. Giving you a little extra responsibility and putting a scare in you seemed to be the best way to do that."

"Why, you conniving... How could you do this? I've been on pins and needles for weeks not knowing if I could even keep my condo. I've heard of some lousy managerial techniques, but this is definitely the worst."

"Now, hold on, Brooke." Milt stood and extended his arms, as if surrendering. "I told you before, and it's still true. You're the best producer in the business, the best to train our new anchor. If you'd stopped to think for even one minute why I'd fire the best, you'd have known I wasn't serious."

"Don't you dare turn this around on me." She blew a long, frustrated breath through her lips. "I know this is petty and childish, but Milt Cramer, right now I'm pretty sure I hate you. Why you think you can toy with people's futures, with their emotions, is a puzzle I'll never understand. If you ever do that again, I'll walk. I mean it, Milt."

She tried to calm down, but her head was spinning. All these weeks, all this worry. And for what? To satisfy a man's urge to play a game. She didn't think she'd ever fully trust Milt again.

"What about Jeremy?" she said. "Are you going to fire him or was that a bluff also?"

"Oh, yeah, he's got to go. Once Channel Seven did the story I wanted Jeremy to cover, my decision was pretty much a done deal."

She closed her eyes, letting Milt's choice sink in. "For one mistake?"

"One major blunder, Brooke, and you know it. It's not just the incident with Davis, although that would be enough. I just don't think Jeremy has what it takes to be an anchor. I want somebody stable, uninvolved, determined to deliver the news no matter what the consequences. I don't want someone who will go all soft when a story hits him hard. I just want someone who'll tell the news."

"It was one time, Milt. You can't overlook one misstep?"

"Come on, Brooke, his delivery is way off.

That little tape you ran isn't the only time I've watched recordings of him. I've arranged several tapings since the last one, and I've been observing his camera presence. He's got a lot of qualities I like. He's personable, good-looking. Lord knows he's got celebrity status, but he's no newsman, and that's what it all boils down to."

Brooke didn't know what else to say. Milt had obviously made up his mind. This would crush Jeremy. He'd invested so much in this opportunity. He'd changed his entire life to make this work.

On a personal level, Brooke was heartsick. Every moment she'd spent with Jeremy had almost become a gift to her. She found herself thinking more and more about one sad and confused little girl who maybe, with a bit more time, might actually need her. And a little boy who just wanted to laugh and have fun without being reminded of a recent sadness. Jeremy's kids were good kids. A woman who'd always believed she would never relate to children, especially someone else's, was discovering that getting close to them wasn't that hard. All that was required was an open heart and a lot of understanding.

But what about giving up her life in Charleston? Maybe there was a way to compromise. As far as Brooke was concerned, it no longer seemed important that she'd have to travel a few miles just for a quart of milk. Not when those few miles would bring her back to a family she knew she'd never forget. Her eyes had been opened to the fact that deep down she wanted what her sister had. Maybe she always had. And now, what would Jeremy do? Go back to Charlotte and become a broadcaster for the Wildcats? Go to Colorado if that's what his kids wanted?

"When are you going to tell him?" she asked Milt.

"Today. I haven't seen him yet, so I'm assuming he's not as obsessed as you are with the news."

"Are you trying to make me angry all over again?" she said. "I was worried and for good reason. Who wouldn't be?"

"You know, Brooke, you should think of that training you gave Jeremy as a positive step for you, too. You can't deny that boning up on all the essential elements of putting the news out every day hasn't made you a better producer. I'm pretty sure some of those details had slipped your mind over the years, but now you'll be even better than before."

Brooke stood. "I have to get out of here, Milt. I'm pretty sure all that flattery is going straight to my head."

He chuckled. "Go on, then. You don't have to tell Jeremy. I'll give him my decision. As far as I'm concerned your responsibility to my grand scheme has ended. So go produce the news."

She walked out of Milt's office feeling as if her world had suddenly crumbled. She hadn't wanted this tutoring job in the first place, but she'd taken it on with a determination to succeed. And now, as Milt just said, her responsibility had ended. But Milt didn't know that the door had been shut on so much more than just her responsibility to Jeremy Crockett's career.

The production meeting wouldn't start for another hour. So Brooke went into her office, left the blinds closed and locked her door. She needed time to think, to prepare for what her encounter with Jeremy would be like when she saw him later. So much had been riding on Jeremy's success. Now, everything depended on how he would handle his failure.

JEREMY ARRIVED AT the station at 9:00 a.m. Even knowing this could be his last day at WJQC, he walked the hallway as if nothing had changed. And it hadn't. The writers were in a production meeting with Brooke. Technicians were examining the equipment in the studio, as they always did. Computers hummed, phones rang and the coffee room buzzed with Monday-morning catch-up. And Jeremy headed to Milt's office.

He was stopped in the hallway by a forceful voice. "I need to talk to you."

He turned and almost bumped into Cissy Littleton. "Okay," he said. "But aren't you supposed to be in the production meeting with Brooke?"

"That's hardly any of your business," she said.

Jeremy tried to keep his jaw from dropping. What had gotten into her? To his knowledge, she had never had an original idea that hadn't come from Brooke. "Fine," he said. "Let's go in the break room and talk."

They sat at a sterile table in the plain room. Jeremy poured a coffee for himself. He didn't offer to do the same for Cissy. So far she hadn't spoken another word.

"What's on your mind, Cissy?" he asked.

"Somebody at this station needs to give it to you straight, Jeremy. And since no one has the guts, I guess it'll have to be me."

He crossed his legs, stared at her. "You have my attention," he said.

"Do you have any idea what harm your presence at this station has caused?"

He knew what trouble he'd gotten into on Wednesday at city hall, but other than that, he didn't know he'd been causing harm in other ways. "Actually, yeah, I remember Wednesday wasn't a red-letter day for me."

"You really blew that interview," she said, almost gleefully. "But I'm talking way back. In fact, the first day you strutted into WJQC as if you owned it, or planned to. People thought you were going to be the savior of the station. The men reacted like you were some kind of god. The women were practically swooning."

Despite Jeremy's recollection being much different, he didn't argue with her. Obviously, Cissy had to get something off her chest.

"I'm not quite sure where this is going, Cissy," he said. "Maybe you should just come out and say what's on your mind."

"Oh, I'm going to do that. Maybe you never thought about this, but you should realize that there are several great people who have worked at this station for years and deserved a shot at the job Milt handed to you on a silver platter."

"I hadn't thought of that," Jeremy said. "I guess I assumed that Milt considered all in-house staff before he offered the job to me."

"You're wrong. For some inexplicable reason, you came across Milt's radar, and he zeroed right in on your popularity as a means to raise our ratings. He never gave anyone else a chance to try out for the anchor job. People you know, people you've gotten close to, wanted that job."

"Tell them they may still have a chance. Milt was pretty sore at me for what I did on Wednesday."

Cissy sputtered a sarcastic laugh. "Like he's

going to fire you! He won't do that. He still thinks you can walk on water."

Jeremy knew Cissy was way off-base. He didn't know what Milt's decision would be today, but he figured he had about a fifty-fifty chance of remaining employed by WJQC. "Would you mind telling me who these people are who wanted the anchor job?" he asked Cissy. "Especially the ones I've gotten close to."

"I guess it can't hurt now. After all, you should be aware of the lives you changed when you got here, the dreams you shattered, the goals you destroyed. Success is more than just boosting the ego of the guy in charge. You can only be successful if you don't step on people on your way up."

"I'm not aware that I stepped on anyone," Jeremy said. "I was looking for a job in broadcasting. Milt offered me this one. I accepted. End of story." He took a deep breath to think about how to phrase his next statement. "Frankly, Cissy, I'm offended by these charges you're making against me. You make it sound like I'm someone who doesn't care who he hurts. I'm not. You're wrong."

"Really? You want to know who wanted that job?"

"Sure. If you want to tell me."

"You're looking at one of them."

He tried to contain his shock. Even if Jeremy hadn't been selected as the new anchor, he doubted Milt would have given Cissy a second thought as the successor to Fred. Maybe there were others at WJQC who would have been capable, but not Cissy. "Did you ask Milt for an audition?" he asked.

"No. Brooke talked me out of it. She said if I wanted an on-air job I should look at another station."

Darn good advice, Jeremy thought.

"Unfortunately, she also talked herself out of trying for the job," Cissy said.

All at once Cissy had grabbed Jeremy's attention as if she'd lit a fire underneath him. Brooke wanted the anchor job? No way. She would have told him. "That's not possible," he said. "Brooke is happy as a producer. She loves that job."

"Brooke doesn't always know what's good for her. We talked about her becoming the anchor. She's talented and experienced and gorgeous. She deserves the job more than I do, but we're friends. If she'd gotten the job she would have taken me with her to be her personal assistant. We would both have gotten promotions and pay raises. But no-o-o… you walked into WJQC with an attitude that told everyone else to take a hike."

"Did Brooke ask Milt for an audition?"

"She couldn't. You tied her hands. Maybe you didn't know it, but she couldn't tell Milt what she wanted, not once she was forced to make a success of you."

"Brooke took that assignment freely. Nobody forced her."

Cissy shook her head as if she couldn't believe Jeremy's words. "You may have been good at catching a football, but you are definitely clueless about people."

"I've about had all I can take of your insults, Cissy. I've been with Brooke for weeks. We've gotten close. I would know if she felt any resentment for helping me."

"She couldn't tell you she resented you, Jeremy. Brooke doesn't keep anything from me. One day she let it slip that Milt said he'd fire her if she didn't make you into an anchor. So not only did she not get a shot at the on-air job herself, she had to worry about losing the job she had." Cissy glared at him. "And she might lose that job, anyway, thanks to your incompetent interviewing technique."

Jeremy experienced a pain greater than any inflicted on him during a football game. His head ached. His stomach roiled. Why hadn't Brooke told him? He would have stepped down immediately if he thought Brooke wanted the anchor job. He would have done anything she asked him to do. He had done anything she asked him to except for last Wednesday.

He swallowed, not trusting himself to speak. He stood, walked around the table. Finally he said, "Do you swear this is the truth, Cissy? That the whole time Brooke was working with me, she was being forced to do it?"

"Now you're beginning to see what you've done, Jeremy. I don't know if you can correct any of it now because we all know you're Milt's golden boy. And the rest of us are just stepping stones for you to get to the top."

"I've got to get out of here," he said.

"What are you going to do?"

"That's the million-dollar question, isn't it?" he said. He left the break room and slammed the door behind him. He hadn't been honest with Cissy. She didn't deserve his honesty. The fact was, he knew exactly what he was going to do.

Milt was at his desk when Jeremy opened the door.

Milt looked up from some papers on his blotter, then set down his pen. "I've been expecting you," he said. "Today's the day we get a lot of things straight."

If Milt only knew the weird irony of those words. When Jeremy came to work this morning, he had no idea just how things would be straightened out, and just how Milt's words would come across as anticlimactic.

"You're right about that, Milt," Jeremy said. "But before you fire me, just one question. Did you force Brooke to train me under the threat of taking away her job?"

Milt's eyes rounded. "Who told you that? Did Brooke…?"

"No, not Brooke." Jeremy clenched his hands at his sides. "Well, did you?"

"Does it matter? You've only benefited

from Brooke's guidance, and she learned a valuable lesson, as well. You've learned a lot in the last weeks…" Milt's smile was smug. "Though not enough."

"I'll take that as a yes," Jeremy said. "For what it's worth, Milt, I'm going to tell you what I think of you. It's the least I'm entitled to after the bashing I've received the last few days."

Milt leaned back, crossed his arms over his chest. "Take your best shot."

"You're a manipulator, Milt. You don't care how you treat people as long as you get the results you want. I don't know why Brooke would want to work with you, but apparently she does. That's her business. But you should know just what a prize you have in that woman. You might try treating her with respect."

"You don't need to stand up for Brooke," Milt said. "She's got the gumption to stand toe-to-toe with anyone in this station. And, for your information, I do appreciate her. She's the best in the business, and I tell her so often enough." Milt raised his hand, pointed his index finger at Jeremy. "And I'll tell you one

other thing. She wouldn't have pulled that un-
professional stunt you did the other day. She
would have done her job."

"Yeah," Jeremy said softly. "I've learned
just how well she does her job." How her job
comes above everything else in her life, he
thought.

"So then," Milt said. "With your brazen
analysis of my personality hanging over our
heads, let's move on to the matter at hand. Am
I going to fire you?"

"The answer to that is no," Jeremy stated.
"You can't fire me because I quit."

"You quit? Are you a darn fool, Crockett? You're giving up that hefty bit of cash
you would have gotten in the buyout if you
were let go. If you walk out that door like this,
you'll be leaving with nothing. You should
have been hoping all night that I would fire
you."

"We'll let our lawyers figure out the details,
Milt. But I wouldn't be so sure that I'll get
nothing. Thanks for the memories and giving
me a shot. And good luck with everything."

Jeremy strode to the door, but before leaving, he turned back to Milt. "As for that replacement, you might give Brooke a try."

"She doesn't want the job!" Milt bellowed. "And I wouldn't give it to her because I'd lose the best dang producer I've ever known."

"Here's another idea, then," Jeremy said. "Cissy Littleton. She's a natural. Good luck, Milt. I'll be watching the news."

He heard Milt holler through the closed door. "You lost two things today, Jeremy. Your job and your ability to know what's good for you."

CHAPTER EIGHTEEN

AS SOON AS Brooke heard the news that Jeremy had quit, she began trying his cell-phone number.

"This is Jeremy. I really want to talk to you, so leave your name and number and I'll call you back."

After hearing the message the fifth time, Brooke wanted to scream.

Finally, at four o'clock in the afternoon, he answered.

"Where have you been?" she asked. "I've been calling you all day."

"I've been meditating. Isn't that what we're supposed to be doing these days? Meditate and eat kale? I haven't mastered the art of kale yet."

"I've been worried sick about you."

"Stop worrying. I'm fine."

Brooke could tell from the sound of his voice that it wasn't true. "You really quit?"

"I did."

"Jeremy, we were so close to the end. You were going on air in just a few days."

"If Milt didn't fire me."

"I doubt he would have fired you. Where was he going to get another anchor by Monday? He backed down on his threat to fire…" She stopped abruptly.

"What were you about to say?" he asked.

"Nothing. Look, there's a place about midway between my place and Hidden Oaks. It's called the Lowcountry Tavern. Is Marta at your house? Can she stay with the children?"

"She's here. I suppose I could get away for a while."

"Great. It's on Route Forty. Just turn right off the main highway when you see the gas station. I'll meet you there at six thirty."

"Okay. But Brooke, I've quit. I said it and I meant it. Nothing will change my mind, and I don't think Milt wants me to change it."

"Just come to the tavern," she said. "We'll talk."

Brooke left WJQC as soon as the news ended. She'd been to the tavern before. It wasn't fancy, but the food was Southern and the drinks were strong. Not that she was going to drink too much. She didn't need a ticket on top of the horrible emptiness she was feeling in the pit of her stomach.

She entered the tavern ten minutes early and found a table in a dark corner. She ordered a white wine and the kind of beer that Jeremy liked. She waited. He was only a few minutes late. He saw her at the table and walked over. He didn't kiss her. They could have been acquaintances renewing an old friendship for all the attention he showed.

Brooke cradled the wineglass between her hands, hoping he couldn't tell that her hands were shaking. "How are you?" she asked.

"I'm okay. Actually I feel like the weight of the world is off my shoulders."

"You didn't have to quit," she said. "Milt may have said he would fire you, but he wouldn't have. You were doing great. When I go over the amount of stuff you learned in such a short time, I'm impressed. I really put you through the ringer, and I'm sorry."

"I hope my quick learning skills made your job a little easier then?" he said. "Well, good. No regrets."

She started to reach for his hand but paused. "Jeremy, what are you going to do now?"

"I've got options," he said. "I'll take a couple of days to make some contacts, see what's out there for a washed-up wide receiver and a never-been news anchor."

His assessment of his choices was like a stab to her heart. "You are not a failure," she said. "You would have made a fine anchor."

"We'll never know, will we?" He took a long sip of his beer. The waitress came and asked if they would like another round. "I think we're done here," Jeremy said. When the waitress left, Jeremy said, "Let's face the facts, Brooke. From the day I walked into WJQC, I've been different things to different people. First I was Milt's ego booster. Then I was your special project. And finally I ended up as Cissy Littleton's punching bag. It's time I went back to being plain old Jeremy Crockett."

Brooke didn't even try to hide her shock. "Cissy? What does she have to do with this?"

Uncertainty clouded Jeremy's usual confident demeanor. She didn't know if he would answer until he finally sighed and said, "She told me everything. About how you and she wanted the anchor job—"

"That's ridiculous. Cissy has a vivid imagination. I never wanted that job."

"Well, maybe Cissy is right. You don't recognize opportunities when they fall in your lap. Maybe you should try out for the position. You would be great at it." He gave her a smug grin. "And I can attest that you know a lot about the news business."

She didn't like this side of Jeremy. But he was hurt. His life had changed, and he didn't know what he was going to do about it. "Who are you going to believe, Jeremy? Cissy, who has an ax to grind about everything at the station, or me, the woman who's been by your side from the beginning?"

"So why were you by my side, Brooke? What was at stake for you in this whole make-Jeremy-great scheme?"

"Nothing. I just wanted you to succeed, and when Milt asked me to counsel you, I was happy to do it. You may not believe it, but some of us at WJQC just want the station to flourish, the ratings to climb. We don't have personal agendas."

He sat back, gave her a penetrating stare that made her uncomfortable. "Really? You had no personal agenda? Not even keeping your job?"

Her jaw dropped. She couldn't even respond to his veiled accusation.

"Cissy told me everything," he said. "I know Milt was going to fire you if you didn't make me into his caricature of the perfect anchor." He stared at her a long moment, then said, "Are you going to deny it? Now would be the time."

She shook her head. "No."

"So here you are, a woman who has probably never watched a football game in her life, who has no idea who Jeremy Crockett is or was. And suddenly you're faced with the almost insurmountable problem of turning him into someone he's not and never will be. And all to keep your job, your precious job that allows you to live six blocks from the Battery and have all the bells and whistles that go with it."

A sense of desperation washed over Brooke. "Okay, you are right about how this started, but I never expected to end up believing you would be perfect for the job. No one's perfect."

"Is that all you never expected to happen, Brooke?"

No. I never expected to fall in love with you. I never thought I would try to reconcile our differences and love your children. I never expected that I might end up thinking I would marry you if you would have me.

But she didn't say any of that. Instead, she cleared her throat and said, "What do you want to hear from me, Jeremy? That I care for you? Because I do. I don't want you to throw away your future because you're angry with me."

"Brooke, I learned more about you and myself in the last few hours than I learned in all those weeks we worked together. I learned that I can't be bought. I can't be a pawn in anyone's game plan. And I can't let my heart overrule my common sense. It all comes down to one thing. I have to be my own man, not yours, not Milt's."

He reached for his wallet, threw a ten-dollar bill on the table and stood. "Nice talking to you, Brooke. In truth, there has been a lot about the last few weeks that has been nice. So don't worry about me. I'll be fine. I have those nice things to think about as I consider my options.

I've been knocked down enough times in my life that I know how to get back up again."

He turned and walked out of the tavern without looking back.

WHEN BROOKE GOT home she did what she and Camryn had done their entire lives. She looked to her twin for comfort and advice. The minute Camryn heard Brooke's voice, she said, "What's wrong?"

"Are you busy?"

"No, of course not."

Baby Grace crying in the background told a truer story than Camryn's words did. "I can call back," Brooke offered.

"Don't do that. Everything is fine here." She paused a moment. "Come here, Esther, take your sister and give her a bottle. Make sure Reed warms it in the microwave for a few seconds." A relaxed sigh was next. "Okay, talk to me."

"I don't think I'm a very good person," Brooke said.

"Don't expect me to agree with you, but why do you believe that?"

"It's Jeremy. I've made him so disappointed

in me that…" Brooke ended the sentence on a giant sob.

"Oh, my gosh, Brooke, you're crying," Camryn said. "I haven't heard you cry since we made that fateful trip to meet our not-so-wonderful biological mother. Something terrible must have happened."

Brooke tried to get control, but once the tears started, they were hard to stop.

"Oh, no," Camryn said. "You were fired. Milt actually fired you."

"No. I almost wish he had. But I still have my job."

"Then Milt fired Jeremy?"

"He told me he was going to but I'm not sure he would have," Brooke said. "But Jeremy learned all about Milt's scheme if I didn't turn Jeremy into the area's number-one news broadcaster. And Jeremy quit. Just walked out a few days before he was due to go on air."

"I guess he just couldn't stand to work for someone who would threaten to fire you, Brooke. He sees Milt for the lowlife he is. How many times have I wished you would do the same thing? Milt is unreasonable. He's—"

"Cam, the reason Jeremy quit was only

partly to do with Milt. He really quit because of me." Brooke reached for a tissue on the end table beside her sofa. She wiped her eyes and then twisted the tissue into a tight little ball and held it in her palm. "I feel so horrible."

"You're going to have to give me more than this, Brooke," Camryn said. "You've been working your butt off to train Jeremy. From what you've told me, he's made numerous romantic gestures toward you. And I don't have to be a genius to know that you're crazy about him."

"I am," Brooke admitted. "For the first time in my life I'm truly in love. With a man who has kids and lives in the country. It doesn't make sense, but I heard love never does. I've also heard that love hurts more than almost anything, and it's true. Hurting someone you love is worse than being hurt yourself."

"So why did Jeremy quit because of you?"

"Because I was never honest with him, not from the start. He kept asking me what was in the training sessions for me. I kept saying things like 'I just wanted to see him succeed' or 'I'm a team player and I would do anything for WJQC.' None of that was true, not at first. I played along with Milt so I wouldn't have to give up a darn thing, so my life could go along as it always had. And you want to know the worst part?"

"Sure, tell me."

"I was never honest about his chances of making it. He worked hard, he tried, but so much was lacking. And because I was desperate to go along with Milt, I kept telling Jeremy he was going to be great." She sniffed, started crying again. "I hate to admit it, but he would have been poor if he'd gone on air to do serious news. And it would have been my fault."

"But you were trying so hard," Camryn said. "Maybe he would have done well."

"I was working hard to prepare him for a job he wasn't suited to," Brooke said. "But I never prepared him for failure because I was always thinking of myself. I was protecting Brooke Montgomery above all else. And now I'm left with the job I thought was so important and suddenly it doesn't seem like it was worth it."

"I'm so sorry, honey," Camryn said. "What are you going to do?"

"What else? I'm going to work tomorrow like

every other day. I think when I left today, Milt and I had formed a kind of understanding."

"And what is Jeremy going to do?"

"I don't know. He says he has options. But none of them include WJQC. And none of them include me." She released a shuddering breath into the phone. "I wish I'd never met him, Cammie. Then I could go on being the selfish person I've always been, not even caring that there are people like Jeremy in the world, nice people with principles."

"You're being too hard on yourself, Brooke. I wish I could help you," Camryn said. "Why don't you come down to the farm this weekend? We'll drink tea or wine if you want to. We'll talk. You can see the girls. The boys will leave us alone, I promise."

Brooke smiled. "Thanks, sis, but I don't think I could stand being around all that wholesomeness right now. I just wouldn't fit in."

Brooke glanced at the clock across the living room. She'd been monopolizing her sister for forty minutes. Camryn was a woman who had much more important things to do than dust her antiques and make sure her work clothes were pressed. She had people who loved and needed her, people who trusted her to tell them the truth and be honest.

Brooke had always thought she was the lucky one—money, success, power, the perfect life of independence and freedom from responsibility. But it turned out that Camryn was the lucky one because she had people, some of them those messy, noisy creatures Brooke had always avoided—kids.

"Thanks for listening to me," she said. "I love you, Cammie. Though I can't imagine why."

"I love you, too. And I can think of a thousand reasons why. Call me tomorrow, please."

"I will. Good night."

When Brooke went to bed that night, she couldn't help challenging the priorities in her life the last few months. She'd spent time and dollars and energy looking for a man—yes, a brother—who might never want to have her in his life. And all the while the man she should have been concentrating on was right before her eyes. And until today, she'd have sworn that he definitely wanted her in his.

CHAPTER NINETEEN

"DADDY, AREN'T YOU going to work today?" Alicia stared at Jeremy as he poured her cereal.

"No, not today," he said for the second day in a row.

"Then why do we have to go to school?" Cody asked.

"Because you're not old enough to make up your mind about things like this."

Alicia scowled at him. "So we have to go to school, but you don't have to go to work?"

"That about sums it up." Jeremy gave each child a glass of orange juice. Both kids ate in silence a moment, crunching and slurping, while staring at their father.

"Did you get fired?" Alicia asked when her bowl was empty.

"No, I did not get fired."

"People who aren't fired go to work," Alicia pointed out.

"I'll stay home with you, Daddy," Cody said. "Then you won't be lonely."

"I'm not lonely," Jeremy lied. He was definitely lonely. His days had gone from too much to do to hours of empty nothingness.

"Maybe now we should get a dog," Cody said. "He could stay with you all day and you could forget about being fired."

"I wasn't fired," Jeremy said again. "Are you guys ready to go? The school bus will be here any minute."

"Did you pack our lunches?" Alicia asked.

Shoot. Something else he'd forgotten. Jeremy went to the refrigerator and yanked out cold cuts, cheese and mustard. Then he took bread from the box on the counter. "I meant to do this last night," he said, while foraging in the cupboard for bags of chips and a box of cookies. He dumped the cookies into his kids' lunch boxes without wrapping them separately. "These might be crumbs by the time you eat them," he said. "Sorry about that."

He put the lunch boxes in backpacks and zipped them up. "Okay, let's go. I'll walk you to the road."

As the bus pulled up, Jeremy leaned over

and kissed each child on the forehead. He always kissed them goodbye, and he finally breathed a sigh of relief at experiencing at least a measure of normalcy in his otherwise emotionally chaotic days. He'd quit WJQC only two days ago, yet it felt like he'd been gone a month. Days were long when you didn't have anything to do.

"Is Brooke coming over?" Cody asked as he climbed the steps to the bus.

"No."

Following her brother, Alicia said, "Are you going to look for another job or are we going to be poor?"

"Don't worry about it," Jeremy said. "Everything is going to be fine."

He walked back up his drive thinking about the long hours ahead of him. Marta would make the beds and tidy the house, stopping at intervals to give him a sympathetically forlorn look. He'd listen to the news on TV, oddly on WJQC. And he'd think about Brooke getting ready for the five o'clock broadcast.

Then he would send Marta on some errand or other. Surely they needed milk or eggs. After she left, he would sit in his office and scroll through the contacts on his cell phone. Who would he call today? Would he finally succeed in making one of those options a reality?

Jeremy only knew two things for certain. He would not go back to WJQC. And he missed Brooke with an ache that wouldn't go away.

"BROOKE, IN MY OFFICE, now."

Brooke barely saw Milt as he clumped past her door, but she definitely heard his booming voice.

"Now, Milt? I'm working on the final lineup for tonight's show."

His voice faded, but only slightly as he continued down the hall. "That's two hours away, so yes, now."

She put her computer on silent mode and stood up. *Might as well get this over with.* She had no idea what complaint Milt was concentrating on today, but whatever it was, he loved telling her about it.

"What is it, Milt?" she asked from the entrance to his office.

"Come in. Sit."

She did.

"I suppose you realize as much as I do that we're having that retirement party for Fred on Friday night?" Milt said.

"Yes. I'm the one who bought the set of golf clubs and a membership to Whispering Pines Country Club."

"Right. I suppose it will be a heartstring-tugging few minutes of airtime on Friday as he says goodbye to his viewers, the ones he has left, anyway."

"He's been a staple of the news hour for years now, Milt. Of course he has an audience that will miss him."

"I've arranged for Dirk Billings to fill in for Fred for next week at least."

"Good choice." Dirk would do a good job. He was thorough and somewhat accomplished on camera. He'd been WJQC's lead remote reporter for a long time. He could be counted on to give a solid performance. But Brooke had never thought his demeanor was conducive to an hour of airtime. And besides, Dirk wasn't interested in the job.

"I've been auditioning applicants for Fred's job for the last two days. We've had lots of tryouts."

"I've seen you in the broadcast booth," Brooke said. "Come up with a keeper yet?"

"Not even close. Ten days, Brooke, and I've got to put Dirk back on the streets." Milt frowned. "I may end up putting that pushy chatterbox assistant of yours on air."

"Up to you, Milt. But my gut instinct is that Cissy isn't ready for prime time."

"Ha! She isn't! All she's got is moxie, and she's driving me to distraction. Can't you keep her busy and out of my hair?"

"I'll see what I can do, but Milt, you don't have any hair…"

Brooke had decided after her meeting with Jeremy at the tavern Monday night that Milt would never push her around again. Maybe that was Jeremy's influence. Maybe she envied the moxie *he'd* displayed by quitting before Milt fired him. Or maybe she'd just had enough of Milt telling her what to do and making the success of WJQC ride on her shoulders. Whatever it was, Brooke was wielding some power at WJQC that she hadn't enjoyed in a while. Too bad all that wielding wasn't making her happy.

Milt sat back, folded his arms across

his chest. "Here's what we're going to do, Brooke…"

She waited while he slowly nodded his head.

"Get Crockett back," he finally said.

"He won't come back."

"Of course he will." Milt tore a piece of paper from a tablet on his desk and scribbled something down. He handed the paper to Brooke. "Show him this."

She stared at the figure on the paper. "Milt, this is a ridiculous amount of money to give an anchor. I know guys who have been at the desk for decades and haven't made this much. Fred, for instance."

"I'm over a barrel, Brooke. I sunk everything into making that jock a newsman, and now I'm left holding an empty bag. I still think he can do this job."

"He doesn't want the job," Brooke stated simply.

"Well, convince him he does! We'll get viewers just because of who he is. I'm not denying that he infuriated me after that stunt at city hall, but I'm willing to overlook it for the sake of the station."

"And maybe for the sake of your own reputation?" Brooke added. "You are, as it seems, a station manager with no five o'clock anchor."

"Whatever. Just go talk to him. You're closer to him than anyone here. He'll listen to you."

He did at one time. Brooke doubted he would again. Besides, she wasn't certain he was right for the job. He could be a novelty, sure, but what kind of staying power did a novelty have? But what if his skills improved? Did she owe it to Jeremy to give him another shot at a position he wanted just a few days ago? He'd be coming back to WJQC with the ball in his court. Milt was begging, and that gave Jeremy strength.

But, bottom line, Brooke was sick and tired of doing Milt Cramer's bidding. She wanted to see Jeremy on her terms for once, not because her egomaniacal boss told her to. "I won't do it, Milt," she said. "There's not enough money in Charleston to make me confront Jeremy with this offer."

Milt made a show of tearing off another piece of paper. "Not even a bonus like this?"

Whew. He was offering her enough to pay back Jeremy the money she owed him and have plenty left over to continue her search for Edward. Brooke tapped the paper on her knee and thought a moment. This would be an excuse for her to see Jeremy again—the only one she could think of. It was a legitimate offer. He could accept or decline. She'd approach him with all honesty, give him her personal and professional opinion of his chances to succeed. And then leave it up to him.

Milt leaned forward. "Well? It's a darn good offer, and you know it, Brooke. Even if Jeremy says no, you can keep the money. No games this time, just you and me working for the good of WJQC, like we used to."

She stood, tucked the offer in her pants pocket. "I'll let you know by the end of the day."

By the end of the day Brooke had given Milt her answer, ordered two pizzas from a restaurant on the way to Hidden Oaks and headed out to the Lowcountry.

BROOKE RANG THE Crockett buzzer on the gate surrounding Jeremy's subdivision. His voice came over the speaker. "Yeah?"

"Hi, it's me, Brooke."

He didn't immediately respond, so she said, "Are you busy?"

"I'm trying to get two kids to do their homework, but I guess I could put down my cattle prod for a good reason."

"Is two pizzas a good reason?"

She heard the kids encouraging him in the background. "Pizza? Let her in, Dad."

"Yeah," Alicia said. "We didn't like those grilled-cheese sandwiches."

The gate slowly opened, and Brooke drove in. Making a few familiar turns, she pulled into Jeremy's drive. Cody burst outside, ran to her car and waited for her to step out. He wrapped his arms around her waist and said, "You have pizza?"

Her heart gave a little kick, and she put her hand on his back. "Yep. How have you been?" she asked.

"Okay. I'm glad you came back."

"Me, too. Did you think I wouldn't?"

"I didn't know. Dad has been kinda weird lately. When I ask him if you're coming over, he just says, 'How would I know?'"

She reached inside the backseat of her car and took out the pizza boxes. "I know I missed your dinnertime, but I figure you must have room for a slice or two."

"Or maybe the whole thing!"

They walked to the house together. Jeremy stood in the doorway. He was dressed in jeans, a red polo shirt, and a pair of casual slip-on loafers. His hair was messy and he sported a five o'clock shadow. He looked like someone she would like to come home to for the rest of her life.

"Here, let me take those." He relieved her of the pizza boxes and stepped aside to let her in.

Alicia came out of the kitchen. "Hi, Brooke. I'm glad you're here." A reserved welcome but a genuine one.

"Hi, Alicia. Everything okay with you?"

"I guess." She looked up at her father. "I poured fruit punch for me and Cody. Can we have pizza now?"

"Get it while it's hot," he said.

"You want some, Brooke?" she asked. "It looks like there's plenty."

"Maybe later," Brooke said. "But you guys go ahead."

The kids hurried to the kitchen, each with a pizza box.

"The kids look good," she said to Jeremy.

"They should. They're getting away with murder since Marta is visiting a friend in Beaufort. Come on in." He walked into the living room and waited for her to find a chair before he sat on the sofa. "So how was work today?" he asked.

"Normal, mostly."

He smiled. She relaxed into the chair.

"I'm surprised you even know what normal is at WJQC."

"How have you been adjusting to a life of leisure?" she asked him, and then felt strange since he had only left his job two days ago. To Brooke, it had seemed much longer.

"I'm not crazy about it," he said. "But I've been following up on some possibilities."

"Really? Have you made any decisions?"

He didn't answer. Just gave her a good, long stare, starting at her hair, which she'd brushed to a shine before leaving the office, and continuing down her face, which suddenly warmed with his attention. She'd also freshened her makeup and hoped the stress of the day didn't show through.

"Dang, but you look good, Brooke," he said.

"I don't mean for that to sound so surprising, but I feel like I haven't seen you in months. The last few days I've been stumbling along without my best friend."

She could have said the same words to him.

He kept his gaze locked on her eyes and then said, "So what brings you out to the country? I can't imagine you've taken a second job as a pizza delivery guy."

She laughed. "No. I'm done with taking on added responsibility in my life." She hoped he would interpret her words as another apology for making him her project. "But I did promise Milt I would do one last thing for him."

Jeremy released a long breath. "Which is?"

"He wants you back, Jeremy. He doesn't know how to ask, or more accurately *beg* you himself." She smiled. "Let's face it. Milt is not a study in gracious Southern manners."

"That's an understatement."

"But he does know effective ways of getting what he wants." She took the piece of paper Milt had given her from her purse. "He didn't ask my opinion of this plan," she said. "He decided on his own that you really can become a good newsman."

"Is that what you think, Brooke?"

"I don't know. I'm inclined to believe that you can do anything you set your mind to. So if WJQC is what you want…"

He slowly shook his head. "It's not."

She had anticipated that answer, but it still stung. She opened the paper and handed it to him. "Maybe you should look at this before you decide for certain."

His eyebrows rose. He blew a low whistle through his lips. "My new salary?"

She nodded.

"Impressive, but honestly not what I made my second year in pro ball."

"Isn't that comparing apples to oranges, Jeremy?"

"Yeah. You're right. Sorry, I don't mean to sound cocky. Besides, my playing days are over. If I could succeed as an anchor, this kind of money would do well for us for years."

"That's right. It would."

"But it's not about the money," he said. "I think I had false illusions about the WJQC job. I could see myself as a legit newsman, recounting events of the day in a serious, confident manner that would endear me to the audience. I didn't know I would pick and choose the stories I would tell. Tug Davis taught me that not all news stories should be told, by me at least."

Jeremy crossed his legs, settled back in the sofa. "Tug is wrong, and I was wrong. If I accept a job, I should do it. But I'm probably not going to change. If it comes down to me telling a hot story versus ruining a person's life, I don't think I would do anything differently.

"I'm not a newsman, Brooke. I'm an ex-jock with two kids to raise and no idea what to do with myself. Quitting football was the right decision, so no regrets there. I'm all those kids have, and I'm going to do my best to be the guiding force for their entire lives. But I have to do something with my time and what talents I have. I have to make myself proud of whatever it is I do, and not just for my kids. For myself, too."

Would he ever be proud of himself as a newsman? Brooke didn't know, but she owed it to him to stand behind him if he wanted to try. "Jeremy, I would help you if you decide to give this another chance. Milt wouldn't be pulling the strings this time. It would just be you and me…testing you, training you, working you hard."

He slowly folded the paper she'd given him and handed it back to her. "Thanks, but no." He looked down at the floor a moment before giving her an intensely honest stare. "I don't know how to put this delicately, Brooke, so I just have to say it. You are part of those illusions I let myself believe in."

She wanted to hold her hand over her heart to keep it from breaking. She had let this man down, and he would probably never forgive her.

"You and a lot of people at WJQC. It's not your fault. It's not even Milt's fault. It's a cutthroat business, and people who decide to join it have to be tough. I always thought I was tough. I could take a hit and get back up. I could stay with a woman who refused to marry me and keep coming back." His lips quirked in an odd grin. "You know, in ten years of professional football I never got one personal foul called against me. That's the way I am. Play fair or don't play at all. I wasn't born that way. Far from it. I learned that from Tug Davis, and I'm sorry that he forgot it.

"So, no, Brooke. I won't be coming back. I'm not cut out for it. Milt will figure something out."

But what about us? Was this it? When she walked out his front door would that be the end of the feelings she'd come to accept she'd never feel in her life? Instead of making Jeremy into the image she wanted for him, had he succeeded in making her into the image he wanted for himself? Play fair or don't play at all. She had certainly taken a step in that direction this week at work.

She took a deep breath and released it, afraid of the way her words would sound coming from her mouth. They were simple words, but would he realize how much she meant them? "Jeremy, I'm so sorry. You're a decent man and no one should try to make you into something you're not."

He stood up then and she did as well, thinking he was ending this conversation. Ending everything. Her chest hurt. No, not her chest, her heart. But he didn't walk her to the door. Instead he wrapped her in a warm, protective hug.

"It's okay, Brooke. For a while I thought I

could be something I'm not. I wanted to be that person, for me, for you. But it never would have worked."

He still had feelings for her. She knew it, but would it be enough?

"I have something for you," he said. "Come with me into my office."

She followed him into the office. He went behind his desk, opened the lap drawer and took out a tablet. "I just got this today," he said. "I really believe it's reliable."

Brooke stared at the name on the tablet. Edward Smith. It was written above an address in the Florida Keys. Her first instinct was to ask what it meant, but then the significance of the name hit her. Edward. He'd found Edward!

Her hand shook so badly she almost dropped the tablet. For a moment she couldn't speak because she couldn't breathe. But after a few seconds she looked at Jeremy, and said, "This is my Edward, Jeremy?"

"I think so," he said. "All the clues fit. He lives at a marina on Sweet Pine Key in Florida."

"But how?"

He came around his desk, took her elbow

and led her to a chair. "Sit down, Brooke. I know this must come as a shock, but remember, I told you I knew some people who might be able to help with the search."

"Yes, but…" She did remember, just like she'd remembered everything she'd heard in the last few months about the whereabouts of her mysterious brother. "But I didn't think…"

"I know." He nodded his head. "At first this seemed like finding a needle in a haystack. The last thing I wanted to do was disappoint you, but consulting with the right person makes a difference."

"Who did you talk to? Why do you think this is truly Edward?"

He sat on the edge of his desk, just a few feet from her. "There's a guy who used to play for the Wildcats. He's older than I am and retired a couple of years ago. But while he played, he started a charity to help out troubled kids, adults, whoever needed guidance.

"His charity became well known in the Carolinas. He was respected by almost everyone who wanted to see these kids turn over a new leaf. He'd get names from cops, social workers who didn't have the resources to follow through on all their cases. Sometimes he even got names and backgrounds from judges."

"And out of all these needy people he remembered crossing paths with Edward?" she asked.

"No. I wish he had. That would eliminate all doubt. But Terry is pretty sure he's found your brother even though he never actually met him. There was a kid's story that crossed Terry's desk over fifteen years ago. Terry was going to pursue the lead and see if he could help this teenage boy out."

"And what happened?"

"The kid was taken in by the very judge who sentenced him, a guy everyone trusted. The judge, whose name is Smith, became quite fond of Edward, who was disguising himself as Jerry Miller. He made the boy serve some time in juvenile detention but kept visiting him. When the boy got out, the judge adopted him."

"That judge's name…" Brooke said. "It's the same name Gabe gave me. I wonder why Gabe couldn't connect the dots."

"Not so surprising. The judge retired more

than fifteen years after adopting Edward. He moved from South Carolina and bought a marina in the Keys. He never kept in contact with his old life. Instead built a new life around this marina, his solitude and Edward, now a grown man. Terry did some digging. They are still together, Judge Smith and his adopted son, Edward."

Brooke's heart pounded. She drew a line with her finger under the address on the tablet. "Do you mean I could go to this marina and find my brother?"

"If that's what you want to do, it's a start."

"If it's what I want to do? Absolutely, it's what I want to do, Jeremy. It's all I've thought of for months." *At least until you came into my life.*

"Just remember," Jeremy said. "You don't know how Edward will react. It's likely he doesn't even know you exist."

"I have to try."

"I know that. I just don't want you to get hurt."

More hurt than I am right now? she thought. This news was a beacon of hope when so much seemed about to be taken from her life.

"I don't know how to thank you, Jeremy." She hugged the tablet to her chest. "This is a miracle and you made it happen." Before she allowed logical thought to cloud her instinct, she went and wrapped her arms around his neck and held him as tightly as she could. He felt so warm, so strong, so good. She didn't want to let go. When he cradled the back of her head in his hand, she wanted to cry.

"How are you going to go about this, Brooke?" he asked against her hair.

"I'll ask Cammie to go with me," she said. "We'll contact Edward together."

"Okay. That's a good plan. I don't know if it would be wise to go alone. The end of this story is so uncertain."

She looked up at him and nodded. "I know." His gaze was soft upon her face and crumpled the last of her resistance. She started to sob. He leaned in and kissed her forehead. Then his lips moved to her eyes, her cheeks. Everywhere his mouth touched her felt like a spark of longing.

She placed her hands on each side of his face, relishing the scratchy ruggedness of his day-old beard. He was as real to her as any person had ever been and yet so special that she almost couldn't believe her luck in having met him.

He drew her closer to his chest. His breath was warm on her moist face. "Brooke, do we know what we're doing?"

And then his mouth was on hers, hungry, insistent, as if he could banish the memory of the last days without her by obliterating everything but the kiss.

She closed her eyes and let touch guide her impulses. The feel of his skin under her palms, the press of his chest against her breasts. "Jeremy, I have to tell you. I…"

"Brooke, I heard from a major Manhattan news station today."

She halted. What was he saying? What did this station have to do with a declaration of love she had to utter? Her eyes blinked open. She waited.

"I applied with the head of their sports division on Monday afternoon. I've known him for a few years. He used to cover Wildcats games. Seemed like a good possibility for me. The guy called back today. The job of color commentator for their professional football games is mine if I want it. I'll be the on-screen broadcaster who tells the intimate details of the players that they want the public to know—their backgrounds, struggles they've known, the good they do in their communities, heck, even the kind of ice cream they like."

She tried to catch her breath. "But you're talking about Manhattan."

"That's right. I'll have to sell my house, relocate. Otherwise I'd be leaving the kids with Marta for too many days each week."

"Relocate?" She knew she was adding very little of substance to what he was telling her, but logical thoughts wouldn't form in her brain. Everything he was saying was like a knife to her heart.

"I'll be good at this job, Brooke. I've always had a way with players, listening to them, helping to heal their wounds, letting them lean on me. It's a role I've always enjoyed, and now I get to find out about these guys on a personal level and get paid for it. I should have done this from the beginning, but I had such unrealistic dreams for myself."

Dreams that I encouraged to keep my job and

earn a big bonus. Besides being devastated at Jeremy's news, Brooke was deeply ashamed.

"But Jeremy," she whispered. "Where does that leave us?"

He shook his head. "I don't know. If you had asked me this question on Monday, I would have said there is no us, but being without you for these last days, seeing you tonight, I have the strongest desire to try again, forget the past. But, Brooke, I don't see how I can."

"What do you mean?"

"I have to do something with my life. I've seen too many ex-players live on their laurels and a pile of money that they thought would never run out. So many of them have been wrong. They've become irresponsible, too self-centered, feeling they're entitled to watch from the sidelines the rest of their lives. I can't be like them. I've got two children who look to me for guidance. What kind of a mentor would I be to my own kids if all I taught them was that a lucky break and some brawny talent was all they needed?"

"You could never be that kind of a father, that kind of a man," Brooke said. "I understand your need to start again, but why can't you do it from here, in a place you've come to love?"

"I do like it here, Brooke, but I haven't been here long enough to build many strong attachments. Frankly, I don't know where I'd start over in this area. My gut instinct tells me to go away."

But what about us? You're the only man I've ever loved. This wasn't about her. It was about Jeremy and how he needed to find a life that he could feel good about for himself and his family, how he needed to recover from thoughts of her and how she'd hurt him. So all she said was "I will miss you." She could have added a thousand words to that simple statement of fact.

He wrapped her in another strong embrace. "And I will miss you. But I know you, Brooke. You will resume the amazing work you do at WJQC. You will continue to become an even more successful producer. Someday I will see your name on one of the biggest and most respected cable news channels that others like you have only dreamed about. You were made for this job. You thrive on the tension, the competition, the split-second decisions." He kissed the top of her head. "I am so proud to know you, Brooke. Admittedly, I disagree with some of the choices you make to get what you want, but I admire your dedication to get it."

How could she argue with him? For more than a decade this job had been her life.

"Daddy! Where are you? We finished our pizza."

Brooke stepped away from Jeremy's arms when she heard Alicia call him. That step would probably turn out to be the longest and most difficult one she would ever take in her life. "I should go," she said.

She slipped her hand in her pocket to feel the paper with the name and address she'd copied down. Her brother's name. Tonight she'd accomplished what her heart had yearned for for so many long months. Only it was Jeremy who had accomplished it for her. The moment when her heart should have been soaring with hope and gratitude, it was breaking, cell by cell, and there was nothing she could do about it.

Alicia and Cody came into the office. "That was great pizza, Brooke," Cody said.

She went down on one knee to look into his

bright blue eyes. "I'm glad you liked it. Can I give you a hug?"

"Sure." He stepped into her arms.

"I think your squeezes are about the best I've ever had," she said.

Next she hugged Alicia. "Call me if you ever want to talk, sweetie."

Alicia's eyes clouded. "Why are you talking this way? Aren't you coming back?"

Brooke glanced at Jeremy before giving Alicia her full attention. "Sometimes even we adults don't know how things are going to turn out. Sometimes we just don't know." She smoothed her hand down Alicia's silky hair. "I have to say goodbye. For now."

"I'm going to walk Brooke to the door," Jeremy said. "I'll be with you kids in a minute. Go upstairs and get ready for your baths."

As she drove away from Jeremy's home, Brooke thought about him and his children, their lives returning to normal while hers would never be the same again.

CHAPTER TWENTY

"ARE YOU SURE it's him?" Camryn sounded skeptical, but Brooke understood her reluctance to believe that Edward had been found.

"As sure as I can be. I know it's hard to picture that he actually exists. I never would have found him if I hadn't confided in Jeremy."

"I'll admit that the story Jeremy gave you is convincing. You must have been so excited."

"Yes, I was." *Unfortunately, my excitement was overshadowed by the horrible sense of loss I was experiencing.* Brooke couldn't dwell on the emptiness in her life right now. Jeremy was making a decision that was right for him, and it didn't include her. Maybe someday... But at this point he'd given her a gift, a miracle actually, that she had been dreaming of for a long time. She loved her adopted mother and father and her heart ached that she couldn't tell them about Edward. Maybe sometime in the future when they wouldn't be so hurt that she'd tried to locate her mother.

"So when are you planning to go to the Keys?" Camryn asked her.

"I've got to clear some time with Milt, but that shouldn't be a problem. He'll be taking a much more active role in producing the news when he hires an anchor, so I'm sure he'll give me leave for a few days." Brooke took a deep breath. "I'm so scared, Camryn. What if Edward doesn't want to know us? What if he is nothing like I've allowed myself to imagine? What if he isn't even nice?"

"I know you, Brooke. Scared or not you're going to follow through with this. Any of those things might be true, but you can't give up now. You wouldn't be Brooke Montgomery if you did."

Cammie was right. No matter what the cost, Brooke would see this through to the end. "You'll go with me, won't you?" Brooke said. "I don't think I can do this without you, Cammie. We need to be together, like we always have been. Say you're coming with me."

Camryn paused a moment. "When are you going?"

"I have some loose ends to tie up, but I was thinking next weekend. Nine days. I'm going to fly to Miami and rent a car. It's not so far to Sweet Pine Key from there."

Camryn's voice fell to an agonized whisper. "Oh, honey… I can't go that soon. I'm still breastfeeding Grace. Reed can do a lot of the chores around here, but I'm afraid he can't take over that one."

"We'll take Gracie with us," Brooke said, knowing it was an impractical solution. Flying with an infant, stopping every couple of hours to feed her, introducing Grace to a different climate in a situation that might prove extremely tense. This was not Camryn's idea of responsible motherhood.

"That's not a good idea," Camryn said. "Perhaps if you put the trip off a couple of months. You've waited this long…"

"No. No way. I'm going. I need to go, Camryn. Things haven't been so great in my life the last few days. I need to know that my search for Edward is finally over."

"What about a friend?" Camryn suggested. "Maybe one of your friends can get some time off work." She made a clicking sound with her tongue as if she was thinking. "I know! What about Jeremy? I realize you said you two had a falling-out, but if he gave you Edward's information, he knows how important this is to you. Maybe inviting him to go will make your situation better."

"No, I can't ask Jeremy," Brooke said. "He's been wonderful but he's leaving the station. He's leaving the Charleston area and taking another job."

"When did this happen?"

"I just found out today." Feeling her throat tighten with another sob, Brooke fought back tears.

"Is this what you meant by your life not being so great lately? I'm so sorry, Brooke. I really thought he could be the one."

On a trembling rush of air, Brooke said, "So did I." She reached for a tissue and blew her nose. "It's okay, Cammie. I understand why you can't go. I'll figure something out. I've got nine days."

"Please find someone to go with you, Brooke," Camryn said. "I know you have an impression of Edward in your mind, but we have no idea if he's the man you want him to be. You need someone with you."

"I'll find someone. In the meantime, I'll be in touch. Kiss the girls for me."

"I love you, Brooke," Camryn said.

"I love you, too. And at least loving you doesn't hurt."

"Oh, sweetie…"

She could barely get the last words out. "I've got to go, Cammie." She couldn't bear to say their usual goodbye.

Brooke disconnected. She turned on her television and immediately turned it off. Watching fictional problems and love affairs wouldn't comfort her tonight. One fact was certain. The next nine days were going to seem like months, but alone or not, she was going to Florida.

"DADDY, WHAT'S THE matter with you?" Alicia stood outside her father's office and scowled at him.

"Nothing, Ally. Everything is fine."

"But you hardly ever play with us anymore."

He wanted to argue that point, but Ally's

comment made him realize that he had been self-absorbed the last few days. "I'm sorry, Ally. I've had a lot on my mind, but that's no excuse. I'll be out to play with you in a minute."

"Cody wants to play *Sorry!* It's his favorite game and yours, too."

Jeremy smiled, something he hadn't done much in the last few days. The idea that a game for six-to-ten-year-olds was his favorite could even bring a grin to his stuck-in-Neutral face. "It's a great game," he said. "I was just catching up on some paperwork."

"And then you'll play with us? It's Saturday and we don't have to go to bed early." Alicia cocked her head to one side. "Do you even remember it's Saturday?" she asked.

"Oh, I do. Who took you guys out for burgers and fries earlier?" He didn't want to be cross with his daughter primarily because she was right. Usually he enjoyed coming up with inventive ways to keep his kids happy and occupied. Lately he just wanted to do his thinking, his regretting, his feeling sorry for himself in the privacy of his office. But that wasn't fair, and he knew it.

He opened his desk drawer and put some blank papers inside to create the image that he'd actually been working. "Let's play that game right now," he said. "Get ready for the tromping of your life, Ally."

She danced ahead of him toward the kitchen, where Marta and Cody were taking cookies from the oven.

"Take the rest of the night off," Jeremy said to his housekeeper. "We're going to have a *Sorry!* marathon."

"And somebody has to eat these cookies," Marta said. "I'm going to my room to watch the Hallmark Channel."

"Call Brooke, Daddy," Alicia said. "I'll bet she'd like the game, too."

"Yeah, call Brooke," Cody said.

"I'm pretty sure Brooke is busy tonight, guys."

"Just call her and ask," Alicia prompted. "You're never grumpy when Brooke is here."

"I'm not grumpy," Jeremy said, forcing himself to smile. A lot of good it did, though.

"Give me your phone," Cody said. "I'll call her. She won't be mad if I call her."

Jeremy stared at his son. "What makes you think she'd be mad if I called her?"

"Just 'cause you've been so grumpy, I guess."

Jeremy took the board game from the kitchen pantry and opened the box. "One more *grumpy* from either one of you and I'm going to watch the Hallmark Channel with Marta."

Thankfully, the threat worked. He didn't know what he would do if the kids kept accusing him of being in a foul mood, especially since he knew it was true. Doggone it, he missed Brooke. He missed talking to her, listening to her, watching her run the station in a way that he never could but made him respect her. He missed seeing her as she opened a door when he knocked. He missed kissing her, holding her, touching her and hearing her sweet sighs.

He'd sealed the job deal with the New York station, so he was committed, but maybe there was a way to salvage what he and Brooke had. Other people made long-distance relationships work. Other people learned to respect the work ethics of their partners even if it seemed impossible. Other couples learned to forgive and start over where they left off. Other partners managed to trust again.

"Come on, Dad," Cody said. "What color do you want to be?"

The answer came naturally. "I'll be blue," he said. He put his token on the starting place and decided that beginning the very next day he was going to think of a way back to Brooke. He had to try. But how he would do it was the biggest puzzle he'd ever faced. He wasn't good at mending relationships. He'd been a part of only one serious love affair, and he hadn't been clever enough to get Lynette to marry him. Maybe help would come from somewhere.

JEREMY FLEW TO New York City on Sunday. For two days he toured the studio, met some production people, had meetings with directors, producers and other athletes who would be his cohosts for a few hours during each football game. He signed contracts, was taken to lunch at the best restaurants. Maybe his personal life was a mess, but when he caught a plane on Wednesday morning, he was certain he'd made the right career decision. Now to do something about that personal problem.

As he drove home from the Charleston airport, he thought of everything he had to do. At the top of his list was talking to his children about making a move to New York. They wouldn't want to do it. They loved their home and the Lowcountry. They claimed they didn't miss snow at all. But, heck they would learn to adjust to New York and apartment living. Lots of kids did. Maybe Cody couldn't get that dog right away...

Jeremy's thoughts were interrupted by his cell phone. Not recognizing the number on his dash screen, he considered not answering, but did, anyway. Maybe it wouldn't be a telemarketer. People could get cell numbers so many ways these days.

"Hello."

"Is this Jeremy Crockett?"

A woman's voice. Soft and kind of sweet, not chirpy, clipped and impersonal like someone who wanted him to buy a time-share. "Yes, this is Jeremy."

"My name is Camryn Bolden. You know my sister..."

He almost ran off the road. Had something happened to Brooke? "I know who you are," he said. "You're Brooke's twin sister." *Now please tell me she's all right before I can't breathe.*

"Yes, that's right."

"Is she…? I mean nothing happened…?" He sounded like a blithering old fool.

"Oh, no. Not at all. She's fine. In fact a bit over the moon because of your help in locating our half brother, Edward."

He let his chest expand with a normal breath. "That was nothing. I knew finding him was important to her."

"She's flying to Miami on Saturday and renting a car to drive to the Keys."

"I thought she might make plans to go down pretty quickly."

Camryn sighed. Jeremy waited.

"Look, I don't know how to say this," Camryn said. "I mean your life is none of my business. But Brooke's is. I worry about her, and I'm worried now."

"Why? Are you concerned that Edward might be a danger to Brooke? I assumed you both would go to Florida since this is a family matter."

Camryn explained in detail why she couldn't accompany her sister. "I even asked her to postpone the trip, but, well, you know my sister."

Yes, he did. Knew her. Loved her. Missed her. *Loved her.* How effortlessly that phrase had popped into his head. "I don't like the idea of her going by herself," Jeremy said.

"Neither do I. That's why I'm calling you today. I know you and my sister have had a falling-out, but I also know how grateful she is for what you did. And I know she trusts you."

"What exactly are you asking, Camryn?"

"I thought maybe you would go with her. I realize it's short notice."

Yes, it was. But Jeremy had just completed everything he absolutely had to do to start his new job, and football season was still a couple of months away. But go with her? He had no way of knowing for certain, but he was quite sure that Brooke hadn't instigated this plan. He also knew that Marta had no plans for the weekend, so he could leave the kids for a couple of days.

Before he could organize his thoughts into a logical progression, his heart started pounding. Just a few days ago he had been pondering ways he might approach Brooke and see if they could work out their differences. He'd even hoped that help would come in one form or another to guide him. Camryn Bolden… perhaps that help had just dialed his phone number.

"Jeremy? Are you still there?"

"Yes. I'm sorry, Camryn. I was just thinking."

"This is a lot to ask. I've tried to come up with someone else that might go with her, but her friends all have jobs and commitments. And frankly, I don't think Brooke would appreciate their input on this matter. She's rather independent."

Jeremy smiled. "She is that."

"But as I said, she trusts you. If you need some time to think about this, you can take a day or two, but flight arrangements have to be made. I might be able to pay for your ticket…"

Jeremy recalled Brooke telling him that her sister was happy but far from wealthy. The woman raised chickens and sold eggs. "That won't be necessary," he said. "Have you mentioned this plan to Brooke?"

"Are you kidding? She would have told me to mind my own business. And maybe she's right."

No, she's not right. Sometimes a well-meaning friend, or sister, can turn problems into solutions.

"I'll do it," Jeremy said. "But don't tell Brooke. Just text me the flight details. I'll book the same time and meet her at the airport. Like you say, she's independent. Let's not give her time to object."

"Oh, Jeremy, thank you." Camryn's voice was breathless with relief. "If you ever need a favor. If you have a pet that needs medical attention, my husband is a vet."

Maybe Cody would get that dog after all.

"Or if you need eggs..." She started laughing, and Jeremy's heart clenched. She sounded so much like her sister.

"Don't worry, Camryn. I'm sure you'll hear from Brooke soon after we land in Miami." *I hope she's thanking you and not reminding you not to interfere again.*

Jeremy disconnected. He was almost at

Hidden Oaks. The first thing he was going to do when he got home was cancel the appointment he'd made with a Realtor. If everything went according to plan, he wouldn't be selling his house after all. But living arrangements were only one of the obstacles he and Brooke faced.

"One step at a time, Crockett," he said to himself. "You have to convince Brooke that a life together isn't just an impossible dream." For the first time in days, Jeremy felt the stirrings of hope. Being with Brooke was suddenly more than a dream. It was the life he wanted. The life he could have if he could just convince her.

CHAPTER TWENTY-ONE

BROOKE PUT THE last of her clothes in the suitcase and snapped the lid shut. She had two hours before her eleven o'clock flight, plenty of time to order an Uber driver, check in at the airport and go through security. She didn't want too much time to spare before the flight, too much time to think.

She certainly hadn't tied up all the loose ends before making this plane reservation. She knew her brother's name—Edward Smith. She knew the name of the marina where he might be living and working. She knew the name of the judge who had supposedly rescued him from a troubled life. She didn't know if the judge's efforts succeeded. She didn't know for certain what Edward did for a living. She didn't even know if he would be in the Keys when she arrived. Everything she was doing today was based on a dream, and she'd learned lately that dreams, unfulfilled ones, often left a person alone and wanting.

The driver dropped Brooke off at the airport at 9:45 a.m. She rolled her suitcase behind her to the security line. She hadn't packed much, not knowing if she would stay a few days or catch the next flight back to Charleston. When she cleared security and approached her gate, she was tense. Nerves tingled in all her extremities. She almost felt nauseous, so she sat in a chair in the waiting area, drew several deep breaths and took out her phone.

I'm here, she texted her sister. The plane is at the runway so we should be boarding.

Her fingers stopped dancing across the keyboard. Her heart stopped beating for a frightening few seconds. She blinked. It couldn't be. Jeremy was walking toward her after leaving a concession shop with snacks in his hand.

She couldn't look away. She was frightened of looking too closely for fear he would shimmer and disappear like a mirage.

He stopped in front of her. "Want some gum?" He unwrapped the package. "I understand it's good for popping ears when we take off."

"We?" she repeated. "Jeremy, what are you doing here?"

He took the seat next to her. "I'm going to Florida to see a guy about renting a boat."

"Jeremy, stop teasing me. I can't take it." Her eyes flooded with tears, and she wasn't sure why they'd begun to fall. Except that Jeremy looked so wonderful in a yellow denim shirt and blue jeans, expensive sneakers on his feet and gum in his hand. She'd never seen a more beautiful sight.

"Okay, I'll stop," he said. "I'm going with you, Brooke. We're going to meet Edward together. I'll be there for support, and I promise to let you do the talking."

"You're going with me? Have you thought this through?" She prayed that he had, every last detail.

"Sure I did. I've got nothing to do the next couple of days. Marta's with the kids. I'm free as a bird." He lifted her hand, brought it to his lips for a warm kiss. His face grew serious. "And, besides, I don't want you to be alone."

"Jeremy, I've suddenly never felt less alone in my life than I do right now."

"Good, because I don't want to think of you

alone just for this trip. I don't want you to be alone ever. Almost as much as I don't want to be alone another day."

As her mind processed his words, her heart soared. "What are you saying?"

"I've got to spell it out?"

She smiled. "Some of us deal in facts, Crockett. We can't work with assumptions."

His grin was sweet and promising and honest and hopeful. And suddenly Brooke believed anything was possible with this best of all men.

"Okay then, Miss News Producer. I'm suggesting that we work out our problems, eliminate the obstacles and pledge to stay together for every wonderful day we can grab between trips from New York to Charleston."

"You've taken the job in New York?"

"I did."

"So you're proposing a long-distance relationship?"

"I am. I realize it didn't work out for me before, but I believe in us, Brooke. I hope you do, too. Enough that you'll give this a shot."

"I want to. But Jeremy, what about…?"

"Your job? You should keep it as long as

you like. Do it however you want. I'll continue to be as proud of you as I am today."

He'd read her mind and answered perfectly. "And what about…?"

"My kids? The two who have decided that I'm a much better man and father and much less grumpy when you're around? Those kids? I'm hoping you'll come home to Hidden Oaks after work most nights and see that they do their homework and take showers and go to bed. Marta will be there if you need help. And if it becomes too much…"

She'd already begun shaking her head. "No, it won't. I love Cody and Alicia."

"I believe you," he said. "But all kids are unpredictable beings, mine included. If you need a break, you can escape to your condo by the Battery for a sleepover. Or go to that chicken farm your sister owns. Or anywhere you want as long as you come back."

Brooke had always admired her sister for knowing what she wanted and settling for nothing less. A fine man, a family, a flock of cooperative chickens. But Brooke had never realized how her goals could be so much like

Camryn's. Well, maybe not the chicken part. But the rest sounded like heaven.

"Jeremy," she said, taking both his hands, "I will always come back."

"Good. Then let's go find us a best man. I hear there might be one waiting in the Keys."

She placed her hands gently on each side of his face and kissed him soundly. She hardly heard the flight attendant announce that boarding had begun.

* * * * *

*For more great romances from
Cynthia Thomason and
Harlequin Heartwarming,
visit www.Harlequin.com today!*

Psst!

We're Getting a Makeover...

STAY TUNED FOR OUR FABULOUS NEW LOOK!

And the very best in romance
from the authors you love!

The wait is almost over!

COMING FEBRUARY 2020

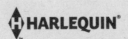

DTCSERIESIFCB1219

Get 4 FREE REWARDS!

We'll send you 2 FREE Books plus 2 FREE Mystery Gifts.

Love Inspired® books feature contemporary inspirational romances with Christian characters facing the challenges of life and love.

FREE
Value Over
$20

ReaderService.com has a new look!

We have refreshed our website and
we want to share our new look with you.
Head over to ReaderService.com
and check it out!

On ReaderService.com, you can:

- Try 2 free books from any series
- Access risk-free special offers
- View your account history & manage payments
- Browse the latest Bonus Bucks catalog

Don't miss out!

If you want to stay up-to-date on the latest at the Reader Service and enjoy more Harlequin content, make sure you've signed up for our monthly News & Notes email newsletter. Sign up online at ReaderService.com.